Full Service Blonde

IMBRIFEX BOOKS

Also by Megan Edwards

Roads from the Ashes:
An Odyssey in Real Life on the Virtual Frontier

Getting Off on Frank Sinatra

Strings: A Love Story

Full Service Blonde

Megan Edwards

A COPPER BLACK MYSTERY

IMBRIFEX BOOKS

IMBRIFEX BOOKS
Published by Flattop Productions, Inc.
8275 S. Eastern Avenue, Suite 200
Las Vegas, NV 89123

This is a work of fiction. All of the characters, organizations and events portrayed
in this novel are either products of the author's imagination or are used fictitiously.
Any resemblance to actual persons, living or dead, businesses, companies, events,
or locales is entirely coincidental.

IMBRIFEX® is a registered trademark of Flattop Productions, Inc.

Printed in the United States of America.

Set in Adobe Caslon, Designed by Sue Campbell
MeganEdwards.com
Imbrifex.com

ISBN 9781945501005 (paperback)
ISBN 9781945501098 (e-book)
ISBN 9781945501104 (audiobook)

Library of Congress Control Number: 2017934397
First Edition: November 2017

For Margaret Sedenquist
Champion
Crusader
Benefactor
Blonde

Full Service Blonde

"The job at the *Bucks County Reporter* is perfect for you."

"It is. You're right."

"Darling, you'll love Pennsylvania!"

"No, Mom. I'm going to Las Vegas."

This little interchange took place last April, right after the letter carrier had dropped off two pristine white envelopes to my parents' house and I had opened them in the kitchen while my mom drank her late-morning coffee.

I remember it as though it happened ten minutes ago. I had graduated from college three years earlier. The internship scene in New York City was getting old, as was commuting from my parents' house in Connecticut.

All at once on that crisp spring morning, I had two genuine full-time job offers. I read them both to my mother, prompting the interchange I reported above.

Things might have been so different. If, for example, the offer from Bucks County had arrived a day earlier instead of in tandem with the one from southern Nevada.

Or maybe if it hadn't been the era of "What Happens in Vegas, Stays in Vegas." If I hadn't seen—and enjoyed—all those seductive commercials promising guilt-free anonymity in Sin City, who knows how I would have responded to the lovely offer of an assistant editorship on the right side of the tracks in Pennsylvania?

But the slogan was ubiquitous and irresistible, and as I reread the letter offering me a position at *The Las Vegas Light*, I could swear it glowed with a hint of neon.

Of course, Mom was right that Pennsylvania was the safer choice. But even she had no inkling then of just how right she was. Even with her often overactive imagination, my worrywart mother couldn't have dreamed up what actually lay in store for me. Looking back, I wonder if things would have been different if she had been able to foretell the future.

Copper, burglars are going to ransack your apartment. A thug in a ski mask is going to slash you with a knife. You're going to get mixed up in murder. And that's not the worst of it. Copper, darling, you're going to make friends with a prostitute!

It wouldn't have mattered. I was twenty-four and itching to build a career. Las Vegas was a beehive of pop culture, and stultifying suburban security held as much appeal as an iron lung. Once I decided to go to Las Vegas, no one could have talked me out of it.

Chapter 1

I carry business cards that read "Copper Black, Assistant Editor." To my parents, they're reassuring proof I'm a bona fide journalist, but what my title really means is that I update show listings and bring caffe lattes to Chris Farr, the arts and entertainment editor. But my parents are in Connecticut, where it's far more satisfying to imagine me interviewing celebrities.

"Copper," my mother will say on the phone, "I read that Bill Clinton was in Las Vegas last week. Did you meet him?"

No, Mom. I was standing in line at Starbucks.

Not that I haven't learned a lot in my nearly eight months in Las Vegas. I know about high pollen counts and flash floods, the shortage of obstetricians, and the abundance of Mormon churches. I'm an expert at giving and following directions using casinos as landmarks. I know that when real Nevadans said "Nevada," the VAD rhymes with MAD. Only newscasters broadcasting from Rockefeller Center say Ne-VAH-da. Well, I used to, too, but I've acclimatized.

Even so, I still have a lot to learn, even about subjects as ordinary as the good old-fashioned Yellow Pages. Remember those big fat books we used to use as booster seats and doorstops? I thought they had died out along with phone booths, but there's a whole bookcase full of them at *The Light*. They've been relegated to the far side of the lunchroom, probably their last stop on the road to extinction, but there they are. I was eating lunch alone that Friday, so out of curiosity, I pulled one out to keep me and my ramen noodles company. I had just returned to my table when a familiar but unwelcome raspy voice fell on my ears.

"Hey, blondie, help me out and turn to 'Entertainers' in the Yellow Pages you've got there."

I looked up to see Ed Bramlett leering at me from his usual spot near the windows. He covers business at *The Light*. Next to him, wearing a similar expression, was J.C. Dillon, who has the local government beat. They both have at least thirty years on me, and they liked nothing better than to see me blush. When I first arrived, they could turn me crimson in a matter of moments, but I've toughened up.

"It's *Copper*," I said, looking back down. "Do you need some entertainment, Ed?" I hoped I sounded sufficiently sarcastic.

"Not when I have you, sweetie," Ed said. J.C. emitted a snort that was supposed to pass for a laugh.

I should have ignored them, but I flipped to the "E" section. I know now that I should not have been expecting discreet ads for piano players, but I was still a Vegas newbie.

"FULL SERVICE BLONDES," read the three-inch headline staring me in the face. I looked up, and Ed smiled triumphantly as I felt my cheeks warming. I am the world's fastest blusher, and I was glad I had worn my hair long that day. It covered my ears, which always heat up even more violently than my face. But I wasn't embarrassed. I was angry. Ed had succeeded in turning me red again.

"It means they bring you coffee," Ed said, and J.C. snorted again. I slapped the phone book shut. Clutching it in one hand and my cup of noodles in the other, I stalked out of the lunchroom.

Back in my cubicle, I turned the pages once again to the letter E. The section dedicated to "Entertainers" went on for at least a hundred pages, and most of the ads were just like the one Ed had needled me with: "Full Service Blondes," "Barely Legal Asians," "College Hardbodies in Short Skirts."

I called David Nussbaum, thanking God as I dialed that at least one of the reporters at *The Light* didn't treat me like an inflatable doll.

"David, this is Copper. I've got some questions about prostitution in Las Vegas. It's illegal, right?"

"Yeah, it's illegal in Clark County. Why?"

"Is it really, though? I mean, there are those trucks that drive up and down the Strip advertising 'Girls direct to your room.' And those guys who snap little cards at you on the sidewalk. And ... well, I'm just flipping through the Yellow Pages, and the section under 'Entertainers' looks a lot like—"

"Call girls."

"Yeah. 'Discreet and Confidential.' 'Full Service.'"

"The ads aren't illegal, even though what they're promoting is. What's ironic is that the legal brothels over in Nye County *can't* advertise like that, even though they pay taxes and follow all the rules. But why are you so interested in prostitution all of a sudden? Thinking of a career change? Tired of being Calendar Girl?"

"Don't start, David." I told him about Ed Bramlett's latest gambit.

"Copper, there is nothing more threatening to an old reporter than young talent. He's just jealous."

"Of the coffee chick whose assignments mostly involve chasing down lounge singers?"

"Of youth. Of beauty. Of a degree from Princeton."

I was so glad David and I had Princeton in common, even though he graduated before I got there. I never fully appreciated the value of old school ties until I got this job. I was still an outsider, but at least there was somebody of the same species in a nearby cubicle.

"Got any good plans for the weekend?" David asked.

"I was thinking about driving up to Zion tomorrow," I said. "I've never been."

"It's really beautiful with snow on the ground. Have fun."

"How about you?" I asked.

"Working."

I really had nothing to complain about. Coffee-bearing Calendar Girls don't have to work on weekends.

I finished my lunch in my cubicle. David said Ed Bramlett would count it as a victory, but I figured screw the old goat. He didn't seem to have the vaguest inkling that I could nail him with a sexual harassment suit, and he was lucky I didn't come to Vegas gunning for sexist pigs. I knew I had to be tough to make it in journalism. I stayed in my cubicle so I could get some work done. I didn't have time to waste sparring with a leathery old misogynist.

Chapter 2

David was right about Zion. It was fantastic, fully deserving of its National Park status. I hiked the Riverside Walk and made it back to my car just in time to see the sun set on a huge red-rock formation called the Temple of Sinawava. The only thing that could have made my day better was if the man who held the keys to my heart had been there with me.

Daniel Garside was the one person who could have kept me on the East Coast. When he got an internship at the National Arboretum after college, I tried to find a job in Washington, D.C. New York was the closest I could get, which at least allowed us to spend a lot of weekends together. I figured we'd find a way to live together once he decided on a graduate school, but then he got a Wilberforce Fellowship and flew off to Costa Rica to study tropical mistletoe. We talked almost every day, but I hadn't seen him in the flesh since February. The countdown to Christmas seemed interminable, but somehow I had to make it through another twelve days.

I had breakfast in the house with my sister-in-law before we both went to work. We watched *The Morning Show* while we ate. Kathie Pitchford was interviewing a woman named Victoria McKimber.

Even though Victoria looked like she was on the wrong side of forty, she had masses of curly platinum blonde hair. It had to be a wig, although her fair skin and blue eyes made me wonder if it might be real. Then again, maybe the fair skin and blue eyes were fake, too. Anyway, she was wearing a tight, low-cut knit top that showed off a pair of casabas that were either very expensive or a sure sign God loved her.

"When you entered American Beauty's Queen of Sales contest, did you tell American Beauty the true nature of your profession?" Kathie asked.

"No," Victoria replied, "and they didn't ask. The contest was open to active distributors of American Beauty products, which I have been for the last ten years."

"So you didn't tell them you work for—"

"That I'm a prostitute? No. There was no reason. Prostitution is legal where I work in Nevada."

"She's a hooker," Sierra said, her mouth full of cinnamon toast. "I knew it. Although she's farther over the hill than most."

"How do you know?" I asked, though I wasn't surprised she did. My sister-in-law had been my main source of information about Nevada culture ever since she and my brother invited me to move into the apartment over their garage.

Sierra's a native. She even worked as an "exotic dancer" after she graduated from Bonanza High School. That's a secret, though, at least as far as my parents are concerned. Sierra's convinced they'd die of blue-blooded shock if they knew their son was married to a woman who used to give lap dances. She's probably right. They have a hard enough time telling their Fairfield County friends that both of their children live in Las Vegas—*by choice!*

"Oh, come on, Copper, look at her. She's closing in on fifty. Most of them are your age—mine at the outside." Sierra turned thirty-two on Halloween.

We kept watching as Kathie elicited all the details of Victoria McKimber's rise to Sales Queen fame. She'd won local and regional contests before heading for Kansas City, where a few days ago she beat out a dozen other American Beauty distributors to win a tiara, a pink Impala, and a year-long contract to star in American Beauty's television commercials.

And now, American Beauty was going to take it all away. Accusing Victoria of concealing information that she knew would damage the company's reputation, American Beauty's top brass had rescinded her crown, cancelled the Chevy, and torn up the contract.

"When I revealed my profession at the first pageant, they were horrified, but they hoped I'd lose the regional competition and just disappear," Victoria told Kathie. "They were total jerks about it. And then I won, so they threatened to take away my distributorship."

"And that's when you hired an attorney?" Kathie asked.

"Yeah, I got a lawyer interested," Victoria said, "and she told them to go pound sand. But now that I've won the crown, they're freaked about one little ol' working girl—" She paused, looked straight at the camera, and shook her mass of blonde curls. With a smile, she went on. "They think I'm out to destroy their brand, so they're pulling out the big guns. But I'm not going down without a fight. This is the United States of America, and I've done nothing illegal."

"Oh, my God," I said, looking at my watch. "I'm late for work."

The one very bad thing about having to bring morning coffee for your boss is that he always knows if you're late. Fortunately, Chris Farr was even later than I was, and his latte was cooling on his desk by the time he arrived.

I was on the phone with a publicist from the Golden Sands when David Nussbaum appeared at my desk.

"Yes," I was saying, "I got the press release on Friday, and it'll be in this week's Dazzle section." I hung up. "The Golden Sands is having open tryouts for a new Golden Girl."

"You get all the fun stories, Copper."

His comment didn't deserve an answer.

"Remember how you were asking about call girls on Friday?" David continued. "Well, I've got to interview one today, and I thought you might like to come along."

"What's the story?"

"She won a national sales contest sponsored by a cosmetics company, and—"

"*Victoria McKimber?*"

"Yeah. How did you know?"

"I saw her on TV this morning," I said. "But she was in New York. She was on *The Morning Show.*"

"She would have been on *Late Night* tonight, but she had to come home."

"Home?"

"Yup, she's one of our own. Works at the Beavertail Ranch in Pahrump."

"I'd love to go, but I can't leave now," I said. "It's Monday, and—"

"I know," David said, "but she doesn't get in until this afternoon. I'm meeting her at the Silverado at five. You can ride with me if you like, and I can bring you back here afterward."

The Silverado is a "locals' casino" a few miles south of the airport. I had never been there even though the person handling their publicity offered me free tickets to a magic show every time I talked to her. I was going to have to skip lunch and talk fast to get all my Monday calls and calendar updates done, but Chris Farr had an editorial meeting at four o'clock. If I got caught up, he wouldn't mind if I left half an hour early.

I was about to meet a real live hooker who was smack in the middle of her fifteen minutes of fame. And for fifteen minutes, the Calendar Girl could feel like a real reporter instead of the title of an old Neil Sedaka song.

David Nussbaum reappeared at my desk just as I was making my last call, and we walked out to the parking lot together. David is an East Coast Jewish preppie who wears tweed jackets, rimless glasses, and Hush Puppies. But instead of the Saab that would complete his Ivy League style, he drives a Jeep, and it isn't one of those upscale soccer mom models. It's a basic canvas-topped Army man vehicle. It's even got two extra gas cans strapped to the back, as though David's never sure when he might get an assignment in the middle of Death Valley.

Not that I think it's fair to judge someone on the car they drive. I mean, I hope no one thinks mine is a four-wheeled personality statement. I drive a white Chrysler minivan, a "Town & Country" I would never in a geologic age have selected for myself. My father chose it using the flawed logic that I'd be safer driving a large vehicle. He drove the thing—"right off the lot"—out to Princeton in October of my senior year. My mom followed in their BMW, and they handed the keys to me over dinner. "Happy Birthday!" they said. My birthday's in March, so the car was definitely a surprise. So was the fact that it looked like the sort of thing a suburban housewife with a large brood might drive.

The supreme uncoolness of my ride was not lost on my best buddy Jessica.

"It looks like a Kotex!" she proclaimed as soon as she saw it. "Big enough for those extra-heavy days!"

She had a voice like an alpenhorn, and I had managed to pause in front of Witherspoon Hall at rush hour.

"Dude! It's a freakin' maxi pad!" she added in a voice that could shatter glass, and that sealed my poor minivan's fate. From then on, it was known as the Maxi Pad. Contrary to my father's safety-conscious thinking, it wasn't really a plus that the car seated seven people with dedicated seat belts, because it could carry at least double that if the riders were willing to share. Whether I liked it or not, I was an instantly popular designated bus driver. By the time I graduated, "the Maxi Pad" had mercifully shrunk to "the Max," and "the Max" it has remained, but only because I'm used to it and no one in Las Vegas knows what it's short for. I'd trade it in for a Jeep like David's in a New York second, but I know it would hurt Dad's feelings. And I have to admit that I like being able to buy bookcases and take them home without renting a truck.

Anyway, David's Jeep was covered in a thin layer of dust, which made me wonder if he might actually get assignments in the howling desert.

"Sorry it's dirty," David said as he opened the passenger door and moved a plastic bag and a stack of mail to the back. "I had to cover the groundbreaking for a housing development in North Las Vegas. No pavement."

We took the freeway south to Blue Diamond Road and arrived at the Silverado with ten minutes to spare.

"I told her I'd meet her in the coffee shop," David said as we wove our way through the slot machines.

The coffee shop was sparsely populated, and even in the dim light it was easy to see that Victoria wasn't there. A hostess showed us to a table near the entrance.

Before we could check the menu, Victoria materialized in front of us, enveloped in a cloud of musky-smelling perfume. She was wearing the same outfit she'd had on for *The Morning Show*: a purple leather miniskirt and a low-cut black leotard top. She'd clipped her hair into one of those deliberately messy up-dos, and she was carrying a zippered shoulder bag big enough to hold a body.

"Victoria McKimber," she said, holding a scarlet-taloned hand out to me.

"Oh! Hi! I'm Copper Black," I said, "and this is—"

"You must be David," Victoria said. "Thanks for coming down here to meet me. I came directly from the airport."

"The pleasure's mine," David said. "Please, have a seat."

"Thanks," Victoria said, but she didn't sit down. Plunking her huge shoulder bag on the table, she rummaged through it and extracted a glasses case. Then she pulled out a package of batteries, a gold cigarette case, a disposable lighter, a notebook, two pens, and a small tape recorder.

I couldn't help staring as she unpacked. She was so ... constructed. Not one square inch of her was accidental, and there were many square inches. She was a lot taller than I'd expected, taller than me, taller than David even. I glanced down and saw that her stiletto heels had something to do with it, but even flat-footed she had to be nearly six feet.

"I hope you won't mind if I record our conversation," Victoria said as she sat down. "My lawyer's advice."

"Not at all," David said, "as long as you don't mind if I do the same."

Victoria laughed, and her laugh struck me as being just as calculated as her appearance. Slightly breathy, intentionally sexy. "Of course not," she said as she snapped batteries into her tape recorder.

Just then, the waitress came back. We all ordered coffee, and David started asking questions.

This wasn't the first time I'd seen David in action. He had invited me to an air show at Nellis Air Force Base when I first started working at *The Light*, and in the last few months I'd tagged along to a motorcycle rally in Laughlin, a bomb scare at a high school, a tour of a gypsum mine, and the opening of a new fire station on the Las Vegas Strip. But as I listened to him talk to Victoria, I realized that this was the first real one-on-one interview I'd watched him do, and he was good. Better than Kathie Pitchford, even. In three minutes, Victoria had repeated everything she'd said on TV, and David was probing deeper.

"How old are you?" he asked.

"Forty-seven," she said. "A prime number."

"And you've been selling American Beauty products since 1999?"

"November of '98. I'm their top distributor in this region. Utah-Nevada-Arizona-New Mexico. And I'm damned if they're going to take that away from me."

"How do you manage it? I mean, isn't your work at the Beavertail a full-time job?"

"Yes, when I'm there, which is usually two weeks a month. I'm due back out there Thursday, as a matter of fact, unless this American Beauty mess blows completely out of control." She sighed a stagy sigh and patted her hair. "I have a partner, and he does all the paperwork. Richard. My husband."

Her *husband?* I stared at Victoria again, and I can't swear my mouth wasn't open. How could a prostitute have a husband? And what kind of husband would a prostitute have?

"Yes, I'm married, honey. Twenty-three years." Victoria patted my hand, and I looked at those talons again. So perfect, and even though her hand had a few ropy veins poking up, it was unblemished and soft.

"You had to know you'd stir up controversy," David was saying, "as soon as they found out."

"If I'd told them at the get-go, they would have barred me from competing while they could still get away with it," Victoria said. "So I kept quiet until I won the first contest. Once the media knew about me, they couldn't ban me without stirring up more controversy." She shrugged. "So they harassed me in every other way they could think of. Followed me whenever I wasn't at the Beavertail, dug into my past, dug into my husband's past—"

"And your motive in all this was—?"

Victoria laughed. "You won't believe this, but at first, it was one lousy case of Forever Young."

"Forever Young?"

"American Beauty's new antiwrinkle face-firming lotion. Any distributor who entered the contest and wrote a 300-word essay about how great Forever Young is would get a whole case. Twenty-four jars. Four hundred dollars retail. Richard figured there was no downside, so he sent off an entry in my name. I didn't even know about it until his essay qualified me for the local pageant."

"What made you go for it?" David said.

"I decided it was my chance to improve the status of working ladies. Get us some respect."

Victoria had a lot to say on the topic of "sex workers' rights," and David let her ramble. At first, I wondered why he was allowing her to run the conversation, but gradually I realized that even though it seemed inefficient, it was a fabulous way to get answers to questions you'd never think to ask. As Victoria regaled us with her grand plan to elevate legal prostitutes to the level of other "personal therapists," she also revealed that her husband had been a mechanic for Nate's Crane until his left elbow was crushed in a construction accident. Their fifteen-year-old son, Jason, also had health problems, and their medical bills had added up to over $76,000 so far this year. There was so much more on David's cassette when he finally clicked off his recorder that I was jealous. He had probably captured a Pulitzer-worthy story on that tape.

The whole time Victoria was talking, my mind kept traveling back to my last semester in college, when I wrote my senior thesis. What I would have given to talk to Victoria back then, while I was struggling to make my case about the motives and fates of women heroines like Cleopatra and Joan of Arc. Victoria McKimber wasn't a real queen or a national hero, but she had all the qualities of a genuine crusader.

My heart beat faster as I wondered whether I could meet her again and interview her myself. Maybe I could give Victoria what she needed—a respectful ear—and get what I wanted, too—a brilliant article that might get picked up by a big-name magazine. I didn't feel right about barging in on David's interview and asking for her phone number, but maybe he would share it with me later.

My mind was still buzzing with hopes and fantasies as David wound things up. He was about to say good-bye when Victoria surprised me.

"Copper, I'm so glad I got to meet you. And I'm wondering—" She paused and shot me a look that almost qualified as shy. "Well, here's the deal. I'm going to the New Moon Ceremony at the Sekhmet Temple tomorrow night. I'd love it if you'd join me."

Shocked by the unexpected invitation, I was still trying to formulate an answer as Victoria went on.

"I'd invite David, too, but men aren't allowed. They can come to the Full Moon Ceremony, but the New Moon is goddesses only."

"I'd love to go," I replied immediately. David shot me a disapproving look, but damn! This was way more than I'd hoped for. I had no idea what a New Moon Ceremony involved, but I wasn't going to let a chance to spend time with Victoria slip by.

"That's great!" Victoria said with a wide smile. "If you meet me here at six tomorrow, I'm happy to drive."

David let me have it on the way back to *The Light*.

"Do you know what you've gotten yourself into?" he asked. "Do you even know where the Sekhmet Temple is?"

I shook my head. "I don't even know *what* it is."

"Then why did you say you'd go?"

"I'm kind of fascinated by her. She's nothing like I expected. And I would really like to know more—"

"Take your own car," David interrupted. "Rule number one is: Stay in control. Don't become part of the story."

I wasn't sure I liked David bossing me around, but I let it slide.

"So where's the temple?" I asked.

"Indian Springs. About forty miles north on Highway 95. You go by the prison, then take a left just past Creech Air Force Base, where the Predator squadron lives."

Chapter 3

When word got out later that day that I was planning to head into the desert with Victoria McKimber, everyone immediately began treating me like a third-grade Girl Scout. It was bad enough that David started spouting safety rules, but at least he had some experience as a journalist. It was Daniel's response that really irked me. Daniel, a botanist studying how the distribution of mistletoe supports the theory of continental drift, knew nothing about journalism, and he had never set foot in Nevada. But that didn't stop him from feeling perfectly entitled to micromanage me by e-mail:

> *Copper, it can't be a good idea to go places with someone like her, and especially not to some weird cult site out in the desert. You worry me, babe. Please don't go.*

Sierra wasn't nearly that polite at dinner.

"You're insane," she said. "Michael, talk some sense into her."

"Sierra's right," he said. "This isn't Disneyland, baby sister, and Ms. McKimber isn't a storybook character."

Damn, he annoys me when he puts on his big brother act. He's only twelve years older than I am, but he's worse than my dad. It doesn't help that he's also an Episcopal priest. He still had his clergyman clothes on.

"I often work with streetwalkers at St. Andrew's," he went on. "If you want to know what their lives are like, just spend some time with me there. You're more than welcome."

"Victoria's not a streetwalker," I said. "She's an activist. She wants to improve the status of sex workers."

It didn't help. Sierra was still upset, and Michael kept right on expressing concern in a patronizing sort of way. Not that it mattered. I was going to the New Moon Ceremony at the Sekhmet Temple the next night, and to hell with all of them.

❖❖❖

Tuesday, December 13

Michael tried to talk me out of going to the temple again before I left for work.

"Sierra's genuinely worried," he said, "and so am I. You're not in New Canaan anymore, Copper."

"I'm not twelve, either."

When I got to *The Light*, it was obvious David had been talking. Everyone in the place seemed to know my plans for the evening. It made things especially tough when I tried to eat in the lunchroom at noon.

"You don't need pointers from an over-the-hill pro, sweetie," Ed Bramlett said. "You should be giving *her* lessons. And I can't believe you're going out to howl at the moon with a bunch of ball-busting dykes."

How did he keep getting away with that vulgar sexist crap? At least Norton Katz was there. He's a dapper older guy who writes a column

about celebrity sightings, and he's amassed a large and loyal following
of spies who keep him informed by phone or e-mail whenever a
newsworthy person appears in a public place. If Jennifer Lopez leaves
a lousy tip in this town, Norton knows within fifteen minutes.

"I met Victoria McKimber once," Norton said. "She was representing American Beauty at a fundraiser for Door of Hope at Caesars
Palace. That lady really knows how to work a room. I wasn't there
three minutes before she was chatting me up. And it got her what
she wanted, too. That was the first time she made my column."

"How long ago was that?"

"Oh, I'd have to check. Off the top of my head, I'd say two years,
maybe three. I hadn't given her a thought until I caught *The Morning
Show* on Monday. Recognized her the minute I saw her, even with
all the extra hair and—"

"Nutcracker tits," Ed said, and that's when I left.

At least being back in my cube gave me a good chance to do
some research. A few clicks and I learned that the Sekhmet Temple
of Goddess Spirituality was built by a woman who wanted to get
pregnant. On a trip to Egypt, she promised the lion-headed goddess
Sekhmet that she'd build her a temple in exchange for a little fertility
magic. Sekhmet obliged within a month, granting the first of three
daughters, but it wasn't until decades later that the woman kept her
end of the bargain. She eventually organized a female work crew and
built a stucco-covered straw-bale sanctuary on a patch of desert not
far from the Nevada Test Site.

Why anyone would ask Sekhmet for help having babies, I can't
figure out. The stories about her make her sound more like a monster
than a baby-loving fertility goddess. When Ra, her Sun God father,
sent her to punish human evil-doers, Sekhmet used her supernatural
strength to rip the humans to shreds. The massacre was so huge and

bloody that it shocked even Ra, who wasn't exactly nonviolent himself. A quick thinker, he filled a vat the size of Lake Nasser with beer and dyed it red to look like blood. Sekhmet drank so much she passed out, and the destruction of mankind was averted. I don't know much about Egyptian religion, but this does not strike me as appropriate behavior for a goddess of sweet motherhood.

As I walked out to the Max that evening, I suddenly remembered that "new moon" would more appropriately be called "no moon." It was going to be as dark as deep space as soon as I left the neon radiance of Las Vegas, and not much warmer. I was glad I had grabbed my ski jacket on my way out the door.

It had come as a big surprise to me that winter is actually cold in southern Nevada. When I arrived last May, I laughed at all the chimneys, figuring they'd been built for looks by homesick New Englanders. Now that I've nearly broken my neck a couple of times slipping on patches of ice created by errant sprinklers, I know better. And even though the portable electric heater in my apartment is powerful enough to keep me from freezing, I'm grateful that Sierra and Michael don't mind sharing their fireplace once in a while.

I slid behind the steering wheel, snapped on my seat belt, and fought off a sudden attack of nerves. Why had Victoria invited me? What happens at a ceremony honoring a deity of mass destruction— in the dark? I checked my cell phone. It was fully charged. My gas tank was full, and as I turned the key in the ignition, I made up my mind to take David's advice. I'd be doing the driving out to Indian Springs.

I arrived at the Silverado with a minute or two to spare and waited at a table in the coffee shop. When the waitress showed up, I ordered coffee. As I sat there, I almost hoped Victoria would stand me up. I was still a little uneasy about driving into the darkness with her.

Whenever I have doubts about whether I should do something a little adventurous, I think about my Aunt Melanie. Back in the middle sixties, when she nineteen or twenty, she spent a heavily chaperoned summer in England with a group from her college.

The day before she flew home from London was a Sunday. Auntie Melanie wanted to visit St. Paul's one last time. Another girl said she'd go with her, and the chaperones decided to let them. At the last minute, the other girl decided not to go.

"But it was my last chance," Auntie Melanie said. "I was already dressed in my hat and gloves."

So, breaking all the rules, she hailed a cab and went on her own. After the service, she stepped out in front of the cathedral. As she stood there hoping a taxi would appear, a young man approached her.

"He was in his twenties, and he was wearing a dark blue three-piece suit," she said. "He bowed slightly and asked me if he could be of service. Well, my first reaction was to step away. This was exactly the reason we had chaperones—to keep us safe from men with bad intentions." She would always chuckle at this point.

"But he kept talking politely while I kept looking around for a cab. He realized I was an American after I spoke a few words. 'A flower of the colonies,' he called me, and we both laughed. We chatted some more. I was about to ask directions to the Underground when he said, 'I know this is terribly forward of me, but would you do me the honor of accompanying me to a garden party this afternoon?'"

Auntie Melanie thought for a moment. The young man seemed decent, and his manners were perfect. She had a hundred dollars in travelers' cheques in her handbag and two ten-pound notes tucked into her bra. When I was a kid, I never let her leave out that part of the story.

"I had money in case I needed to get a ride back to London," she would tell me, "but I still should have said no."

"Then why did you go?" I would always ask. I could answer the question myself, but I loved hearing her say the words.

"I seized the opportunity!" When I was little, she would grab me and hold me tight. "It was too precious to let it get away!"

And oh, was it ever. Christopher Drummond drove Auntie Melanie to a palatial manor in Windsor in his shiny green Jaguar E-Type.

"With the top down," Auntie Melanie said. "It was a beautiful day, and he loaned me his college scarf."

All this would have made my aunt's story more than enough to enchant me, but there was more. At the party, Christopher Drummond introduced my aunt to Princess Margaret!

"Oh, she was beautiful!" my aunt would say. "And she was wearing the most glamorous pink straw hat. I was so glad I was dressed for church, and that I had learned how to curtsey."

And then she would show me how to curtsey, "because you just never know when you might need to."

While curtseying was not a skill I'd be likely to need at the New Moon Ceremony, I reminded myself about the other lesson from my aunt's story. Spending a few hours with a prostitute at a cult site in the desert was an opportunity I might never have again.

Just then I saw her, over near the roulette table. She was dressed all in black spandex except for a wide silver belt cinched tight around her waist. Two women were talking to her, and a guy in a cowboy hat. *Oh, my God.* She was signing autographs.

"Copper!" Victoria said as soon as she saw me. "I'm so glad you could make it!" She sat down, reached across the table, and patted my hand.

"Would you like some coffee?" I asked, "Or do we need to get going?"

"I'm fine," she said, "but finish yours. We've got plenty of time."

I took a sip and watched her as she pulled a little mirror out of her huge shoulder bag and checked her makeup.

"The Sekhmet Temple's my church," she said, putting the mirror away and zipping her bag up. "I don't get out there very often, but it's always there for me. Supportive, nonjudgmental. I grew up Catholic, but …" she paused and smiled. "Let's just say I'm even less salvageable than Mary Magdalene."

"Thank you for inviting me," I said. "I'm still pretty new in town, and—"

"It's totally my pleasure, Copper," Victoria said. "I was hoping we could talk some more. I wanted to …" She hesitated as I took my last swallow of coffee. "Maybe we should get going. We can talk while we drive."

"Oh—" I paused. "I'd like to drive, if you don't mind. I've got my laptop in my car, and—"

Much to my relief, Victoria agreed immediately.

"But there's some stuff in my car I need to take along," she said. So after I'd paid for my coffee, we took a detour by her blue Taurus. She pulled a cardboard box full of files from its trunk, and we loaded it into the Max. Following her directions, I headed north on Interstate 15 and then out into the desert on Highway 95. On the way, Victoria did most of the talking, filling me in on more of her views about women, sex workers, prostitution laws, and the "misogynistic double standards pervading our entire socio-political landscape."

She really talked like that. It was weird to hear that kind of dialogue coming from a platinum-blonde prostitute who sold lipsticks, and I was surprised to find I agreed with her more than I disagreed. I've never understood why people keep trying to make laws about what consenting adults do in private, and it seems to me that governments would be better off regulating and taxing prostitution than wasting money trying to stamp it out. Victoria still struck me as an exhibitionistic media hound, but I found myself admiring her courage. She was standing up to the bigwigs at American Beauty and to their high-powered lawyers, and she was standing on principle. The owner of the Beavertail wanted her to shut up, too.

"I knew I was setting myself up for a public lynching when I went to Albuquerque for the regional pageant," Victoria said. "But I also figured it was my big chance to really—finally—make a difference. You shouldn't have to keep it a secret if you're a sex worker. You should be able to tell people and feel proud that you're in a profession that helps people. It's kind of like teaching, or nursing." I could see her looking at me in my peripheral vision, seeing what I thought of this argument and calculating what she would say next.

"And even if you do nothing more than provide pleasure and entertainment," she went on, "what's so bad about that? Isn't that what actors do, and singers? How come only prostitutes get treated like lepers?"

I said nothing, but my mind was whirling. I didn't know whether I agreed with Victoria's reasoning, but I didn't want to argue with her. I just wanted her to keep talking.

"Sometimes I think it's hopeless," Victoria said, "and these days I worry a lot about my husband and my son. Richard—that's my husband—he totally has my back, but he's a private kind of guy, and now he avoids going outside the house or answering the phone. And we're both worried about our son—"

Victoria paused. We both sat silent for a few seconds. I could tell Victoria was struggling with what to say next.

"Copper, I've got to finish what I started. Otherwise—well, what did I do any of this for? Meeting you was a sign. You showed up unexpectedly, like a spirit guide or—" She stopped herself. "I'm sorry. That's just what the Crone Witch would say."

The Crone Witch? Who—or what—was that? Where was this conversation going? Maybe my family and coworkers were right. I had no business heading out into the desert with—

"What I mean is, you came on your own time yesterday," Victoria said. "You must really be interested in the issues."

"I am," I said slowly, buying myself time while I considered what to say next. "But I don't know if—"

"Is David your boyfriend?"

"What? No!"

"Well, he likes you. That's pretty obvious."

I could feel a blush creeping up my cheeks, and I hoped it didn't show in the dark.

"He's just a colleague," I said. "We went to the same college."

"I wish you were writing the story," Victoria said.

"David's an excellent writer. He'll do a good job."

"He's a guy. Even my husband doesn't always understand."

God, how could her husband *ever* understand? I wondered. I just couldn't get my head around the idea of multiple sex partners. I've never bought into the "save yourself for marriage" credo, but I've always been a serial monogamist. So, pretty much, have my friends. It's always been kind of an unwritten rule that you don't warm the sheets with a new flame until you've shown the old one the door. It's a mix of morality, self-image, and fear of disease, I think. It's bad karma to cheat, unpleasant to be labeled a slut, and getting herpes is an obvious downer. But here was Victoria, a married mother, sharing her assets with all comers. Her marriage seemed to be intact, and she didn't seem the least bit worried about being damned to hell or any other dire moral consequence. I was dying to know more about what went on inside her head, but I didn't feel comfortable enough to ask, at least not yet.

"Everybody always says men can separate sex from love with no trouble," Victoria said, "but that's not what they do at all. They just divide women into two categories. The ones they can take home to Mama, and the ones they can't."

And which are you? I wondered. Does your husband's mama know what you do?

"Do you believe in love?" I asked.

Victoria was silent a moment before she answered.

"No. I don't believe in love."

Well, that explains how you do your job, I thought.

"Do you believe in toothaches?" she asked.

"What?" I glanced at her. "I don't think pain is something you believe in. It just happens."

"That's how I feel about love. It isn't a matter of belief. It shows up and—eats you alive."

We were both silent a moment.

"Everything I do, I do for love," Victoria said. "I do it for my husband and my kid, but the world thinks I do it for money." She laughed. "Actually, they're right. I *do it* for money."

"It's a business," I said, trying to keep her talking without injecting my own views into the conversation.

"Yes. It's a business. And I care about my clients the same way a lawyer or a doctor cares. I don't take them home with me, but I care."

"Who are they?" I asked.

"Your dad, your uncle, your brother."

My brother. I sincerely doubted it. My dad? Never!

"So—ordinary guys."

"And some not so ordinary. I just spent a few weeks teaching a half-paralyzed bull rider how to have sex again. His fiancée sent me flowers."

She shrugged.

"And some are disgusting, frankly. Smelly, perverted, violent—you name it. But talk to a public defender sometime. They get bad guys for clients, too. It doesn't make their work less valuable."

"What about romance?" I said. "Do you believe in that?"

"Of course. What would life be without wine and roses?"

I didn't say anything.

"The only real difference between a traditional date and a date at a brothel is honesty."

She paused, but I still didn't have anything to say.

"Think about it, Copper," she said. "A guy buys you dinner and a movie. He's expecting sex in exchange, right?"

"Maybe," I said.

"No maybe about it. He does. But he never knows if he's going to get it, and that's why so many guys like brothels. No games. You pay to play, and everybody gets lucky. And let me tell you, I get a lot more than food and a flick for a f—for my services."

I found myself resisting her logic. I hadn't worked out a coherent argument, but I knew there was more to dating than negotiating for sex. My relationship with Daniel certainly had a lot more to it. We'd hammered it out on many levels, and we were even beginning to think in the long term.

"Here's the turnoff," Victoria said. "Make a left."

The night was as black as I had predicted when we parked in a dirt lot near the highway. I followed Victoria up a sloping path, straining to see well enough to avoid running into a cactus or stepping on a snake. Then, as we crested the low hill, there it was, lighting up the desert for at least a hundred yards in every direction.

The Sekhmet Temple is a small, gazebo-like structure that looks like it's made of adobe. It has four archways open to the four directions, and the roof is a lattice dome formed out of curved copper piping. The fire blazing in the central hearth turned the interior bright gold, and the flames cast long, dancing shadows across the sand outside.

Outside the temple and not too far away, another fire was burning in a pit. This one had a big cauldron suspended over it, and a woman in a purple cape was stirring its contents with a long wooden stick. More women were sitting on logs. One or two sported similar long cloaks, but the others were dressed more like Victoria and me, in jeans and jackets.

One of the women stood up immediately when she saw us. She was tall, and the word that popped into my head was "stunning." She had long, straight, bleached blonde hair and a model's body. Her leather jacket was unzipped, and two perfect globes pushed out a V-necked ribbed sweater underneath it. Her skintight jeans were low enough to expose her navel, which was practically at my eye level. It was pierced with a diamond stud.

"Good," she said. "You made it."

"Hi, Heather," Victoria said. "This is Copper."

Heather surprised me with a fast hug instead of a handshake. She was wearing the same musky perfume Victoria had on.

"Heather's my other business partner," Victoria said. "We met at the Beavertail some years back, and now Heather's our CFO."

"She makes it sound so corporate," Heather said, "but yeah, I'm the bean counter. Math and money have always been my strong suits."

And here I was thinking her looks were her major asset.

Just then, two more women appeared, both swathed in black cloaks. One was young and dark haired, and the other, silver-headed and sixtyish, was smoking a cigar and leaning on a cane.

"It's the Crone Witch," Victoria whispered, "and that's Moon Raven with her. Her apprentice."

The Crone Witch! She was a real person, and she looked like a grandmother. Somehow that helped me relax a little. The Crone Witch hobbled over to an upended log that had been sawn into a sort of chair. Moon Raven helped her settle into it and relit her cigar.

"So," the Crone Witch said after a thoughtful puff, "I see we have a visitor."

I was surprised to find out that the Crone Witch was a chatty extrovert. Her real name was Paula, and she was originally from Norwalk, Connecticut. That gave us a few things in common, like her niece went to New Canaan High School a few years before me and had Mr. McNabb for biology.

The only thing Egyptian about the New Moon Ceremony was the big black fiberglass statue of Sekhmet standing against one wall of the temple. Everything else reminded me of the year my college roommate dabbled in witchcraft, which she insisted the rest of us call "Wicca." Annie spent nearly two semesters collecting odd-smelling herbs in baby food jars and murmuring, "So mote it be." She asked me along to ceremonies a number of times, but I never went. It always seemed too silly.

Now I think maybe I should have swallowed my pride. I loved the Crone Witch's ritual from the beginning, when she threw down her cane and galloped around the outside of the temple "casting the circle." The rest of us, ringing the hearth inside, held hands and listened to her feral incantations answer the bark of a distant coyote.

At St. Mark's in New Canaan, religion followed a boring old script in a book. It was pleasant in a Shakespearean sort of way, but the only real spontaneity I can remember is when people told Pope jokes at coffee hour. Even at the tender age of twelve, when I knelt in front of the bishop for my confirmation, I had the sneaking suspicion that the Episcopal Church was just a politically correct social club for wealthy white people in designer clothes.

But out there in the desert, holding hands with a hooker while a witch darted by outside, I suddenly realized what I had been longing for when I read fairy tales and Tolkien, which is what I did all the time growing up. I wanted something more dangerous than an extra-large slug of communion wine. I wanted wildness. I wanted a true feeling of connection with the divine, and shouldn't that be a little scary? The fierce lion-headed goddess was beginning to make sense to me. If I'm going to have a deity on my side, she might as well have fangs.

Not that the rest of the ceremony had anything to do with violence. It was warm and personal, in fact. We held hands. We repeated the Crone Witch's affirmations for energy, creativity, and neighborly love. At one point, we faced each person in turn and shouted her name three times.

"Victoria! Victoria! Victoria!"

I was really jealous of that name. It sounds so powerful—in a totally different way from mine.

"Copper! Copper! Copper!"

I don't hate my name, and I dearly loved the great-aunt who had it before me. It's just that everyone always cracks jokes about how I should have gone into law enforcement. Fortunately, the Crone Witch said you can call yourself whatever you want, and if I ever go to her temple again, I'm going to pick a name that doesn't sound like a cry for help when you shout it.

At the end of the ceremony, the Crone Witch announced it was time to cackle.

"Yes, I said *cackle*," she repeated when she noticed my surprise. "Long and loud. Let the goddess cackle through you."

As the hyena-like hoots and squawks of a dozen women rose through the open roof of the Sekhmet Temple, I couldn't help thinking that Ed Bramlett hadn't been too far off the mark. On the other hand, I couldn't help admiring a religion that requires its worshippers to laugh.

When the rites were complete, and after we'd sampled the lentil soup that had been simmering in the big pot over the fire outside, I followed Victoria and Heather back to the parking area, where Heather stopped by a black pickup and unlocked the door.

"It was nice to meet you, Copper," she said. "Thank you so much for helping Victoria."

As soon as we climbed back into the Max, I turned to Victoria.

"I'm sorry," she said before I could get a word out. "Heather assumed I'd already asked you."

"Asked me what?" I said as Victoria leaned between the seats and pulled her cardboard box forward.

"I wasn't sure what I was going to do with this box tonight," she said, pulling out a fat manila folder and opening it on her lap. It was overflowing with newspaper clippings and Xeroxed pages.

"What is it?" I said.

"Pretty much everything that's happened since my husband wrote that winning essay," Victoria said. "That got me my first TV interview, and it's been a whirlwind ever since I won the local pageant. Copies of all the newspaper stories, web pages, threatening letters, memos, some tapes, my notes, my lawyer's notes …" She sighed. "I've got a battle royale ahead of me. American Beauty has an army of attorneys determined to shut me up, and they've got publicists telling their side of the story. It's David and Goliath, and sometimes I wonder if it's worth it." She stuffed the file back into the box and looked at me. "A big part of me wanted to lug all this stuff up the hill and chuck it into the fire."

"You mean just give up?" I said.

"Yeah, and get on with my life. Take care of my family. This is really hard on them, and it's not their battle." She paused and looked at me again. Our eyes met. "I think if I hadn't met you, I really would have burned the box."

"What do I have to do with it?"

"You're a journalist, you're a woman, and I think you might care," Victoria said. "If I give you my files, will you tell my story?"

I stared at Victoria. If I hadn't been so surprised, I would have cackled.

Chapter 4

On our way back from the Sekhmet Temple, Victoria told me that she was expected back at the Beavertail Ranch on Thursday, and she wouldn't be off again until New Year's Eve.

"Once you check in for work, you don't leave the ranch until your next break," she said. "I wanted to be off for Christmas, but nobody wants to work on Christmas. So we had a lottery, and I had to settle for taking New Year's off."

I don't know what my face was saying, but it made Victoria smile. "I think of it as working on a cruise ship. If I were a massage therapist on the *Emerald Princess*, wouldn't this all sound perfectly normal?"

Victoria didn't seem to expect an answer, so I didn't say anything.

"I started working at the Beavertail after Richard's accident," she continued. "When we first started talking about it, it was just a joke. But I don't have a college degree, and I'm over forty. Makes it tough in this town. I couldn't find a job worth doing that paid more than eight bucks an hour."

"What about your beauty business?"

"It's funny how things worked out. Four years ago, Richard brought home a good paycheck. American Beauty bought us a few extras, like dinner at Andre's or a trip to Tahoe. A good little housewife hobby—that's all it was. I sold lipsticks to girls I met at the gym or the beauty salon.

"Then came the midnight call from University Medical Center. Richard was working late on a crane at the Fashion Show Mall. A metal beam fell on his arm, and it almost had to be amputated. He'll never have total use of his left hand again, and he still needs more surgeries on his elbow."

"May I ask you something?" I said.

"Anything you want."

"What does your son think?"

Victoria didn't say anything for a minute or two.

"Up until a few days ago, Jason thought I worked as a massage therapist on a cruise ship."

"And now?"

"I had to tell him. I couldn't let him find out on TV or from kids at school." She paused, and when she looked at me, her eyes were glistening with unshed tears. "The toughest part wasn't telling him, though. The toughest part was admitting I lied in the first place." She paused and wiped her eyes with the back of her hand. "That poor kid. And I can't even be home with him for Christmas."

"Do you have plans for New Year's?" I asked.

"I have plans for a better new year," Victoria said. "Everything will be better once American Beauty coughs up a good settlement."

Back at the Silverado, I pulled in next to Victoria's blue Taurus.

"We have a lot more talking to do, Copper," she said. "We can do it by phone, or you'd be more than welcome to come out to Pahrump."

As curious as I was about the Beavertail, I decided to go with the telephone idea. Victoria said she'd call me around ten on Sunday morning, when she'd be "off shift." I drove home, debating the whole way about whether I'd tell David Nussbaum about the box behind my seat.

❖❖❖

Thursday, December 15

Wednesday disappeared in a hectic blur of holiday updates, but Thursday started off quietly. Not long after I arrived at work, Chris Farr asked me if I wanted to write a movie review. The regular reviewer's father had come down with meningitis in Colorado. It wasn't a sure thing, because the reviewer had an intern. But if the intern was too busy, I would get to go to an advance screening of an independent flick called *Toto Too* at the Village Square. The Village Square is one of the few theaters in Las Vegas that shows stuff besides the latest blockbusters. I had never heard of *Toto Too*, but a review with my byline would make a nice addition to my portfolio.

Everything settled down into the usual routine after that, but a triple latte had given me an energy boost. I was alert enough to realize I had better read Victoria's files before Daniel flew in from Costa Rica and my parents arrived from Connecticut.

Christmas hadn't started out as a family reunion. My original plan was to go to Costa Rica for a week, but Daniel had never been to Las Vegas, and we decided that New Year's on the Strip was too good to pass up. Then Sierra asked my parents to come for Thanksgiving, but they'd already decided to spend it in Rhode Island with my mother's sister. So now everybody would end up here on December 23rd—God, it was only a week away. Thinking about Daniel brought a warm glow to my belly. Thinking about Mom and Dad turned the glow into a knot.

Just before I left for the day, David Nussbaum stopped by my cube.

"I'm glad I caught you," he said. "I've been swamped all day, but I wanted to ask you how things went Tuesday night."

"I liked the Sekhmet Temple," I said, still unsure whether I should tell him about Victoria's box of documents. "Everyone was really friendly." I paused. "I like Victoria, too. I think she deserves a lot of respect for what she's doing."

"Maybe," David said. "Or maybe she just likes all the attention."

"There's a lot more to her than that," I said. "I'll keep you posted. I'm talking with her again on Sunday."

David raised his eyebrows.

"I'm only taking your advice, David," I said. "Remember how you told me that the best way to move up is to sell a good freelance piece?"

"Just be careful. Victoria's got an agenda."

So do I, I thought, but all I did was nod.

Chapter 5

Friday, December 16

No more than two minutes after I arrived at work, David Nussbaum appeared at my desk and said, "The Alliance for the Homeless is holding a press conference this morning."

"I know," I said. "Say hi to my brother for me."

The Alliance for the Homeless is Michael's big community project. He and his fellow board members were finally ready to announce that they had succeeded in acquiring a piece of land for a new service center across from Willow Lake, a wastewater treatment plant in the old part of Las Vegas. Tonight, they were holding something they were billing as a "gala" in a big white tent they had pitched on the property.

"You can say hi yourself," David said. "You're going with me."

"What are you talking about?" I said. "I'm not going to any press conference. It's bad enough that I have to go to the party tonight."

"You have to come," David said. "Chris's orders."

Just then, my phone rang. It was Chris Farr.

"David Nussbaum needs you to help him cover a press conference, Copper. We're in good shape here. Get David what he needs, then you can take the rest of the day off."

"I'll meet you in the lobby in half an hour," David said when Chris hung up. "The conference starts at eleven."

It was very, very weird. Why was the arts and entertainment editor sending his Calendar Girl to hear about the plight of Las Vegas's homeless population? And where did David Nussbaum get off ordering me around? The guy was way too pushy, and he also talked way too loud.

As we climbed into his Jeep, David said, "Copper, I really am covering the press conference, and I really do want you to come with me, but I also have something to tell you."

Weirder and weirder, I thought. David hadn't even put the key into the ignition.

"I had to check out a police investigation early this morning," he said. "Down near Blue Diamond Road. A jogger found a body just before dawn. Have you heard about it?"

"What? No."

David paused and locked his door. He reached up and adjusted his rearview mirror. Then he sighed and looked at me.

"I thought there was a chance you hadn't, even though it was a freaking media circus. I wanted to be the one to tell you if I could."

I stared at him.

"Who was it?" I asked.

"Victoria McKimber."

What?

Was I hearing right? Victoria *McKimber?* How could she be dead? She was just riding in my car on Tuesday night. She was fine! She had plans!

"Victoria is *dead?*" I said. "What happened?"

"There still has to be an autopsy, but it looks like she bled to death," David said.

Nothing was making any sense. What was Victoria even doing on Blue Diamond Road? She was supposed to be at the Beavertail.

"I'm so sorry, Copper," David went on. "I know you were getting to know her. It's such a shock."

"How could she bleed to death?" I interrupted. Was she shot?"

"No, no gunshot wound, but that's the only thing that's clear. She might have been hit by a car, or she might have been beaten.

"God. She told me she had enemies, but—"

"They're still trying to figure out whether she was killed where she was found or just dumped there."

"So she was murdered?"

"Not necessarily. It could have been an accident."

"I don't know," I said. "Like I said, she had enemies."

"The police will sort it out," David said.

"What do you think?"

"I don't know. All we can do is give the detectives a chance to do their work."

I didn't say anything.

"Anyway, I really am sorry," David said. "It's always hard when you know a victim. And I can see you liked her."

"I don't know if I liked her. But I did respect her."

❖ ❖ ❖

I was grateful that the press conference was unpleasant enough to take my mind off Victoria's death. The Alliance for the Homeless had been trying to close the deal on its godforsaken piece of land for over a year. The property was a large desolate triangle wedged between railroad tracks and the wastewater treatment plant. The only "improvements" on the property were a warehouse with a caved-in roof and a dilapidated trailer. The police swarmed the place every few days to evict homeless men, and every so often there'd be a fistfight. You'd think the city and the county and the other powers that be would be thrilled that a nice nonprofit organization wanted to invest in a piece of land less inviting than the surface of Mars. It was crazy that they were giving Michael and his well-intentioned colleagues such a hard time, when all they wanted to do was clean up an eyesore and get some homeless people off the streets.

The press conference was held on the property, which had been spiffed up considerably for the party later that day. Sierra was one of the organizers, and she'd been complaining all week about how hard it was to cover up oily dirt. They'd had to rent at least an acre of Astroturf. Fortunately, the big white tent hid the crappy buildings pretty well, and with the forest of potted palms they'd trucked in, the whole place would look pretty decent after dark.

Things were going okay until a gadfly columnist from the *Las Vegas Herald-Dispatch* asked a question that made everyone in front of the microphones stop smiling.

"What happens if the deal doesn't close?" Randolph Berman asked.

"It's as good as closed," said the woman standing next to Michael. She was wearing a rust-red power suit that almost exactly matched her hair. "If it weren't, we wouldn't be going ahead with the gala tonight."

"Don't you lose your funding on December 31st?"

"We aren't losing any funding, and—"

"Let me say something," Michael interrupted. My brother smiled beatifically and took his time before he spoke. It's his favorite tactic for calming difficult situations.

"Mr. Berman," he said after a long minute. "It's true that the final documents haven't been executed, but this has been a complex transaction. Everything will be finalized tomorrow, and the Alliance for the Homeless will at last be able to—"

"But Reverend Black—"

Michael has always hated being called Reverend, but he didn't let it ruffle him. He just started talking again in his Sermon on the Mount voice.

"We are grateful to all of you for joining us here this morning, and we're looking forward to an even happier day when we open our new service center's doors. Now, if you'll join me in prayer—"

He pulled it off. Michael actually made Randy Berman shut up. The only sad part was that the stories in tomorrow's papers, including David's, wouldn't be about the Alliance's altruistic plans, but rather about all the legal and financial troubles.

"I have to write about it, Copper," David said as we left in his Jeep. "The land isn't theirs, and it's true that the matching grant money disappears at the end of the year. That's not much more than a week away, if you subtract holidays and weekends. The deal was supposed to close over a month ago, and it still hasn't. I'm sorry, but that's—"

"I know. You don't have to tell me. That's the story."

And then, damn it, I cried. I don't even know why. I didn't give a rat's ass about the Alliance for the Homeless, and I hardly knew Victoria. I couldn't believe it, but I also couldn't help it. I sat there snuffling, and I didn't even have a Kleenex.

"*Cleopatra must die.*"

I didn't mean to say it out loud, but the words popped out.

"What?" David asked.

"Oh, nothing," I said, still sniffling. "It was just the name of my—no really, nothing." But I'd said too much. David was staring at me.

"'Cleopatra Must Die' was the title of my senior thesis."

"That sounds like a history topic. I thought you majored in English."

"I did. It was about—do you really want to hear this?"

"I do."

"Cleopatra, Joan of Arc, Antigone—strong women …"

"Who die," David finished.

I nodded. "I tried to make the case that as literary characters, they're killed off to maintain the status quo."

"I guess they are," David said. "Uppity women, all of them."

"Yeah, I admit it. It was a feminist rant, and I'm not even sure I proved my point, but—"

"Victoria."

Fresh tears sprang to my eyes. I nodded, unable to speak.

"You're right," David said. "She was trying to disturb the status quo."

"And she's dead," I said. "Just like she would have been in a play by George Bernard Shaw."

We just sat there for a minute or two.

When I finally stopped hiccupping, David said, "Have you ever been to the Art House?"

"No," I said, but I knew about it. The Art House is a trendy downtown restaurant favored by people who work for the city and county.

"Want to grab a bite to eat?" David asked, and I readily agreed.

I felt better as soon as I walked inside. The lunch rush hadn't begun, and the hostess told us to sit wherever we liked. David ushered me to a booth in the corner. A big framed print of Marilyn Monroe trying to keep her dress from flying up hung over the table. Another dead woman, I thought, but I refused to let it bother me. It was time to pull myself together and act like a grownup.

"What do you want to drink?"

"Iced tea," I said. Later, when I took a sip, I realized he'd ordered the "Long Island" kind.

"You don't have to drink it," David said, "but I thought you could use it."

He was right, even though it was only 11:30.

◈◈◈

At home, I was immediately tempted to zone out on beer and DVDs. I wished I didn't have to go to the gala, but I had promised Michael and Sierra I'd play handmaiden to the celebrity guest. It was going to be Wayne Newton, but he had cancelled a week earlier. His replacement was a Cuban singer-comedian-dancer named Mirandela, and I was supposed to hold her pink guitar while she struck a photogenic pose with a decorated shovel.

God! I couldn't help wondering why I wasn't teaching kindergarten in Connecticut.

That always works. Whenever I picture myself wearing a denim smock and asking a roomful of five-year-olds whether they have to go "Number One or Number Two," I come to my senses. Victoria's demise had been a shock, but I had to get used to things like sudden death if I was going to make it as a journalist.

Limiting myself to one pale ale, I started organizing all the stuff in the box Victoria had given me. It didn't take long to think she really might have been a victim of foul play. American Beauty's executives and attorneys had been trying very hard to shut Victoria up. There were several cease and desist orders in one of the folders, and a restraining order requiring her to stay away from American Beauty headquarters. Newspaper articles quoting American Beauty repre-sentatives accused Victoria of pandering and illegal solicitation—an obvious smear campaign. All that effort had to be expensive. Killing her and making it look like an accident would be an effective and permanent way to silence her.

I also discovered that Victoria was in an ongoing feud with the owner of the Beavertail Ranch, a guy named Kent Freeman. He had made it clear in a couple of terse memos that he didn't like the kind of publicity Victoria was generating for the brothel, and he had even threatened to bar her from working there. What if his next step had been to dispatch someone to take care of things?

The more I read, the more I realized that I should still write Victoria's story. It was the least I could do for her, I thought, but I knew that was only partly true. Victoria deserved an advocate, but I was also thinking about my journalism career. Truth be told, Victoria's story might well be more compelling now that she was dead.

Except I needed to know more, and that meant I had to find out how to reach Heather, the woman I had met at the Sekhmet Temple. She'd not only be able to answer my questions, but she'd have good reason to want to know what really happened to her business partner.

Chapter 6

Around five, I had to start worrying about how I looked. I wouldn't have cared very much, but the San Marino, a new casino out at Lake Las Vegas, was sending a limo to pick us up. Sierra said there might be photographers because the San Marino was hoping to get some publicity for helping out the Alliance. Fortunately, I had recently acquired the most awesome little black dress in the universe, and I also had a new little plastic clip that was guaranteed to trap my hair in a perfect French twist.

I was ready at six, but the limo still hadn't arrived twenty minutes later. Leaving me to wait for it, Michael and Sierra took off in Michael's Jetta. I wasn't happy about being left behind until I met the limo driver. He was about my age, and his name was Adrian. He was very apologetic about the delay.

"I was taking care of a spoiled Japanese whale," he said, and I was grateful I'd been in Las Vegas long enough to know he wasn't talking about a decomposing marine mammal.

"Don't worry about it," I said. "High rollers are bigger tippers than I'm going to be."

I kind of wanted to ride in the front seat with him so we could chat, but I was afraid it might look wrong when we arrived at the gala. It turned out we could chat anyway through the window behind his head.

"Help yourself to a drink," Adrian said as he got onto the freeway and headed north. "Because of the whale, the bar's better stocked than usual." What the heck, I figured, and I poured a slug from a Johnnie Walker bottle with a blue label.

"So how long you been living in Vegas?" Adrian asked.

"How do you know I'm not a native?" I said.

"You aren't, are you?"

"No."

"This job teaches you things," Adrian said.

I'd finished my Scotch by the time Adrian pulled the limo up to the Astroturf in front of the white tent. I had imagined that there would be strobes flashing when I got out, but I was wrong. Nobody seemed to notice my arrival, and that was actually a good thing because when I stood up, I was suddenly aware that I hadn't put much besides alcohol into my stomach all day.

"I'll be over there," Adrian said as he shut the door. He pointed to a dusty lot where other cars were parked. "We can leave any time you want to," he added, taking my elbow. "Are you okay?"

"I'm fine," I said, but I think I was wobbling a little as I went to look for Michael.

When I found him, he was talking to David Nussbaum.

"What are you doing here?" I said. "I thought things like this were Alexandra Leonard's beat."

"They are, but she got food poisoning at the St. Jude's Christmas party. So here I am."

Just then the red-haired woman who'd been on stage at the press conference grabbed Michael's arm. She was wearing a black cocktail dress remarkably like my own, and I could swear she'd used the same kind of clip on her hair.

"Ozzie's here," she said, and no further words were necessary to spirit my brother away to greet the mayor.

"Do you know who she is?" David asked as we watched them shake hands with Oswald Brightman and his wife.

"An Alliance board member, I assume."

"Her name's Julia Saxon," David said, and I turned to him with my mouth open.

"Julia Saxon? Really?" The name was all over the files in Victoria's cardboard box.

"Yeah, but lots of people have other names for her."

"She was Victoria McKimber's lawyer."

"Doesn't surprise me," David said. "Las Vegas is a very small town." He draped his arm around my shoulders and added, "That's why you see so many people with teeth marks on their asses."

I had no idea what he was talking about, and my head was beginning to ache.

"I'm supposed to find Mirandela," I said. "I'm her keeper tonight."

"I'm not sure you have that assignment anymore," David said, pointing to Julia again. She was greeting Mirandela and a paunchy guy in a baby blue tux as they stepped out of a lime green limo.

"I didn't want the damn job, anyway," I said, surprised at the flash of anger I felt. "I've got to go find my sister-in-law. I'm supposed to be helping her."

My new job was to inform guests of their table assignments, and as I sat matching names with numbers, I was amazed at how many names I recognized. David was right. Las Vegas is a small town, but its global reputation makes everyone think it's on a par with New York.

I kind of wished I could sit with David for dinner, but my assigned seat was at the head table with the board members, and David had to sit with the "press corps," a small cadre that included the society columnist from the *Herald-Dispatch* and a freelance writer who hands out black business cards embossed in gold with her one and only name: Xenobia. Xenobia has got to be at least eighty-five years old. I've seen her at practically every opening I've attended, always clad in the same purple sequined dress and matching feather boa. A walking Las Vegas history book, she's probably entertaining to talk to, but it takes a stronger constitution than mine to hold up against her perfume. I sat down next to her once at a restaurant opening, realizing a little too late why that particular chair was vacant in a filled-to-capacity room.

I wasn't sitting next to Julia at the head table, but Michael was, and he introduced us. As soon as he had to leave, I took his place.

"I'm so sorry about Victoria McKimber," I said.

That really got Julia's attention. Up to then, she'd been far more interested in chatting with Mirandela, who was sitting on her left.

"You knew Victoria?" she said, and my brain had to work fast. This was my big chance to come off like a real journalist.

"I interviewed her on Monday," I said, "for a story I'm working on for a—a major magazine. I was supposed to meet her again on Sunday—"

"What magazine?" Julia interrupted.

"*Esquire*," I lied. "Victoria gave me an exclusive, and that's why I wanted to talk to you. I've got all her files, and—"

Julia looked at me hard, and there was lots of activity behind her eyes. When she spoke again, she was much friendlier.

"Copper, we should have lunch sometime," she said. "I've really enjoyed working with your brother, and I'd love to have the chance to get to know you better, too."

After she gave me her card, and I'd written my phone number on another, Julia took a big drink of merlot and refilled both our glasses from the bottle on the table.

"Victoria didn't give you any tape recordings by any chance, did she?"

"I haven't come across any so far," I said, remembering the tiny recorder Victoria used the first time I met her. "But I think there are things like that in the files I have. I'll keep an eye out as I work my way through them."

"Thanks," Julia said, patting my arm. "I love your dress, Copper," she added.

"Thanks," I said. "AmaroDolce at the Caesars Forum Shops."

"Hey, I got mine there, too," Julia said. "It's a great store."

Meeting Julia made the Alliance dinner well worth the effort, even though my headache was worse than ever by the time I left. Sierra joined me in the limo for the trip home, and another shot of Scotch from the blue-labeled bottle didn't help.

"So what were you talking to Julia about?" Sierra asked.

"Victoria McKimber."

"Be careful, Copper," Sierra said. "It's really risky to poke around things like that in this town. I'm not joking. Everybody's connected here, and everybody's got turf to protect. You could make some dangerous enemies without even knowing it."

The window behind Adrian's head was open.

"Where'd you go to high school?" he asked.

Then he and Sierra spent the rest of the trip talking about old prom queens at Bonanza.

❖❖❖

Saturday, December 17

It was past midnight, and I was exhausted, but sleep was out of the question. A cat was yowling outside the window next to my bed, which opens out onto the garage roof. Burying my head under two pillows didn't succeed in drowning it out, so I finally gave up. I opened the window and stuck my head out, but before I could pull it back in, the cat was on my shoulder.

It was little thing—almost a kitten, really—a gray tabby with the most perfectly symmetrical face and huge green eyes. I was surprised. I'd thought a horny old tomcat was making all the racket.

I didn't have any milk, but the cat happily gobbled up a whole can of tuna and half a carton of yogurt. After that, I didn't know what to do. I couldn't bring myself to throw it out into the cold again, even though it probably had fleas. I finally made a bed out of a plastic bin and a beach towel, but all it wanted to do was sit in my lap, knead my thigh, and purr.

I finally fell asleep, and when I woke up around eight o'clock, there was a cat on my chest. After I tossed it out onto the garage roof, I threw on some sweats and went into the house to have breakfast with Michael and Sierra. Sierra watches a lot of cooking shows and owns at least fifty thousand cookbooks. She "creates something" most Saturdays, and I was hoping a big serving of something rich and buttery might take the edge off my hangover. She makes good coffee, too.

"How are you feeling this morning?" Sierra asked as she pulled breakfast out of the oven. "I'm surprised you're up."

"A cat did it," I said.

"What cat?"

"One that yowled on the garage roof until I let it in."

"Did you feed it?"

"A whole can of tuna and half a container of yogurt."

"It's yours."

"What if I don't want it?"

"Doesn't have much to do with it," Sierra said. "If the cat wants you, you don't have a chance." She sighed. "I'm jealous. No cat's tried to adopt me since Sammy. I still miss him."

Sammy the Siamese disappeared over a year ago, and suspicion hangs heavily over a big German shepherd two blocks over.

"How bad are the stories?" I asked Michael, who was buried in the first section of *The Light*.

"Oh, we'll survive. Thanks to Julia. She's got a backup plan she says is just as good as the original. The worst that can happen is that we'll build our service center on the north side of Las Vegas instead of downtown."

"Why hasn't the deal closed? I thought you had all the zoning issues dealt with a month ago."

"It's complicated," Michael said, "because we're dealing with two different owners. Most of the land is owned by Paragon Properties, but like a lot of parcels in downtown Las Vegas, a little slice of it is owned by somebody else. Those people still haven't signed off, but Julia's getting it straightened out. She's a real mover and shaker."

Mover and shaker. I've always hated phrases like that, and I was mildly surprised to hear it out of Michael's mouth. Did it mean I'd soon be hearing him describe people as *having juice*? Ugh. On the other hand, juice is exactly what Julia Saxon seemed to have. I couldn't wait to have lunch with her.

Chapter 7

When I checked my email, I found a message from Heather, Victoria's business partner, whom I'd met at the Sekhmet Temple. Victoria must have given her my email address, or at least mentioned that I work for *The Light*. Heather asked if I'd be willing to get together to talk about Victoria, which was exactly what I had in mind. Unfortunately, she was in Reno on business, and she wouldn't be getting back to Las Vegas until Monday.

Heather ended her message with a sentence that made me even more interested in meeting her: "Unless we do something, those bastards at the Beavertail are going to get away with it."

I called David on his cell phone, hoping I wouldn't wake him up or disturb the breakfast phase of an overnight date. He was someplace noisy, though, and I asked him for a copy of the police report about Victoria's death.

"Are you still playing sleuth?" he asked.

"Somebody should be," I said, and I told him about Heather's message.

"The police are investigating, Copper," he said. "Her death really could have been accidental."

"Sure."

"Come on, Copper. Give them a chance. It takes time."

"She had enemies, and she was a prostitute. Cops don't care about people like her."

David ignored me and went on.

"For one thing, they have to work with the Nye County Sheriff. Victoria was supposed to be at the Beavertail when she turned up dead. They have to look into the possibility she died there and then got dumped over here."

David said he'd copy the police report and leave it on my desk.

"But you already know more than what's in it," he added.

As I continued looking through Victoria's files, I came across an audio tape. I didn't have a chance to check it, but I wondered if it was the one Julia Saxon wanted. What I did learn was that the madam at the Beavertail Ranch was named Bernice Broyhill. Victoria had written her two letters, one explaining about the beauty contest and another asking for her support in her feud with Kent Freeman, the Beavertail's owner.

Bernice liked to issue commands on pink Post-It notes: "See me today noon," and "See me ASAP." Only one was more revealing: "See me re: Marks this p.m."

Marks. That was a name I recognized. But then, everybody in Las Vegas knows that name. Charlie Marks has practically been deified for reinventing the Strip and building one blockbuster hotel after another. But why would a guy who owns megaresorts frequent a brothel? Surely he could afford full service blondes direct to his room! It can't be him, I decided. Must be some other Marks.

On the Beavertail's website, I found Bernice Broyhill listed as "shift manager" along with the great news that she was happy to give free tours, "Ladies welcome!" I was more than half tempted to drive to Pahrump and take her up on the offer.

I'd been to Pahrump only once before, when Michael and Sierra took me to the Pahrump Valley Winery for dinner when I first arrived in Las Vegas. "Going over the hump," they called it, because we had to cross the Spring Mountains to get there. They didn't mention anything about brothels, though, and it wasn't until two months later that I learned that Pahrump's X-rated attractions were hidden on the south side of town in their own little unmarked bordello zone. Fortunately, the Beavertail's website provided directions: "West on Highway 160, south on Gamebird Road, east on Homestead to the end. Our doors are always open."

They should have added, "And we'll leave the red light on for you."

❖ ❖ ❖

After thinking things over and realizing that Sierra's breakfast had done a good job of making me human again, I decided to go to Pahrump. Even if I didn't find anything out about Victoria, I'd never have a better chance to see the inside of a cathouse. I had Christmas shopping to do, but it would have to wait. As Auntie Melanie would say, the opportunity was too precious to let it get away.

When I opened my apartment door to leave, I almost stepped on the perfectly dissected interior organs of a large rodent. The cat wasn't gone after all. She'd brought me a gift. Sierra would have called it true love, but all I could say was, "Yuck!" I decided to give the cat a name, though: Sekhmet.

As I headed south on the freeway, I realized I would be driving very near the spot where Victoria's body was found. I wondered if I'd be able to find it, and that thought was enough to pull me off of Blue Diamond Road when I got to Grand Canyon Drive. David had told me the site was less than a quarter mile south, on the right hand side of the road. The pavement ended a few hundred feet from Blue Diamond, and the ditches on both sides of the road had standing water in them. The sky was clear now, but there had obviously been a cloudburst in the area sometime recently. I bumped on down the gravel, and sure enough, I soon spied festoons of yellow caution tape.

I pulled off the road where several cars were parked and joined a few other gawkers watching three men in jeans, sweatshirts, and baseball caps. One was poking around in a creosote bush, and the other two were squatting over a big black stain on the ground. Their gloves, clipboards, measuring tapes, plastic bags, cameras, and little flags made it obvious they were on official business, even though they weren't wearing uniforms.

David was right, I thought as I surveyed the scene. There was a lot of blood. At least I assumed it was blood that had created the big black stain.

"Fuckin' drunk drivers," the man standing next to me said. He was a bearded guy of about fifty wearing a Harley-Davidson T-shirt. "Las Vegas is a dangerous place to be a pedestrian, even way out here."

"You think it was an accident?" I said.

"Happens all the time," the Harley guy said. "Some asshole hit her, realized there were no witnesses, and took off."

It made sense except for one small problem. Victoria was supposed to be at the Beavertail, not alone on an isolated desert road.

❖❖❖

I hung around a little while longer, watching the investigators take pictures and put dirt samples into little bags. One of them mixed up something I guessed was plaster of paris and poured it into a muddy rut. I was tempted to try to talk to them, but when the Harley guy asked them if they had any leads, the one who seemed to be in charge brushed him off with a well-rehearsed line that went something like, "We don't have any information at this time."

I had walked back to the Max before I remembered the digital camera in my backpack. Figuring photos would make a good addition to the article I was planning to write, I walked back and snapped a few pictures of the scene before heading over the Spring Mountains to Pahrump.

❖ ❖ ❖

The cloudburst had dropped a picturesque layer of snow on the rocks and juniper trees at the summit, and I enjoyed a brief feeling of Christmas before descending into the wide dry valley on the other side.

I knew I had arrived at my destination when I caught sight of its tall sign, a cutout of a woman's leg in a fishnet stocking. It had a flashing red light at the top, like the ones at railroad crossings. Under the leg were placards saying "Welcome," "Sports Bar," and "Truck Parking." As I slowed, I saw another sign pounded into the gravel parking lot. "Free Tours. Ladies Welcome."

Beyond the parking lot stood the Beavertail itself. I have no idea what I expected a bordello to look like, but it wasn't trailers. Or maybe they were mobile homes. Whatever their official designation, about eight of them had been dragged there, plunked down to form a big square, and painted a dainty shade of lavender. The trailer facing the parking lot had a big silver Christmas wreath hanging on its door. A potted poinsettia stood on each side of the wooden steps leading up to it.

I decided to park across the road. As I did, a truck from a Las Vegas glass company pulled into the Beavertail's parking lot. A man in white overalls climbed out and disappeared through the door with the Christmas wreath. There was no other activity, just four cars in the parking lot.

God. I wasn't sure I could do this alone. On the other hand, that was the only way I could do it at all. David wouldn't have come with me unless the newspaper told him to, and my brother would have had an aneurysm if he had known where I was. Anyway, what was the worst that could happen? In a few days, somebody would report a white Chrysler minivan abandoned out on Homestead Road, and the search for my body would begin.

When I finally got up enough nerve to approach the front door of the Beavertail, it swung open and almost hit me. The man in white overalls brushed past me like I wasn't there, and I found myself face to face with a woman who reminded me of my college Shakespeare professor. Her graying brown hair was pulled up in a librarian's bun, and she was wearing a tweedy suit and a high-necked white blouse.

"Kin ah help you?" she asked, and all thoughts of my Shakespeare professor vanished. Her voice was rough from a century or two of smoking, and she had a truck stop waitress drawl. As I stared at her, she gave me a quick head-to-toe once-over.

"I—I'm here for the tour," I said. Her eyes were still appraising my chest.

"Oh!" the woman said, shifting her gaze to my face. "Sure, hon. Come on in."

She held the door open, and I walked into the whitest room I'd ever seen. Everything was white: the floor, the ceiling, the sofas, the fireplace, the plaster statue of Venus. Even the Christmas tree next to the fireplace was white, and so was the flower arrangement on the white piano, a big urn of fake lilies. There was a faint smell of chemical lemon in the air, like someone had just mopped the floor. Through the window on the back wall, I could see the courtyard formed by the assembled trailers. A white gazebo with a hot tub stood in the center of it.

"Please, have a seat," the woman said, motioning toward a pristine brocade sofa. "Ah'll be back in a jiff."

I didn't sit. I'd caught sight of a small framed placard propped up next to the flower arrangement, and I moved closer to the piano so I could read it. "Menu of Services," it said, and the list began with "Straight Lay." I was pondering what "Extreme French" might be when the woman in the tweedy suit came back.

"Ah'm Bernice Broyhill," she said, holding out her right hand.

"Copper Black," I said, shaking it.

"You want a tour?" she asked, as though she couldn't quite believe it.

"Yes, I—" And if I'd had the chance, I think I would have said, "I'm a reporter." But Bernice was already talking again.

"If you're wonderin' why there aren't any prices on our menu," she said, launching into a sing-songy spiel, "it's because our ladies are independent contractors. Their rates are *in-tar-ly* between themselves and the gentlemen. So are the services they provide. How they accommodate their clients is *in-tar-ly* up to them. Some of our ladies are world famous for their specialties."

Bernice then explained that if I'd been a "gentleman," she would have called a "lineup," and I would have chosen a "lady to party with."

"And if you weren't *quaht* ready to party, you'd be welcome to have a drink in the bar and socialize awhile," she said. She crossed the room and pushed open a saloon-style door. "We're proud of our new sports bar," she continued as she held it open, "and we have a full kitchen and a *gen-you-wine* Core-don Blue chef. If the gentlemen want to party in one of our bungalows, we serve them steak and lobster—real *gore-may* meals."

Bernice kept yakking a mile a minute as she showed me pictures of the bungalows, which were really just more trailers on the other side of the gazebo. Each one had a different theme, like "Psychedelic Sixties" and "Arthur & Guenevere." Then she led me down a hall that looked exactly like a motel except for some artsy black-and-white photos of nude women on the walls. The smell of disinfectant was a little stronger, reminding me of the rest home where my great-grandmother spent her final decade. Just the smell, though. I'm pretty sure Great Grammie's place didn't have a dungeon with shackles attached to the wall or a whirlpool room decorated with Budweiser posters.

"These are our public rooms," Bernice explained as we moved from one to the next. "All our ladies can use them. Their own rooms are *in-tar-ly* private, of course."

I was beginning to wonder if there was anyone else in the building when a door opened and a woman in a skimpy hot-pink tank top and a G-string emerged and walked toward us. Stretched across her obviously augmented breasts was the word "JUICY" spelled out in rhinestones. She was tan and slim and pretty, although I noticed she was missing teeth on both sides of her mouth when she smiled. I couldn't help turning to watch her when she passed, and from the back, it looked like she had nothing on below the waist.

Bernice had launched into a new line of patter about health and cleanliness standards by this time, explaining how nobody had ever contracted a sexually transmitted disease in a legal Nevada brothel. Opening the door of a large closet, she pulled out a plastic bag.

"We call this a trick pack," she said. "The ladies pick one up when they have a client. It's got a sheet, a condom, a towel, and a washrag." When she closed the closet door, I noticed that next to it was a bookcase full of shoes. At least thirty pairs were all lined up neatly, eight-inch stiletto heels facing out. *Slut shoes,* we called them in college, and I almost laughed as I realized just how accurate we had been.

As we rounded the corner and headed back into the living room, Bernice's cell phone rang. She looked at it before she answered, and she wasn't too happy about what her caller ID revealed.

"I've been trying to reach you all morning, Kent," she said. "The glass man was here." She turned away from me. "Close to two grand," I could still hear her say, "and there's only eight hundred in Victoria's account—okay, okay, just git your butt over here, and you can decide for yourself." Bernice snapped her phone shut.

"Sorry," she said. "Where were we?"

And here's where I was either very brave, or very stupid, or both.

"Were you talking about Victoria McKimber?" I asked.

Bernice stared at me.

"I knew her," I said.

"We're all very sorry about her death," Bernice said, her surprise quickly hardening into suspicion.

"Do you know what really happened? I mean, she was supposed to be here when—"

"She was hit by a car," Bernice replied quickly. "A terrible accident."

"I'm not so sure," I said. "I know that's one possibility, but I was hoping you—"

"You've got a lot of nerve coming here and conning me into a tour," Bernice interrupted. "Who are you, anyway?"

"I told you, I—" but Bernice was barking into her cell phone.

"Parlor, Bill," she said. "*Now.*"

Almost immediately, the bar door burst open, and a muscled guy in a black leather jacket was practically on top of me.

"I'm gonna need some *ah-dee*," Bernice said, and while I was still figuring out that she was talking to me, she barked again. "Yer driver's license. Hand it over."

Bill intentionally slid his hand to his hip, pushing his jacket back. Stuck in the waistband of his jeans was a big handgun—the kind hit men use in Mafia movies. Dangling from his belt was a pair of handcuffs.

I didn't waste any time digging my driver's license out of my wallet. Bernice snatched it from my hand and disappeared. Bill moved closer, enveloping me in a disgusting miasma of old cigarettes, breath mints, and sweat. I was just envisioning the cops examining my abandoned body when Bernice came back and slapped my license into my palm. She nodded at Bill, and suddenly I was out in the parking lot.

"Where's your car?" Bill said, his hand gripping my upper arm firmly enough to leave bruises.

"Over there," I said nodding across the street. He marched me to the edge of the road.

"Get in it," he said. "Drive away. Don't *ever* come back." Then he leaned closer. What now? I thought, but when he spoke, he was almost kind.

"You look like a nice girl," he said. "This is a very dangerous place for nice girls."

If he was trying to scare me, it worked. I got in my minivan and drove down Homestead Road so fast I missed the first stop sign and almost hit an old man on a bike. After that, I pulled into the parking lot at the Pair-a-Dice Casino. I needed to calm down, and I knew there would be a coffee shop inside where I could sit until I stopped shaking. As I walked into the smoky darkness, I couldn't help thinking that teaching kindergarten in Connecticut wasn't such a bad idea after all.

An order of fries and a Diet Coke went a long way toward settling my nerves, though I barely touched either of them. I mostly watched legions of blue-haired bingo players mill around while I eavesdropped on a conversation two waitresses were having about their boyfriends. It was all so ordinary that it helped me forget I'd just been evicted from a whorehouse.

When I left the Pair-a-Dice, my plan was to go back to Las Vegas and go Christmas shopping. But as I was driving, I kept thinking about how convenient it was for American Beauty that Victoria was dead. Bernice Broyhill didn't seem exactly broken up, either, and Bill the bouncer looked like he'd make a capable hit man.

I kept seeing the look on Bill's face. He wasn't only trying to scare me. He was trying to warn me.

Warnings. That's all I was getting from everybody—David, Sierra, Michael, Daniel. Except for Heather, not a single person thought I should pursue the truth about Victoria's death.

And maybe I was nuts to think I had something to gain from "poking into things," as Sierra put it. Daniel and my parents would arrive in a few days. It would be Christmas, for God's sake. What was wrong with me? Shouldn't I be at the Caesars Forum Shops buying my mom a big bottle of some new fragrance sensation? I hadn't gotten anything for Daniel yet, either, and I didn't even have a Christmas dress. I love Christmas, and I had never let the holidays go by without acquiring an appropriately festive dress.

The trouble was, I couldn't stop thinking about Victoria, and it went way beyond wanting to be a journalist. I didn't think Victoria was a saint, but she did have a mission. And it was a noble one, I reminded myself. She wanted respect for who and what she was, and she wanted to extend it to all women like her. David might say it was just attention-seeking self-aggrandizement, but I knew he was wrong. I hadn't gotten much of a chance to know Victoria, but it was enough for me to see the crusader in her. She was a natural leader who might have actually been able to reverse an age-old tide of public condemnation and ridicule. And now she was dead. It was awfully convenient for the brothel and American Beauty, but nobody seemed to find that the least bit suspicious. Nobody but me.

Unless her husband cared. I didn't know anything about Richard McKimber except that his left arm was a mess and that he wrote a good essay about Forever Young antiwrinkle cream. Did he miss Victoria horribly? Did he want to wreak revenge on her killer? Or was it just the opposite? Maybe he hated being married to one of Bernice's "ladies." Maybe he took out a huge life insurance policy a couple of weeks ago. Okay, okay, so I've watched too many *Law & Order* reruns.

Anyway, I made a plan. I knew where Victoria lived because her address was in her files: 1075 Chantilly Court. It wasn't far from the big truck stop on Blue Diamond Road, according to my Las Vegas road atlas. There was no harm in driving by, right? At the very least, I could see what kind of house she lived in.

And then—I swore—I was going to do my Christmas shopping.

Chapter 8

I don't know what kind of house I expected Victoria's to be, but—like the brothel—it surprised me. First off, it was in a gated community. Lots of people in Las Vegas live in such enclaves, but I hadn't been inside many of them. Michael and Sierra live in an older section of town that looks more like Anytown, U.S.A. Okay, the house next door to theirs has glitter on the roof, Ionic columns framing the front door, and faux Bernini statuary in the front yard. But if you discount that, ignore the palm trees and cactus, and look at the rest of the block, you might almost think you were in New Jersey.

"Riviera Palms," on the other hand—that was the name engraved on a metal plaque next to the radio-controlled gate at the entrance to Victoria's development—was a collection of newish beige stucco two-stories with red tile roofs. The development looked reasonably nice except for some ugly white water stains along the bottom edges of the perimeter wall and one patch of spray-painted graffiti.

The gate was closed, not surprisingly, although a small pedestrian gate was standing ajar. I was about to park and walk in when a blue sedan pulled up and the gate opened. The car moved through the gate, and before it closed, a crappy-looking pickup truck zipped through behind it. I thought for sure the person in the blue sedan would leap out and confront the man in the pickup. I mean, isn't the point of security gates to keep out burglars and riffraff? But no fisticuffs broke out, so when a white SUV pulled up and opened the gate, I slipped in behind it. Somehow, getting strong-armed out of a brothel had amped up my nerve. Maybe I had what it took to be a real journalist, after all.

I drove along Riviera Lane, which was lined on both sides by nearly identical houses, some with lawns but most with gravel front yards punctuated with prickly desert plants and an amazing assortment of electrically powered Christmas decorations. The place looked deserted, but I knew that was just an illusion. Everybody in Las Vegas keeps their garage doors closed and their drapes drawn, even when they're home. Las Vegas just isn't a porch-sitting kind of town.

Chantilly Court was a four-house cul-de-sac. Number 1075 looked like all the others except the garage door was open. The inside was shadowy, but I could see that it was so full of brown cardboard boxes that there was no room left over for even one car. Victoria's dark blue Taurus was parked in the driveway. A hose was stretched across the driveway, and a pile of stuff—an umbrella, some bags, a folding chair—was lying on the concrete next to the trunk.

Just as I pulled to a stop across the street, a tall man in jeans, a plaid shirt, and a baseball cap emerged from between the stacks of boxes in the open garage. He had a scrubby gray mustache, and he walked like a TV cowboy.

The man sauntered—or maybe it was a limp that made his hips swagger—over to the side of the house and leaned into a shrub. Water shot out of the hose, making it flop around like a snake. He picked it up and aimed it on the front wheel of Victoria's car. As the water hit it, a stream of muddy water flowed down the driveway toward the gutter.

I watched him, realizing as I did that I had not bothered to think about what I might say to introduce myself. It was possible Victoria had told him about me, and just as possible that she hadn't had the chance or inclination.

Before I lost my nerve, I unfastened my seat belt and opened my door. The man jerked his head up. He hadn't noticed me before.

He kept spraying the front wheel as I crossed the street, but he stopped when I got to the back bumper.

"Hello?" he said. He flipped something on the hose nozzle and killed the spray. He tossed the hose into the gravel yard, wiped his hand on his jeans, and turned to face me. "Can I help you somehow?"

"I'm Copper Black," I said. "I knew Victoria."

He squinted at me.

"You worked with her?"

"No!" I said, a little too quickly. "No, I just met her a few days ago. I work for the newspaper."

"Aw, hell," the man said, waving his right hand dismissively. "Can't you just leave us alone?" He pulled a bandana out of his back pocket and started wiping the driver's side mirror of Victoria's car.

"It's not for the paper," I said. "I'm not here for the paper."

"I don't care why you're here," the man said. "I just want you to leave."

He sounded more weary than angry.

"Are you Richard McKimber?" I asked.

The man didn't answer. He stopped wiping the mirror and draped the bandana over its bracket. He pulled a pack of cigarettes out of his shirt pocket and extracted a cigarette using his teeth. Then he pulled a lighter out of his jeans. He did everything with his right hand. His left arm hung pretty much useless at his side.

"Yeah," he said, and he took a long drag on his cigarette. "What do you want?"

It was a reasonable question, and I had no idea how to answer it. Fortunately, I didn't have to. A skinny teenage boy on a skateboard careened around the corner, a brown paper bag the size and shape of a six-pack tucked under his arm. He caught air going over the curb, flipped his skateboard up and caught it in his free hand. He peered at me from under the hood of a gray sweatshirt before he vanished through the front door. It slammed behind him, making the Christmas wreath almost jump off its hook.

"God damn it," Richard muttered under his breath. He threw his cigarette onto the concrete and ground it out with the toe of his boot.

He turned and moved back into the garage. He poked his head out before he disappeared among the boxes.

"I'll be right back," he said.

Encouraged because he seemed to expect me to stick around, I stayed glued to my spot on the driveway and surveyed the scene. From where I was standing, I could see the pile of stuff next to the car's back end. As I looked at it, I suddenly recognized Victoria's big shoulder bag, the same one she had brought with her to the Silverado when I met her there with David. It was open. I inched a little closer. Inside the big bag was a smaller zipper bag, also open. Inside that was Victoria's little tape recorder, which she also had with her the first time we met.

What if I took it? I wondered. It would be easy enough. There might be useful stuff on it, maybe even whatever it was that Julia Saxon wanted. The thought was enough to add theft to my bold moves and sins. Hoping desperately that no one was observing me from behind any of the drawn shades in neighboring houses, I moved forward, bent down, and pulled the small zipper bag out from between a hairbrush and a couple of magazines. It was bigger than I thought, and there was more in it than just the recorder, but I managed to shove it into my backpack.

I stood up, but before I could breathe a sigh of relief, a black sedan rolled up next to the opposite curb. The driver's window slid down, and an arm holding a video camera emerged. I jumped out of range, but whoever was filming seemed more interested in Victoria's car and the garage than in me, capturing Richard when he reappeared between the boxes. Richard paused when he saw the car and squinted at the camera. Then, without a word, he picked up his hose and turned on the spray.

"Strike three on two counts!" a high-pitched man's voice shrieked from the black car. "This tape is going straight to the board!"

Richards said nothing. He just slowly raised his hose nozzle.

"Son of a bitch!" the voice shrieked as the spray reached the car's window. "You're gonna be sorry, asshole!" Lurching into reverse, the car screeched backward. After a spastic turn across the lawn on the corner, it disappeared down Riviera Lane.

Richard turned the hose back on the wheels of Victoria's car. He glanced at me, and the look on my face was enough to make him smile.

"Don't worry, darlin'," he said. "Just swattin' a fly."

Richard shut off the flow of water.

"He's just one of my charming neighbors," he said. "And here's a piece of advice: Never buy a house that comes with a ho moaners association."

Ho moaners? It took me a second. Oh, duh! *Homeowners.* Richard dropped the hose on the concrete and moved a little closer to me.

"Victoria loved the idea of a gated community, but I hate little twerps who make rules against washing your own car on your own property."

"That's it?" I managed to ask. "You washed your car?"

Richard nodded. "And they don't think I should store boxes in my garage, either, or allow FedEx to pick up packages. 'Conducting a business,' they call it, but I say they should mind their own." He paused. "What's your name again?"

"Copper," I said. "Copper Black."

"And why—?"

"Victoria's funeral," I said in a burst of inspiration. "I'd like to attend. I was hoping—"

"Funeral?" Richard stared at me, his eyes hardening again. "You think we can have a funeral? It'd be a goddamn circus."

"I'm sorry."

Richard didn't say anything.

"I'm very sorry for your loss." It was all I could think of to say, but I felt like an idiot repeating the most overused phrase on network television.

"I really am," I added.

And I really was, but repeating it didn't make it sound any more sincere.

"You have no idea," Richard said. "You better just go."

The weariness in his voice was unmistakable, and it made me feel even sorrier.

"Okay," I said. "Thanks, Mr. McKimber."

Clutching my backpack to my chest, I turned to walk back to my car.

"Wait just a second."

I froze, then looked back over my shoulder to see Richard walking across the street to join me.

"My kid and I'll go out to the Sekhmet Temple someday and scatter her ashes," Richard said. "It's what she would have wanted." He sighed heavily. "But I don't know when. They haven't released her body yet."

Guilt enveloped me as I climbed into my car. Richard seemed like a nice enough guy, and here I was, stealing Victoria's tape recorder while pretending to offer my condolences.

But I wasn't pretending, I told myself as I headed toward the freeway. I really was sorry.

❖❖❖

By the time I got home around seven, I had actually managed to do some Christmas shopping at the Forum Shops. I got Daniel a pocket knife inlaid with lapis and malachite, but when I thought about it, I wasn't sure it would be a good gift for someone traveling by airplane. Also, when I looked at it again, it seemed kind of feminine. Daniel was a lot of things, but feminine wasn't one of them. God! Six more days. I wondered how I was going to survive.

Anyway, when I got home, I decided to stop in the vicarage—that's what I call Michael and Sierra's house—just to say hello. The front door was unlocked, so I walked in. The living room was dark, but I was pretty sure Sierra was home because her car was in the driveway. A light was on in the kitchen, so I headed in there.

Sierra obviously hadn't heard me come in, because I surprised her when I stepped onto the linoleum and the floor squeaked.

"Holy crap, Copper! Don't you believe in knocking?"

I knew the minute I heard "crap" that I was in trouble. Sierra does a good job of keeping her language finishing-school perfect except when she gets into one of her moods.

Then I saw the cat food, a brand new box of Kitty Yum Yum. Then I saw the cat. *My* cat! She was curled up in Sierra's lap, and Sierra was fastening a little jeweled collar around her neck. I didn't say anything—I know from experience to shut up when Sierra's demons are at large. But it pissed me off! She'd hijacked Sekhmet! It's not like I really wanted a cat, but she was mine! She could have at least asked.

"Delilah," Sierra said. "That's what I'm going to call her."

It took every ounce of self-control I possessed not to say something a lot more colorful than "crap."

"I already named her," I said, as evenly as possible. "Didn't I tell you? She's Sekhmet."

"Yeah, but Delilah's a lot nicer," Sierra said. "And she purrs when I call her that. You can call her whatever you want, but she's Delilah as far as I'm concerned."

I'd like to call *you* whatever I want, I fumed to myself, but I kept quiet. I'm glad I did, because just then, Sierra burst into tears.

When Sierra cries, there's nothing subtle about it. She doesn't do a little quiet sniffling behind a tissue. She wails. She moans. She could hire herself out as a professional mourner. It's the Greek in her, I guess. Her mother was a local, but her father moved to Las Vegas from some island in the Aegean and opened Nick's Taverna on Paradise Road. Nikos Dendrakis died when Sierra was nine, but he obviously had already taught her everything she needed to know about being a Greek drama queen.

It's possible that Sierra's mother contributed to her histrionic talents, but I never met her. She died about five years ago, not long before Sierra met Michael. From the pictures I've seen and what Sierra has said, she was half hippie and half go-go dancer in the seventies. Her name—or at least the name she went by—was Meadow, and she's the one who insisted on giving Sierra her flower-child name. Her father wanted to call her Christina, but her mother wouldn't agree to anything but Sierra Dawn. After Nick was killed by a drunk driving a stolen car, Meadow sold the restaurant. She disappeared into the Golden Gate casino on Fremont Street, where she parked herself in front of a slot machine, gained fifty pounds, and took a couple of decades to smoke herself to death. For all practical purposes, Sierra was parentless after her father's death, although her mother did manage to pay off the mortgage on this house. Sierra calls it her dowry.

Anyway, what was I supposed to do when a full-grown woman started sobbing for no apparent reason? It's not like I'd had an exactly easy day myself. It would have been nice if my sister-in-law had said something like "How are you?" instead of "Holy crap!" Not to mention asking permission before appropriating my cat.

"What's wrong?" I managed to ask in between her bellows. "Are you okay?"

"What does it look like?" Sierra wailed. "Does this look like 'okay' to you?"

"No. What's wrong?"

More shrieks. More sobs.

"Please just go a-*wa-a-a-y*."

That was enough for me. I figured I'd call Michael on his cell phone and let him know Sierra was having a meltdown, but his Jetta was just pulling into the driveway as I stepped outside.

"Hi, Copper," Michael said as he got out of the car. "How are you?"

"I'm okay, but your wife isn't."

"Be nice," Michael said. "Sierra's under a lot of stress right now."

"Why don't you tell *her* to be nice?"

Michael sighed heavily, retrieved a grocery bag from the trunk of his car, and headed into the house. I climbed the stairs to my apartment, and when I got inside, I opened the window that looks over the garage roof. It was chilly, but it would be worth it if Sekhmet showed up. Sierra herself said it's the cat who decides.

I was exhausted, but I forced myself to empty out the contents of Victoria's zipper bag onto my coffee table. In addition to the little tape recorder, I found three beat-up tampons, an American Beauty lipstick, a bottle of Claritin tablets, an old point-and-click camera, a handful of Canadian change, two condoms in gold foil wrappers, a few crumpled-up store receipts, and a tube of something called Wet Willie. By the time I was finished, I wished I had worn latex gloves.

I told myself I should listen to the tape in Victoria's recorder, but after I'd changed into my sweats and had a beer, I was just too fried. Instead, I logged on to check my email and see if Daniel might be around. One nice thing about Costa Rica was that there was only a two-hour time difference. Another nice thing was that Daniel's landlord had a high-speed Internet connection, so we could actually talk instead of just instant messaging.

Daniel was online, so I rang him up.

"Danno!" I said.

"Babe!" he said.

"I miss you!"

"Six days!"

"Can't wait!"

"What's up?" Daniel asked, and that's when I made my giant mistake. I told him how I had turned myself into a thief.

"You're insane," he said as soon as he learned that I had visited the McKimber house and stolen Victoria's bag.

"I am not insane, Daniel," I said in as restrained a voice as I could manage. "I am concerned. I am diligent. I am thorough. I am determined. I am—"

"You're hot," Daniel interrupted. "You're sexy."

"Shut up!" I said.

"I miss you. I want you."

"Don't try to change the subject."

"What's the subject?"

"My investigation into Victoria McKimber's death. I think I'm really making progress."

"You're really making me crazy."

Ordinarily, I would have played the game. I missed Daniel. I lusted after him. I couldn't wait to rip his clothes off. I had even reserved a room for us at the Golden Nugget. My parents were going to stay in the house with Michael and Sierra, and my apartment was way too nearby for Daniel and me to enjoy ourselves. And we were definitely going to enjoy ourselves.

"You don't take me seriously, do you?" I said.

"Sure I do, babe," Daniel said. "I'm sitting here totally naked. And—um—ready."

"I am, too!" I was supposed to say, but "I'm really tired, Daniel" is what came out. "I guess I'm going to have to get some sleep."

There was a long silence.

"Whatever," Daniel finally said.

I logged off and drank another beer while watching a terrible version of *A Christmas Carol* where Scrooge is a woman who owns a pawn shop and the Ghost of Christmas Past looks alarmingly like Richard Simmons. But I still wasn't ready to fall asleep. Part of the problem was that the room was too cold, but I was still hoping Sekhmet would show up.

Damn. Things really weren't going the way I'd planned, but I had decided one thing. Instead of a Christmas dress, I was going to get some Christmas "club wear." Las Vegas is packed with stores that sell stuff to make you look like a sex machine, and I was going to need some assistance in patching things up properly with Daniel. He would definitely prefer something skimpy and stretchy to something taffeta-stiff and demure.

Las Vegas was creeping up on me. Now that I'd lived here a few months—and been to a brothel—I felt far more capable of breaking commandments. I'm not talking about the Big Ten. I mean all those awful little ones that had kept me from showing more cleavage and saying "fuck" every once in a while.

Chapter 9

Sekhmet came home! And she wasn't wearing the jeweled collar! The cat was on my bed when I woke up. She was really back, and after I got up she stretched out on top of my TV as though she'd been doing it for years. So there, Sierra, I couldn't help thinking. Eat your sorry heart out.

I made some coffee and thought about going to church. When I do, I go to St. Andrew's, my brother's church in North Las Vegas. It's not that I really like going to church or that I get anything spiritual out of it, but when I first moved to Las Vegas, it was church or no social life at all. So I went to the eleven o'clock service a few times, even though I was the only one of my kind in attendance. Most of the people who go to St. Andrew's are ninety and white, forty and Filipino, or homeless. I have to give Michael a lot of credit for shepherding that flock. He does a lot more than hand out wafers and wine. He's always looking for housing, finding medical care, and rescuing abandoned babies. This is no exaggeration. About a week after Thanksgiving, somebody left a little boy in a shopping cart on the church doorstep. Really, sometimes I think Michael is a saint.

But that didn't make him a great landlord. And he was definitely my landlord, not my host. I'd been paying rent since the day I moved in. I think if you pay rent, you should get to do what you want. I would never have agreed to being a long-term houseguest. I don't always like to make my bed, and I also like to share it with a naked man from time to time. Shouldn't rent give me the privilege? It was fair-market rent, too! Sierra works for a real estate company and would never have agreed to anything less. I was paying the same goddamn rent they would have gotten if they'd advertised in *The Light*. But even so, I could never convince them to keep a landlord-like distance. They truly believed they had my best interests at heart when they checked up on me and reported on my activities to Mom and Dad.

I decided to skip church. There was film in the camera I found in Victoria's zipper bag. I decided to take it to the one-hour film place at the drugstore on Charleston and see if there were any pictures on it. Then I'd go to the Starbucks at the Howard Hughes Center, commandeer a whole big table, and set up shop with my laptop and Victoria's files. I needed to get a better handle on all the stuff she had given me, and I couldn't do that without serious coffee. Also, I've always liked working in public. I don't know why. I just do.

When I walked outside with all my stuff, Sierra was just walking outside, too. Michael had to get up in time for the eight o'clock service, but Sierra always slept in and joined him at eleven.

"Delilah is gone," she said. "I guess she decided not to adopt either of us."

"We'll see," I said, deciding to take the high road and not gloat.

"I'm really sorry," Sierra said.

I couldn't tell whether she was disappointed because Sekhmet had disappeared or whether she was apologizing for crying yesterday, but I didn't ask for clarification.

"Will you go to church with me?" she asked. I looked at her. I was pretty sure she'd been crying again, even though her makeup was perfect. It's hard to disguise puffy red eyes. Her shoulders drooped a little, and she looked like a puppy whose owner had just walked out the door.

"Okay," I said, glad that I'd slipped into black pants instead of torn jeans. "But I'll take my own car. I've got errands to do afterward."

"Okay," she said. "See you there."

Driving up to St. Andrew's, I actually found myself looking forward to the service. Advent is my favorite liturgical season. I like the anticipatory feel of it, and I like the purple candles on the advent wreath. All four would be lit today, which meant Daniel's advent was nigh—only five more days! The church was fuller than usual, too. I'd say there were close to eighty people there, which for St. Andrew's is a mob. The soup kitchen gets swarmed every day, but even a sip of wine isn't enough to get the chow-line folks into a room where a collection basket is passed.

One time I helped count the collection, and the take was so pathetic I suggested the church might do better putting a couple of slot machines next to the baptismal font. Now that I think about it, video poker in every pew would definitely do the trick. But St. Andrew's is a "mission," which means that the other Episcopal churches in Nevada have to share their booty to keep it going. For all I know, the more prosperous ones actually do have gambling machines in their sanctuaries, but more than likely, they just count some God-fearing casino owners among their members. At least I hope so. I hope the Catholics and Mormons don't have them all.

Because I've always had trouble sitting through sermons, I'd long ago cultivated the habit of taking books to church with me. I knew I couldn't get away with a magazine, but tastefully applied black paper had done an excellent job of making my mom's ancient copy of *Valley of the Dolls* look like a Bible when I was in fifth grade.

Since church had been a last-minute decision that morning, I didn't have a book. Desperate for something to get me through the service, I'd grabbed a spiral-bound calendar from Victoria's document box. It didn't look like a Bible, but it didn't look like the *National Enquirer*, either. With luck, Sierra wouldn't find it too sacrilegious. She was nowhere to be seen, anyway, I noticed as I walked down the center aisle in search of her. I took a seat in an empty pew several rows from the front, and by the time the organist started grinding out the first bars of "Come Thou Long Expected Jesus," she still hadn't appeared.

Church services would be much easier to endure if there wasn't so much physical activity. Just when you get all nice and comfortable, you have to stand up and sing a hymn or kneel down to say a prayer. Today, the transitions were particularly inconvenient because Victoria had stuck a newspaper clipping inside the calendar. It fell out when I stood up and flew under the pew in front of me. I fished it out from between the feet of an old lady with tattoos of barbed wire around both of her ankles. I read it during the epistle.

"POLICE SEIZE MARKS COMPUTER" read the headline on a story from *The Light* dated last March 25th. Bobby Marks, Charlie Marks's brother, apparently enjoyed looking at pictures of underage girls. Only the first page of the story was there, but it looked like Bobby had been caught red-handed with some pretty damning evidence on his super-duper Mac. The story also mentioned that he had three kids: a teenage son from a previous marriage and two little daughters from a new teenage wife.

I didn't know Charlie Marks had a brother, much less a depraved one. I'd heard Charlie's daughter had been kidnapped once, but lots of money had gotten her back alive and installed her abductors in sandy graves somewhere west of Red Rock Canyon. Well, that last part is a rumor, but David Nussbaum told me it was probably true because no other relatives of Charlie Marks had been snatched since. Word gets around, David said, to the people who need to know. David had never mentioned Bobby, however. I decided to find out why.

Michael delivered a sermon about looking for God in unexpected places. Michael is a talented preacher, and I did my best to pay attention, but my mind wandered first to the Beavertail and then to Victoria. I spent the rest of the service wondering whether I would be able to craft a story that would do her justice—or even make sense. After we closed the service with "Oh, Come, Oh, Come, Emanuel," which I have to admit I love and which at least one other person sang with me, I dutifully retired to the parish hall. The "hall" was really a trailer that used to be the office on a construction site. I poured myself a Styrofoam cup of thin coffee from a dented percolator on a rickety folding table, but I didn't have to drink it because Sierra never showed up. Michael was into a heavy conversation with the old lady with ankle tattoos, and a homeless man wearing a sleeping bag with two armholes cut in the sides was next in line. I dumped the coffee into the trash and slipped outside. Sierra's car wasn't there. What was wrong with her? She'd asked me to come to church with her, but then she didn't come herself! What the hell was her problem?

At Starbucks, I got a table to myself, but a guy with a big mustard-colored unibrow kept staring at me. He had his laptop open, and I could see a Playboy sticker on the top. If there's one thing I detest, it's guys who display bunny logos. As far as I'm concerned, that's as big a turnoff as bad breath. Damn. It was only a matter of time until the creep thought up some excuse to talk to me. I wished I was wrong, because I didn't really want to leave. I had all of Victoria's stuff nicely arranged on my table, and I'd actually been making some headway organizing it. Besides, I had just gotten another eggnog latte.

Fortunately, I remembered a technique honed to perfection by my best friend in college. Jessica was a red-haired amazon who attracted weirdos by the battalion. "When a creep's eyeing you, get on the phone," she'd say. "You still have to use a crowbar on the determined ones, but it gets rid of the wimps."

I had a new wireless headset I used for talking with Daniel over the Internet—one of those things you see supergeeks walking around with in the supermarket while they buy their Tater Tots. I usually avoided using mine in public, but I slapped that thing on and began an intense one-sided conversation with my screen saver. It worked. The eyebrow took his bunny sticker to a table where he could stare at a heavily pierced teenager in a hanky top that was failing to cover a pair of breasts the size of volleyballs.

That's another thing I had come to know and love about Las Vegas: hall-of-fame hooters wherever you turn. From the car wash to the dentist's office, I was always surrounded by awesome racks, and I didn't think it was coincidental that the Yellow Pages listed an amazing number of plastic surgeons. Damn it! Daniel was going to love Las Vegas.

But I couldn't think about Daniel right then. I had to stay in Hercule Poirot mode. I'd made myself a list of suspects—anybody who might have benefited from Victoria's death. Now if I could just get them all into a grand old manor house or a snowbound train, I was sure I'd be able to trick the guilty party into confessing with some clever banter. Not that I'd want to be cooped up with a bunch of whoremongers and a sex deviant, not to mention a slick-haired weasel and a pudgy dough boy.

That's what the two guys in the pictures on Victoria's camera looked like. There were three shots of them on the film I got developed, and I was almost positive they worked for American Beauty. The reason I thought so was that the pictures were date-stamped, and the date matched an entry on Victoria's calendar:

December 15 — 10:00 a.m. — Meet AB reps at Pair-a-Dice Casino – Rick Mack (V.P.), Duncan Frazier (attorney?)

Casino designers often don't have a lot of imagination, so the pictures could easily have been taken in the same coffee shop at the Pair-a-Dice in Pahrump where I recovered after being thrown out of the brothel. The two guys were sitting at a table with folders and papers in front of them. The best evidence, though, was the little tape recorder in the corner of the picture. It looked just like Victoria's. I remembered her lawyer had told her to tape everything that might end up in a court case, so I was pretty sure the weasel and the dough boy worked for American Beauty, although I had no idea who was who.

There were only two other pictures on the film, and they were a mystery. They showed close-ups of a face, one with the lips curled and teeth bared, and the other with the tongue sticking out. They had the same date stamp as the other two—December 15—but I had no idea who that face belonged to. Whoever it was had a chipped tooth on the left side. It was pointy, like a cat's.

When I left Starbucks, I rewound the tape in Victoria's tape recorder and then listened to it as I drove to Tacos Mérida for a quick bite to eat. The conversation seemed to match what I had seen in the photos. Victoria had spoken with two men, and the background noise sounded like a casino coffee shop. Both men chose their words carefully, which I chalked up to the presence of the tape recorder. One of them did most of the talking, and he kept referring to a "settlement package" American Beauty wanted Victoria to accept. Victoria kept saying that she'd have to consult her lawyer, and the men kept telling her that the offer would expire if she didn't act immediately. All three of them kept referring to numbers and details on papers that must have been on the table, and I made a mental note to look at everything from American Beauty in Victoria's files again.

I kept hoping I'd hear a direct threat against Victoria, but there were none. The closest thing to coercion was when one of the men said, "You should consider your family, Ms. McKimber. You have it in your power to keep them out of harm's way."

The phrase struck me as odd because it was so commonly used by politicians and newscasters to talk about soldiers in the line of fire. While Victoria's husband and son might suffer humiliation from her public appearances, their lives weren't at risk.

After two tacos and a *horchata* at Tacos Mérida, I headed home. I listened to the rest of the tape on the way, but it was all small talk. I clicked the recorder off and parked on the street to keep the driveway clear. Unless both cars were in the garage, Michael and Sierra weren't home yet.

As soon as I got to the bottom of my stairs, I saw that the door to my apartment was standing open. My first thought was, "Damn that Sierra! How dare she go into my place without asking?" Yes, it could have been Michael, but I was still kind of irked at Sierra for conning me into going to church and then bagging out herself.

The lights were off. When I stepped onto the rug inside the door, something crunched under my feet. I flipped the light switch.

My whole place—which is really one big L-shaped room and a bathroom—was a disaster area. Every drawer had been pulled out of my dresser and kitchen cabinets and dumped upside down. The crunching noise at the front door came from the shattered remains of a globe lamp that had sat on an orange crate next to my sofa. The sofa cushions had been pulled out. The mattress was half off the bed, and the bedding was in a pile on the floor.

I stood gaping at the scene for a while. Then I backed up, turned the light off, shut the door, and retreated down the stairs. Not knowing what else to do, I headed into the vicarage. I wasn't sure whether anybody was home, but I had a key. At least I could collect my thoughts, I figured, and decide what to do next.

The door was unlocked, which instantly made me nervous. Had the big house been ransacked, too? Were the bad guys maybe still lurking around? But a light was on in the kitchen, and the living room looked the same as always. I was still carrying my laptop bag and my backpack. I dumped them on the sofa. I was about to yell, "Anybody home?" when I heard voices coming from the master bedroom in its own little suite off the entry hall.

Before I could make my presence known, I heard Sierra crying. *Again!* I couldn't resist moving a little closer and listening.

"I don't know! *I don't know!*" I heard her wail. "I know I'm a horrible person for feeling this way, but I can't help it!"

"Sweetheart, sweetheart," Michael said. "Calm down. We don't have to do anything we don't feel completely right about."

"What's—his—name?" she sobbed.

"The nurses are calling him Sam. But we could name him whatever we want. He's not even two years old."

"Oh, God, Michael!" Sierra began wailing again. "*Oh, God!* All I want is to be a mom. Is that so selfish?"

"Of course it's not selfish, sweetheart," Michael said. "Of course it's not."

"*Of—my—own—baby!*"

More wails. More sounds of my brother trying to comfort her.

Well, at least now I know what her problem is, I thought. She'd been trying to get pregnant, and I had no idea.

"A lot of couples have their own children after they adopt," Michael said. "That's all I was thinking."

"I know—I know—I know," Sierra sobbed. "And I know this baby needs us—and I know—"

Loud wails.

"It's okay. It's okay."

"It's not okay! God's giving us a baby, and I—don't—want—it!"

More sobbing. More wailing.

I started tiptoeing back to the front door. I'll go outside, I thought, and make a racket coming back in. That way—

But I was too late. I had just put my hand on the doorknob when I heard the bedroom door open and shut.

"Oh!" Michael said, and the look on my face when I turned toward him told him everything he needed to know.

"You heard," he said.

"I didn't mean to," I said. "I swear. I just—"

"It's been tough, Copper," Michael said. "Really tough."

"Yeah, well—"

"Come on," he said. "Let's go into the kitchen where we can talk."

"No—I've got to show you something," I said. "I have a big problem."

"You, too?" he said, and the look on his face was so tragic I almost felt like hugging him. "Copper—can't it wait?"

"No," I said. "I'm afraid it can't."

❖ ❖ ❖

It took about five minutes for Michael to survey the wreckage in my apartment, turn white, call 9-1-1 on his cell phone, and go back into the house to give Sierra the news. I heard sirens about the same time Sierra burst out the front door in the ratty old bathrobe she wears to sulk in.

"How could you do this to us, Copper?" she shrieked. "How could you? I told you not to go poking around where you don't belong! I warned you!"

I have to give Michael credit for trying to calm her down.

"This isn't Copper's fault, sweetheart," he said, putting his arms around her shoulders. "For all we know, this could be the work of the same burglars who hit Hans and Dustin's house a couple of months ago."

Hans and Dustin live around the corner. They're an aging gay couple who own a wedding chapel on North Las Vegas Boulevard, and whoever broke into their house stole Mr. Simms, their forty-three-year-old Brazilian macaw, along with their extensive and supposedly world-renowned collection of Liberace memorabilia. The burglary practically killed Dustin, who immediately had a major asthma attack and spent nearly a week in intensive care. Mr. Simms and the Liberace stuff are still unaccounted for.

Just then, not one but two Metro police cars pulled into the driveway, each with one policeman inside. Sierra retreated into the house, and Michael explained the situation to the cop who was in charge, a guy about my age but an inch or so shorter. He looked like a brown-haired Richie Rich with muscles, and he made his uniform look remarkably cute, especially the black turtleneck with "LVMPD" embroidered on the neck in gold. Michael and I showed him the wreckage indoors while the other cop, an older, sandy-haired guy with a brush cut, clicked on a flashlight and said he'd look around outside.

"Did you go inside?" the young cop asked. "Was anyone here?"

"I don't know," I said. "I didn't go past the door."

"Good decision," the cop said, unsnapping the leather holster on his belt. He pulled out his gun.

"Wait here," he said. Ready to shoot anything that moved, he checked out the kitchen nook and the bathroom.

"Can you see what's missing?" he asked when he got back to the door. I started to walk inside, but he stopped me.

"Just look from here," he said. "I'm calling Crime Scene Investigation. They'll see what evidence they can collect. You don't want to disturb anything until they're done."

While the cop went back to his car to make the call, I perused the scene as carefully as I could without stepping beyond the doorway.

Everything was messed up pretty thoroughly, but nothing seemed to be missing. I could even see my great-grandmother's string of pearls lying on the floor next to my dresser. Those are probably the most valuable things I own. My TV looked fine, but the books on the shelves next to it were all on the floor.

"Do you think they might actually catch whoever did this?" I asked Michael.

"Not a chance," he said. "St. Andrew's has been burglarized at least six times in the past two years, and all we've ever seen is a police report."

"What's the point, then?" I said.

"Well, the report will come in handy if there's anything worth collecting insurance on."

We went back downstairs.

"It doesn't look like anything's been taken," I said. "At least nothing I can see."

While the cop was still writing, the crime scene investigators arrived, a man and a woman in blue jeans. They dusted for fingerprints and took a bunch of pictures. They didn't say much, and when they were done, the cop told us it was okay to clean up. Then he gave me a piece of paper that explained my rights as a victim.

"A detective will be assigned to your case," he said. "You can call this number after two weeks if you haven't heard anything."

Two weeks. That'd be next year. It felt like a long way off.

"You better sleep in the house tonight, Copper," Michael said after everyone had left. "I'm pretty sure the sheets are clean in the guest room."

I was happy to accept his invitation. I went back up to the apartment to dig through my clothes and find some sweats to wear and a T-shirt to sleep in. My bathroom cabinets had been emptied onto the floor, but my toothbrush was miraculously untouched in a glass on the edge of the sink. I grabbed it and picked my way back across my apartment, trying to avoid doing further damage.

I still didn't see anything missing, though—just broken. I was going to need a new coffeemaker, some new wineglasses, a new lamp, and—damn it—a new tacky Las Vegas souvenir ashtray that says "Dan's Butts" on it. I got that for Daniel the first time I went to Fremont Street, but since I never got around to mailing it, I was planning to give it to him for Christmas. He doesn't smoke tobacco, but I thought it might come in handy for other flammable plants.

By the time I got back into the vicarage, Michael was in the kitchen halfway through a glass of something poured from a spherical bottle with a stopper shaped like a horse.

"It's expensive bourbon Dad left the last time he was here," Michael said.

I might have known. My father is one of the world's great consumers of designer alcohol. When I was thirteen, my best friend and I got drunk one day after school on the best-tasting booze we could find in the liquor cabinet. When my dad got home, he was angrier about his empty bottle of limited-edition fifty-year-old Grand Marnier than he was about the two eighth-grade girls throwing up in the downstairs bathroom.

"I was saving it for a special occasion, and I figure this qualifies," Michael said. "Want some?"

I shrugged and nodded. "Where's Sierra?"

"In bed." He poured a hefty slug of bourbon into a juice glass and pushed it toward me.

"Is she okay?"

"I think she will be." He sighed. "Copper, are you sure you didn't do something to cause this?"

"Don't tell me *you're* going to start in on me! I'm the victim here!"

Michael sighed. "Oh, calm down. It's rough on all of us."

"Well, it doesn't help to make accusations! And anyway, I'm moving out right after Christmas. I never should have—"

"Truce!" Michael said, raising his glass. He pushed my glass a little closer, and I finally picked it up. He clinked his against it, and we both drank. I managed to suppress a cough.

"First thing tomorrow," Michael said, "I'll get the locks changed."

I took my T-shirt down the hall and tried to settle into the guest room." It was really just Sierra's childhood bedroom, and it still looked like a kid's room. I don't mean a high school kid, either. I mean a kid who still plays with My Little Ponies. The four-poster bed had a pink net canopy with sparkles, and there were glow-in-the-dark stars on the ceiling. At least thirty-five Barbies were lined up on a shelf over a little lavender desk with rainbow decals, and a big ugly bunny the color of Pepto-Bismol gave me the evil eye from the corner. Either Sierra was trying to pickle her youth, or she was too lazy to redecorate. Even the air smelled like it had been in here since the eighties.

Chapter 10

Monday, December 19

I woke up before six, and as I lay there under the pink tulle feeling the gaze of thirty-five Barbies and an oversize midway rabbit, I swore I'd be back in my own bed that night.

Michael and Sierra weren't up, so I tiptoed into the kitchen and managed to make coffee without creating too much of a racket. Mug in hand, I headed outside and up the stairs to my apartment. Everything looked just as bad as it had the night before, but in a strange way, that was a relief. When somebody invades your space, it's hard to banish the thought that they might come back. Even so, I would never sleep in that horror of a guest room again. My neck was sore from the bouncy pillow, and no burglar could ever be as scary as that hideous buck-toothed bunny.

By the time I had cleared a swath down the middle of the room and put my sofa and bed back together, it was nearly eight o'clock. I still had time to shower and get to work by nine, which would be only half an hour late. I better call Chris, though, I thought, if only to tell him to pick up his own latte.

My cell phone, I suddenly remembered, was in my backpack, which was still on the sofa in the vicarage. I hadn't given it a thought since the afternoon before.

I could hear Michael and Sierra talking in the kitchen as I crossed the living room and retrieved my backpack and laptop bag. It sounded like a continuation of the conversation I'd accidentally overheard yesterday, so I decided to creep away quietly. This time I made it back out the door without attracting their notice.

Back in my apartment, I fished out my cell phone. Six messages! *Damn!* I'd set the thing on silent while I was at Starbucks and had forgotten to turn the ringer back on.

The first two messages were hang-ups. The next one was from David Nussbaum.

"Copper! Are you okay? Give me a call!"

The one after that was from David, too.

"Copper! Please call me!"

The fifth message was from Chris Farr.

"Copper, I'm sorry to hear about your apartment. If you need some time this morning, it's fine. If you can make it in by eleven, I think we can get everything covered."

The sixth call was David again.

"Copper! Where are you? Call me!"

I called David on his cell phone.

"About time!" he said, his mouth full of something. "Are you okay?"

"I'm fine," I said. "How did you know?"

David laughed. "I keep forgetting what a newbie you are. Haven't you ever heard of police scanners?"

"Oh," I said, feeling stupid. "You have one at home?"

"Yup."

"And Chris Farr does, too?"

"No. I called him."

"Thanks, I guess."

"Tell me what happened."

I told him, declined his repeated offers of help, and hung up. Then I called Chris to let him know I'd be in by eleven. Finally, I started putting my kitchen back together, which mostly meant filling my trash can with broken glass. If I accomplished nothing else today, I told myself, I'd at least buy a new coffeemaker. With coffee and clean sheets, I'd be as happy as Goldilocks.

But first I had to get through a day's work. When I got to *The Light*, I went into the lunchroom to get a cup of coffee, and Ed Bramlett was there. That was no surprise. The only time Ed wasn't in the lunchroom was when he was out on the "smokers' patio." I couldn't understand how he stayed employed. He never seemed to do any work, and when he walked over to tease me, I smelled alcohol on his breath. I had to take a drug test in order to work at *The Light*, but that old bastard carried a flask in his back pocket. It clanked every time he sat down on a hard chair.

"Welcome to Las Vegas, blondie," he said, way too loud. He slapped me on the back way too hard, and I almost dropped my coffee cup. "Getting your place tossed makes you a bona fide local. Is it true they didn't take anything?"

"I don't think so," I said. "I'm not sure."

"Good thing you weren't there," he said, "or there'd be a headline about a kidnapping on the front page this morning: POLICE PROBE BLONDE SNATCH."

I was too stunned by his vulgarity even to blush. I just took my coffee and left. Back in my cube I debated whether to file a complaint about sexual harassment. I didn't want to. I hadn't been working at the paper very long, and the last thing I wanted was to get labeled a troublemaker or a whiner or the chick who couldn't take a little joking around. And also, Chris Farr was a very nice boss. I didn't want to make his life difficult.

I decided to wait until next time. I was too busy to mess around with a bunch of paperwork just then, anyway. Christmas was less than a week away, and I still hadn't done much shopping. Add in the stuff I needed to buy to make my apartment livable again, and Ed Bramlett's comeuppance would just have to wait. Anyway, I didn't really mind eating lunch in my cubicle, and I could bring my own coffee from Starbucks. If I steered clear of the lunchroom entirely—problem solved.

Once I'd made all my calendar calls, Chris asked me to rewrite some of the copy for production shows. I decided to start with *Hombre* because it was one of the few shows I'd actually seen. *Hombre* is put on by a troupe of meaty hunks from Argentina who are supposed to attract the "girls' night out" crowd. I was halfway finished writing a bunch of hyperbolic superlatives about buffed-up male strippers when David Nussbaum appeared at my desk.

"Tell me about it," he said.

"About what?" I said.

"You know," he said.

"So do you. My apartment got ransacked. End of story."

"Nothing's missing?"

"Not that I've determined so far. They just broke stuff."

"Copper, doesn't that bother you?"

"That they broke stuff? Sure it bothers me."

"That they didn't take anything."

"Obviously I don't have anything worth stealing."

David pushed a stack of papers aside and perched a thigh on the edge of my desk.

"Think, Copper. What do you have that somebody wants?"

"Look, David. I have work to do."

"I'm not leaving."

"Why do you care?" I asked.

"I do care. I'm worried. Where are you staying tonight?"

"My place. My brother had the locks changed."

"Copper—" He paused and looked at me. "Copper, can't you stay somewhere else for a few nights?"

"I stayed in my brother's house last night. I'm not doing that anymore. The room is—uncomfortable."

"You want to stay with me?"

I stared at him. Up to then we'd only been work buddies. I'd never even been to his house, although I knew it was somewhere on the south side of town.

"What are you suggesting, exactly?"

"Oh, come on. I've got a dedicated guest room. It's yours if you want it. And I hope you do."

"Well—" I looked at him again. There was no denying he was worried. It was actually kind of sweet. "Okay," I said.

"Really?" David asked. "You mean it?"

"Yeah," I said. "Are you sure you do?"

But David was already scribbling something in a spiral notebook. When he was done, he ripped out the page and handed it to me.

"Directions," he said. "When do you want to come over?"

"I could bring dinner if you like," I said. "I could get subs at Capriotti's or something."

So it was set. I was bringing sandwiches and showing up around seven with my toothbrush. David Nussbaum and I were having a slumber party.

❖❖❖

I couldn't believe it, but I had actually gotten all my calls made and blurb-writing done, and it was only four o'clock. I had arrived so late that I thought for sure I'd be slaving away until at least six, but I guess that just showed how inefficient I usually was. I was embarrassed to admit it, but the thought of going over to David's house—and spending the night—had gotten me, well, kind of super motivated. I wished I always felt that way. If I always got all my work done in four hours, I could spend the rest of the day working on projects that might turn me into a real journalist.

I was really curious about David. I'd never seen him on his own turf, or even off duty. I was dying to see what his house was like. 782 Palm Treasure Drive. I printed out an Internet map to go along with David's directions. He lived in Green Valley, which was on the other side of town from where I lived. Sierra had dragged me down there a few weeks earlier to see a cactus garden decorated with a couple million strings of Christmas lights, but otherwise it was new territory for me.

❖❖❖

David's guest room had no pink tulle, no Barbies, and—thank you, Jesus—no big ugly rabbit. That didn't mean it wasn't weird, though. It was weird because it wasn't really a guest room. It was his wife's office.

Yes! David had a wife! Not an ex-wife, either. Though she didn't live there anymore, they were still married. There was even a wedding picture hanging in a little alcove—a shrine!—next to the front door. I couldn't help noticing it when I walked in.

David saw me checking it out, but he didn't say anything except, "Here's the guest room. The bathroom's the next door on the right."

We walked into the "guest room" together, and David started unfolding a sofa bed. I might have helped, but I was too busy eying the straw hat sitting on the desk. It had three red flowers on the brim, and right next to it was a sewing machine.

"You *sew?*" I asked.

"No."

"Are you married?"

"Sort of."

Fortunately, I had brought a six-pack along with the sandwiches, and by the time I'd sucked down two and David had sucked down three, he was a little more forthcoming.

"I'm not really married anymore, Copper," he said.

"There's nothing gray about being married, David," I said. "Either you are or you aren't. No fudge room."

"She moved back to New York. We'll get a divorce."

"It's in process?"

"No, but—"

"You're married, dude."

"Well, yes, if you're going to get technical about it."

"It's not 'getting technical.' It's the bald truth." I pulled the last beer out of the carton. "You want this?"

"Sure, unless you do."

I did, but I twisted off the cap and gave it to David anyway. Two beers really ought to be my limit, especially on a weeknight.

"So why did somebody toss your apartment?"

"Nice try, David," I said. "But first you have to tell me about her."

"We met in high school but never really hooked up. We met up again after college. She wanted to get married."

"You didn't?"

"Not as much as she did, but yeah. I did."

"What happened?"

"Hell, I don't know. I'm just glad we hadn't gotten around to having kids before the magma burst forth."

"Is she Jewish?"

"What does that have to do with anything?"

"Well, is she?"

"Yeah."

"Your parents approved?"

"They loved her. They're still baffled, but they don't understand any relationship that isn't 'happily ever after.' They met in eighth grade, and they're still madly in love."

It sounded like my parents. They met in college, and even after nearly four decades, they still patted each other's bottoms and held hands when they watched a movie.

"Do you have anything else to drink?" I asked. I was thinking of maybe a Coke, but David rummaged in the refrigerator and pulled out a bottle of wine.

"Cold Chianti," he said. "Okay? Or I've got some vodka around here somewhere."

I should have said no to the Chianti. The more I drank, the more I wanted to tell David that I suspected Richard McKimber was the burglar who had trashed my apartment. I'd been thinking about it all day, and that was the only explanation that made sense. Richard had figured out that I'd stolen Victoria's camera and recorder. Somehow he'd broken in, even though he had only one working arm. Somehow he'd found out where I lived. That was the part I found scariest, and every sip of wine was making it worse.

I looked at David, who was making inroads on his own glass of Chianti. He was a friend. He had lots more experience with stuff like this than I did. He was even worried about me.

But I still couldn't bring myself to tell him about my theories. Gotta be tough, I kept telling myself. Gotta be independent and capable. This is my project and my story, and it's going to take more than a little break-in to scare me into giving it up. Yeah! Copper Black, fearless Girl Reporter. That's me.

"What are you thinking about, Copper?"

"Oh!" I said, jarred from my private pep talk. "Nothing."

"You know, it might be a good idea if you stayed here a few more nights."

"I don't know," I said, but actually I was glad he was offering.

"Just do it. I've got the space, and—"

"It'd only be until Friday. I've got hotel reservations after that. I've got—someone coming for Christmas."

David looked at me, and I know I was blushing. He smiled.

"Copper, are you married?"

Chapter 11

The bed wasn't too uncomfortable, even though it was a fold-out. I had remembered to bring my own pillow, so I don't know why I woke up early, but I did. It was still dark.

Actually, I do know why I woke up. The dream I was having was tiring me out, and I had to wake up to rest. I was at a big crowded house party with Victoria, who didn't know anybody except me. She wanted a glass of wine, but I couldn't find a glass, even though everyone in the place was drinking and there were dozens of cupboards and pantries full of every other kind of glassware. I finally found two little flower vases I thought might suffice, but then I couldn't find any wine, even though there had been dozens of bottles sitting around while I was looking for glasses. I searched for what seemed like hours, and when I finally made my way back through the crowd to where I'd left Victoria, she was gone.

I was exhausted, but I decided I'd better shake it off. There were only five days left until Christmas, and I was feeling homeless. And if I was homeless, where did that leave my cat? I hated the thought of her coming to my window and finding no one there. She'd probably go back to Sierra, which was probably the best thing for her, anyway.

Sierra had maternal instincts. I was beginning to think I had no instincts at all. Hell, even in my dreams I couldn't figure anything out.

❖❖❖

David was in the kitchen making coffee when I went in around six thirty. He looked very cozy in a white terry cloth bathrobe. His hair was still damp and curled in cute little ringlets all over his head. I'd just thrown on some sweats. I hadn't had a shower yet.

"Sleep okay?" he asked.

"Yeah, thanks," I said. "Did you?"

"As well as I ever do," he said, "which is not very well. I'm a midnight pacer. But it's not all bad. I get some of my best writing done in the middle of the night."

He opened the cupboard over the dishwasher and pulled out two mugs, one that said "Caesars," and one that said "Harrah's."

"Black, right?" he asked. He filled the Caesars mug and held it out to me.

"Yeah. Thanks."

Taking a sip, I walked over to the vertical blinds covering a sliding glass door. I peeked between two slats.

"The backyard," David said. "Such as it is."

He yanked on the chain, and the blinds slid aside. In early morning half-light, I found myself staring at a bare concrete patio and a backyard surrounded by a cinder-block wall. The patio was dotted with clay pots. Some were broken, and the rest had the remains of dead plants in them. A dry birdbath stood at the edge of the patio, and beyond that lay a dead lawn surrounded by half a dozen dead trees, even more dead shrubs, a bed of dead rosebushes, and a little arbor covered with a dead vine. It was without exception the most extinct backyard I had ever seen.

"God! What happened?"

"I stopped watering."

"Sorry. Stupid question," I said, but it actually wasn't. The front yard had a happy-looking shade tree, some nicely trimmed shrubs, and a lawn that obviously got mowed regularly.

"It was Rebecca's backyard," David said. "She did all the landscaping. Did her best to make it look like home."

"So—when she left, you just—"

"I'm not proud of turning off the water, but I was angry. The trouble is, it only takes a couple of weeks, and *wham!*" He shrugged. "It looks like I've been doing atomic testing." He yanked the chain again. "So I keep the blinds pulled."

"Do you still love her?"

"Copper, I've got to get to work."

"Yeah. Just keep those blinds drawn. That takes care of everything."

"Copper—"

"I'm sorry, David," I said. "I'm sorry. I didn't mean to—"

"Yeah, you did," he said. "But it's okay. I do compartmentalize. Makes life livable."

I could have kicked myself. Here was a nice guy who had invited me into his private space, and I was picking on him for things I knew nothing about.

❖❖❖

It felt odd to have David Nussbaum's house key on my key ring, and even odder to have made plans to have dinner with him. And the oddest part about it was that it didn't seem odd at all. It felt easy and comfortable and nice. Like I had a real friend.

Of course, that nice feeling got shot to hell as soon as I got to work. Ed Bramlett was lying in wait for me next to the mail room, which was packed with all the people checking their boxes on their way to their cubes.

"So you've hooked up with Dave Nussbaum!" he practically shouted. The mail room crowd instantly fell silent. I'm sure I turned red, but I didn't say anything. I just pushed past him and headed for my cube.

"We had a pool on who the lucky son of a bitch was going to be, and I won!" he called after me. "Fifty bucks, just in time for Christmas! I owe you one, blondie!"

Fortunately, Chris Farr was in the mail room crowd.

He was right behind me when I got to my desk.

"I'm sorry, Copper," he said.

"Thanks," I said, "but you're not the one who should be apologizing."

"I know that." He moved inside the cube. "And I don't think an apology is enough, anyway. The situation has gone way beyond that. I just want you to know that I'm aware of it and—"

He paused and looked at me for a moment. He had a naturally happy face, but right now it looked pretty glum.

"Copper, you've got grounds for a sexual harassment case, and I'll support you if you want to begin doing something about it."

"Yeah," I said. "Thanks, but—" I hesitated, but I couldn't hold myself back. "I just wish Ed would eat shit and die."

Chris didn't say anything for a minute or two. He just stood there, shifting his weight from foot to foot.

"Copper, can you hang in until after the holidays? Things'll be different then, I promise."

It was what I'd been planning all along, so it wasn't difficult to say yes.

"And in the meantime, you can have more time at lunch if you want. So you can eat off campus, I mean. If it helps."

I couldn't see why anything would change after the holidays, but Chris seemed to know what was going on. And longer lunch hours! I wasn't going to complain about that!

Five minutes after he left my cube, Chris came back.

"You still want to do that movie review?" he asked.

"Sure!" I said.

"Great! It's screening tomorrow morning at ten at the Village Square over on West Sahara. You can go directly there in the morning. If you make it in here by one, that'll be fine."

As soon as Chris left, my office phone rang.

"Copper Black?" asked a woman's voice. "This is Heather Vetra. Victoria McKimber's partner. I met you at the Sekhmet Temple—"

"Oh!" I said. "Yes!"

"I need to talk to you," she said. "Have you got some time this afternoon?"

I hesitated.

"It's about Victoria," she said. "I know who killed her."

Whoa. This was a woman who got straight to the point.

"Shouldn't you call the police?" I said.

"I want to talk to you first. In person."

I hesitated again, debating whether I should meet with Heather or call the police myself.

"Okay," I said finally. "Where?"

"My rig's parked at the Silverado RV Resort," she said.

"Your rig?"

"My trailer."

After confirming that the Silverado RV Resort was next door to the Silverado Casino where I'd first met Victoria, I agreed to meet Heather at her place at five thirty.

As soon as I hung up, my cell phone rang. It was Michael.

"What's going on, Copper? Are you coming home tonight?"

"I think I'll stay with my friend this week," I said.

"Oh," Michael said. I knew he wanted to say more. I could almost feel him biting his tongue.

"Hey, I'll come by this evening," I added quickly.

"Why don't you stay for dinner?"

I agreed to dinner after telling Michael I had an appointment after work and I might be late. Then I called David to let him know he was on his own. Damn. The day was not turning out the way I thought it would. Again.

I managed to leave work a few minutes early, and when I pulled through *The Light*'s security gate onto Bonanza Road, I noticed a silver Lexus pull out behind me from a parking place on the street. It followed me onto Interstate 15, where I shrugged off the notion that it might be tailing me. Stop being paranoid, I told myself, and I turned on the radio. Traffic was moving nicely, and it looked like I'd make it to the Silverado RV Resort with time to spare.

Down around Spring Mountain, I revised my prediction. A sea of red taillights stretched in front of me, and traffic slowed to a crawl. Time to escape, I told myself, and I eased into the right lane, exited, and continued heading south on Dean Martin Drive.

I was making good progress when I caught sight of a silver Lexus in my rearview mirror. Was it the same one I'd noticed earlier in front of *The Light*? Once again, I told myself to stop being paranoid.

I paralleled the freeway as I closed in on Blue Diamond Road. I had just stopped for a red light at Russell when—*wham!* My head slammed against the headrest. Something had hit me from behind! I looked in my rearview mirror. It was the silver Lexus.

As soon as the light turned green, I crossed the intersection and pulled off the pavement. The Lexus pulled in behind me. As I watched in my rearview mirror, both doors opened, and a man emerged from each. Both were wearing raincoats, gloves, and sunglasses. It wasn't raining, not even a little, and the sun had already gone down. They started walking forward, one on either side of the Max. They'd gotten about as far as the side door when I broke out in goose pimples. These guys had followed me, rear-ended me, and now they were surrounding me. Maybe I was paranoid, but just as the one on my left reached for my door handle, I stomped on the accelerator. The Max lurched forward, spitting out a spray of gravel as it jumped back onto the pavement. Fortunately, the road was empty as I careened back into the traffic lane and shot forward. In my mirror, I caught one last glimpse of the two men, backlit by their own headlights. One of them was talking into a cell phone.

Not knowing what else to do, I headed in the direction of the Silverado. I kept checking my mirror, but there was no sign of the silver Lexus. When I reached the casino, I pulled into the parking lot near the entrance. Casinos are always crawling with security guards, and I felt safe enough to get out and have a look at my back bumper. Fortunately, the damage was minimal—just a slight dent. The tailgate wasn't damaged, and the taillights were intact. I wished I'd caught the license number on the silver Lexus, but I began to relax. I wasn't hurt, and nobody was following me now. It was just an accident, I reassured myself. Just a fender bender. My heart rate returned to a more normal pace as I drove over to the Silverado RV Resort to find Heather.

As I rolled through the gates, I realized that I had never been inside a trailer park before. Since the only knowledge I had of such developments was a tornado joke or two, I was under the impression that trailer parks were pretty much hillbilly parking lots set up on cheap real estate in heavy weather zones. So when I saw the word "resort" on the Silverado's sign, I was ready to snicker. What makes a trailer park a "resort?" Flush outhouses? Storm cellars with minibars?

Well, I was as wrong about RV parks as I had been about brothels. The Silverado RV Resort was about as far removed from my notions of a trailer park as the MGM Grand is from Motel 6. The "office" was a grand white edifice with Corinthian columns and a copper dome. Through the oversize double doors, I could see a huge crystal chandelier and slick marble floors. I drove past perfectly manicured lawns and trimmed hedges as I looked for Heather's space. I counted two water-spouting dolphins, one golf course, three swimming pools, and four tennis courts. The spaces—hundreds of them—were occupied by an astonishing array of mobile living arrangements, and none of them qualified as trashy. They were all new, and most were huge.

I was creeping along a row looking for Heather's space when a posse of energetic speed walkers strode past me, arms and calves pumping in synchrony. They were all in spandex, they all looked like Jane Fonda, and they blew by me like I was parked. Another stereotype crushed. These were no Cheetos-munching couch potatoes. With their sleek thighs and color-perfect hairdos, these ladies were proud-stepping advertisements for the "active adult lifestyle" that I thought was a myth. I was still watching them strut around a corner when I realized I had arrived at space A-422.

I recognized Heather's pickup. It was the same black Ford she had been driving the night I met her at the Sekhmet Temple, only now it was parked in front of a big white trailer with an awning on one side. There was just enough room next to the truck for me to pull off the street.

Heather opened the trailer's side door before I could knock. She was holding a pink hairbrush and a tiny long-haired dog. New Age-y music was playing in the background.

"Hey, Copper," she said. "Glad you found me okay. Come on in."

She held the screen door open for me, and I climbed inside.

"I was just finishing up with Topanga here," Heather continued. "If I don't brush her every day, she starts looking like something a cat would cough up."

As if in protest, Topanga whimpered and struggled to free herself from Heather's grasp.

"She likes you," Heather said, holding tighter until the dog gave up and went limp. While Heather was occupied with grooming Topanga, I checked out my surroundings. I was standing in a dining-living-kitchen area that was far nicer than my apartment. An oriental carpet covered the hardwood floor. Two candles in glass chimneys flickered on the dining table, and next to them, a little oil burner filled the air with some exotic scent—sandalwood, maybe, or patchouli.

"Have a seat," Heather said. "I'm almost done, then I'll make some coffee or something."

I sat down on the sofa, which was partly covered with a fluffy white sheepskin. Next to me was a book bound in red leather. Its gold-edged pages made me guess it was a Bible, but when I turned it over, gold embossed letters read "The Iliad."

"You're reading Homer?" I asked, trying not to sound surprised. A bookmark with a purple tassel stuck out about a third of the way through.

"Yeah," Heather said. "It's all part of my grand self-improvement scheme. I'm reading all the classics."

"Wow," I said. "Impressive."

"You've done it, haven't you? In college, I mean?"

"Sort of," I said, thinking back to my freshman humanities course.

"Well, you're lucky you had a kindly professor to explain things. I thought I'd be reading about the Trojan horse, and instead I'm slogging through a bunch of bullshit about Achilles sulking in his tent because some dude stole his girlfriend."

"Maybe you should try *The Odyssey*," I said.

"I already read that," she said. "But come on. The guy spends seven years with a sexy nymph on a private island while his wife stays home and does his job? More macho bullshit. Then he comes home, and she gives him a hero's welcome. *Please!*"

She petted Topanga, and Topanga licked her cheek.

"I did like the part where the old dog stayed alive to see Ulysses one last time. That made me cry." She kissed the little dog and let her go. Topanga hit the floor running, launched herself from the rug, landed in my lap, and attacked my face with her tongue. She was so quick—and I was so surprised—that she even managed to lick the inside of my mouth.

"You like dogs, I hope," Heather said.

"Love them," I said, easing Topanga back onto the floor. "They beat men all to hell."

Heather ran her hands through her long bleached-blonde hair and wound it in her fingers before she let it go. She was silhouetted by the candles on the table, and I wished I looked that good in a belly-baring tank top and low-rise jeans. How old was she? I wondered. Thirty, maybe? Thirty-five? I really couldn't tell.

"Want some coffee?" Heather asked. "Or I've got some sparkling cider if you'd like that better."

"Coffee's fine," I said. In fact, it sounded great. I was still feeling edgy from my experience with the silver Lexus and the two guys in raincoats.

After Heather poured us each a gold-rimmed china cup of coffee—we both liked it black—she sat down in the chair facing me.

"I think Bobby Marks killed Victoria," she said. "Or somebody did it for him. He had motive, and he had opportunity. He also has enough money to pay a hit man and shut people up. That's what the Beavertail doesn't want you to know."

"Bobby Marks, the brother of Charlie Marks," I said, sort of as a question, but mostly just to fill the silence.

"That's the bastard," Heather said. "He's a Beavertail regular. Has been since before I started working there. He always asks for the newest turnout."

"Turnout?"

"The newest arrival," Heather said. "The new girl, the one he can intimidate. Because he's really a rapist. He's just figured out a way to do it legally."

I didn't know what to say, but Heather didn't seem to need me to fill in the gaps.

"It happened to my friend Tasha. She got the Marks treatment when she turned out a few years ago. A concussion and three cracked ribs. Not to mention a couple of other assaults that are supposed to be the lady's choice."

I looked blank, so Heather continued.

"Anal sex. Very few girls have it on their regular menus."

"Oh," I said, feeling decidedly ignorant. "Then why—?"

"Why does a shithead like Bobby get away with it?" Heather finished my question accurately. "The Golden Rule: the shithead with the gold makes the rules."

Topanga scratched at the door to the front end of the trailer, and Heather got up and opened it. Through it, I could see a small hallway and a bedroom. The little dog ran through and leapt onto the bed.

"She's spoiled," Heather said. "That's her bed. If I'm lucky, she lets me share it at night."

Leaving the door open, she sat down again.

"I got the whole story from Tasha. Last Thursday, the day before Victoria's body was found, Bobby showed up at the Beavertail around noon. His usual deal was to pick a girl, go to a bungalow, and stay as long as he wanted, sometimes all night. He'd drop between ten and fifteen grand every time he showed up, and I think there was more to it than that. I think he had Kent's—the owner's—head in a vise somehow. Blackmail maybe, I don't know. Something that let him get away with murder.

"Anyway, around three in the afternoon a chair flew through the bungalow's picture window. Tiffany—that's the girl Bobby was with—ran outside, with Victoria right behind her. Bobby ran out after them. He was bleeding and screaming.

"Within half an hour, everything was quiet again. Tiffany was in her room. Bobby was gone. No one ever saw Victoria again."

"He kidnapped her?"

"It's pretty obvious he did. Bobby hated Victoria. She was always looking out for the ladies and cramping his style. Kent and Bernice didn't like her, either, but they cut her slack because she also kept the ladies in line. It was like a cold war, always about ready to explode." She shook her head like she was trying to get rid of the memory. "Anyway, Tiffany told Tasha that when Victoria came to check on her, Bobby grabbed a fire extinguisher and sprayed it at her. Victoria picked up a chair and hit Bobby on the head. Bobby grabbed it and threw it at Victoria, only it went through the window instead."

"Do the cops know this?" I asked.

Heather snorted. "They could if they wanted to."

"You could tell them, couldn't you?"

"I could," Heather said. "But I prefer to do things that actually make a difference. Like tell you."

"Me?" I said.

"Yeah. The press. That's what Victoria would have done."

I sat there a moment, trying to feel like I really was "the press." But the more I tried, the more I felt like an imposter. I wasn't even taking notes.

Chapter 12

"You know what Victoria and I used to say to each other?" Heather said.

I looked at her. She was fighting back tears.

"God, we said it practically every day. 'We've got to leave the life before the life leaves us.' I had no idea how prophetic that would be."

"Why did you leave?"

"I had a Japanese client when I worked at the Beavertail. He showed up like clockwork, once a month. Liked blow jobs. Really liked mine." Heather pulled her legs up and hugged her knees. "He was a perfect client. Good hygiene. Great tipper. The other girls were jealous.

"One day he asked me if I'd go on a trip to Japan with him. A week—all expenses paid—plus twenty grand. I'd have my own room, fly first class, and all I had to do was—what I always did for him. It was totally against the rules, but the offer was too good to pass up."

Heather jumped up and reached above the sofa to open a cabinet. She pulled out a framed photograph.

"My daughter," she said, turning it toward me.

It was a lovely portrait of a tiny, fairylike child with white-blonde hair. She was sitting in a little rocking chair and holding a china doll.

"She's beautiful," I said. "What's her name?"

"Hayley," Heather said. She reached into the cupboard again and pulled out another picture.

The child was wearing the same smile, but in this picture, her eye sockets were hollow, and there were dark circles under them. She was wearing a knit cap and striped pajamas.

"My sweet little bald baby," Heather said. "That picture was taken three weeks before she died."

I didn't know what to say.

"Leukemia. We lived in Fallon."

I looked at her blankly.

"Oh. You don't know about Fallon's reputation for killing kids."

I shook my head.

"The desert has a thousand evil secrets," she said. "In Fallon, it's contaminated water. It's killed a generation of babies."

"I'm so sorry," I said. "I'm—I can't imagine—"

"Sick kids. That's what Victoria and I had in common. Big incentive to make a lot of money. That's why I took Aki up on his offer. I figured if I didn't tell anybody, the risk was pretty minimal, and it would buy good stuff for Hayley and my mom—she took care of Hayley when I was working.

"I told Bernice I was going to L.A. to look into new treatments for Hayley, which wasn't a total lie. I never got any farther than that, because the first night out, I almost died."

"Wow. What happened?"

"Fuck you," Heather said.

"What? I—"

"Most people call it fugu. Big Japanese delicacy."

"Blowfish?"

"Yeah. Aki and I went to this fancy dinner party at a mansion someplace in the hills, and he insisted I try everything. Afterward, I went to bed in a guest house next to the swimming pool. I almost didn't wake up. Blowfish poisoning is usually fatal, but I guess I didn't eat much, and it only paralyzed me for a few hours. Anyway, the house was empty by the time my legs would work again, and I had to hitch a ride with a FedEx driver to get out of there."

"I never went back to work at the Beavertail," Heather continued. "I never heard from Aki again, either. For all I know, he died. Hell, maybe everybody at the party did. All I cared about was that I was alive." She paused, and her mouth turned up in a faint smile. "And Aki gave me five grand up front. It wasn't enough to make up for nearly killing me, but it was still five grand. I took it as a sign to get out of the Beavertail while I was still breathing." Heather stood up and shuddered a little.

"Hey, do you have a boyfriend?" she asked, forcing a cheerful note into her voice.

"Yeah," I said. "Long-distance. But he's coming here for Christmas and New Year's."

"Come with me." Heather opened a door leading to the back end of the trailer. She flipped on an overhead light and beckoned to me to follow her.

I found myself in an elaborately decorated, fully stocked store. I stood there speechless, trying to take it all in. Clothing racks lined the side walls packed tight with dresses and sparkly outfits made of satin, lace, spandex, tulle, and feathers. Spike-heeled boots and shoes lined shelves above the racks. Display cases held corsets, bras, panties, garter belts, cosmetics, jewelry, gloves, whips, belts, chains, and an awesome array of what Daniel called self-diddling toys. A magazine rack was stocked with what looked like catalogues, and a cash register sat on a desk against the back wall, which was otherwise completely bare.

Oh, because the wall was a door, I figured out as I stared at it longer. The whole back end of the trailer could open up like a garage. And everything inside was held down with straps and bungee cords and wire fasteners to keep the merchandise in place while the rig was rolling down the road. Heather lived in a traveling store.

"My place of business," Heather said as I ogled the display in front of me. "As you can see, American Beauty is only one of the lines we carry."

I was too dumbfounded to speak until my eyes fell on a small framed certificate attached to the wall above the light switch:

This is to certify that Heather C. Vetra has qualified for and become a member of Mensa, the High IQ Society, it read.

"You belong to Mensa?" I asked.

Heather laughed.

"Yeah," she said. "That's part of my grand self-improvement plan, too. I knew I'd never get to do the college thing, but for Mensa, all you have to do is pass the test, and you get the privilege of buying a nice certificate suitable for framing."

She walked over to one of the clothing racks and unfastened the strap that was holding everything in place.

"It's pretty impressive," I said, referring to the store.

"Not really," Heather said, misunderstanding my comment. "Mensa isn't what you think. When I joined, I had no idea it was just a drinking club for fat Scrabble players."

She pulled a strapless bronze satin minidress from the rack and continued working her way along it.

"But the cool thing is, they're just thrilled that a former working girl has joined their ranks. They treat me like a celebrity, and—"

Heather's voice caught, and she paused before continuing. "I'm sorry. It's just that I never got to tell Victoria."

"That you joined Mensa?" I asked.

"No. She knew about that. It was her idea. She said Mensa membership was the poor woman's Harvard degree—elitist proof you have a brain for only fifty-nine bucks a year. I just never got to tell her that they've invited me to give the keynote speech at their next convention."

Heather retrieved a pair of translucent stiletto-heeled shoes from the shelf above the rack and moved to one of the cases full of lingerie.

"In Detroit, next July," she continued. "There are supposed to be people there from all over the world."

Heather extracted a garter belt and a pair of stockings with sparkles. "I had no idea what 'keynote' meant, so I looked it up in the dictionary," she said. "That didn't help much, so I figure I'll talk about whatever I want."

Heather moved back toward me.

"I'm pretty sure I can keep them entertained with blow jobs and blowfish," she said.

"I'm pretty sure you're right," I said, wondering whether the fat Scrabble players had any idea what they were in for.

Heather held up the satin dress.

"Ready to try something on?" she asked. "This'd look great with your coloring."

"Um," I said, caught off guard. "Um."

"Well, you don't *have* to. I just thought you might be going clubbing when your boyfriend's in town."

I looked at the dress. Daniel would love it, and my parents would be shocked. It was perfect!

"I'd love to try it on," I said.

Heather walked to the end of one of the cases and untied a curtain that ran on a track on the ceiling.

"Voilà!" she said, pulling the curtain on the track. "Your dressing room!" She pulled a small stool from under the desk and set it inside the space created by the curtain. "Just let me know if you need another size," she said, "although I'm pretty sure I got it right."

While I was removing my slacks and sweater, Heather kept talking through the curtain.

"Victoria and I met at the Beavertail Ranch," she said. "I'd been working there a year or so when she arrived, and we hit it off pretty quickly. We had a lot in common. Even beyond our sick kids."

The dress fit remarkably well, and so did the shoes. I pulled the curtain aside and saw that Heather had opened up a three-paneled mirror on the far wall. As I teetered toward it, she laughed.

"You need some walking lessons," she said.

I stared at myself in the mirror.

"You look great," she said, matter-of-factly. "I knew Isabella Ponti was the designer for you." I stared some more as Heather gathered my hair and clipped it up on top of my head. She was right. The dress needed an up-do to look right.

"It was really our grand schemes that brought us together," Heather continued. "We used to talk about how someday I'd own a bank, and I'd finance her run for governor of Nevada. I was always into the money side of things. Victoria was more into social change."

Heather kept talking while I changed back into my regular clothes.

"What really happened is that we went into business together—selling cosmetics to the working ladies of Nevada. That's how we began, anyway."

I stepped back outside the curtain. Heather was folding my dress into a large shopping bag. She added the garter belt, the sparkly stockings, the shoes, three hairclips, a necklace, and a variety of American Beauty products. I was dreading what it was all going to cost, but I was determined to pay it no matter what. The price of information, I told myself.

"At first, Victoria and I made the rounds of all the houses in Nevada selling American Beauty stuff—taking turns when we were off from the Beavertail. Then we realized that clothes were what the girls really wanted. It's not hard to buy working clothes if you're near Las Vegas, but try shopping for a garter belt in Winnemucca, or even a decent bra. Yeah, you can order stuff online, but there's nothing like trying things on. And you can't tell quality from a website. Believe me, there's a lot of crap out there, and a lot of rip-off artists. We were providing a real service—designer clothes and lingerie right to your door. By the time I stopped working at the Beavertail, I couldn't cram enough inventory into my car." She spread her arms out. "So we got this trailer. Traveling store and home sweet home."

Back in Heather's living room-dining room-kitchen, we sat down again. As if on cue, Topanga bolted out of the bedroom, sprang into Heather's lap, circled a few times, and fell down in a limp pile, her head hanging over Heather's knees.

"Victoria could've left the Beavertail when I did," Heather said, brushing her bangs out of her eyes. "We both said we would leave when the store could support us, but we didn't. I had to almost die, and Victoria—" She paused as tears welled up in her eyes, and it took her a second to be able to talk again. "She couldn't escape. The bastards got her." She wiped her eyes and looked at me. Her mascara was smudged.

"Bastards?" I said. "More than one?"

"Kent Freeman, the Beavertail's owner. Bernice Broyhill, the madam. They're glad she's dead. Besides her feud with Bobby, they hated all the headlines Victoria was generating. Most businesses love publicity, but not brothels. They're afraid it will rile up the Bible thumpers and get them outlawed."

"American Beauty must be glad she's gone, too."

"Yeah. Those bastards are terrified that their apple pie reputation will be ruined now that people know it's popular with whores." She rolled her eyes. "They lucked out as much as the Beavertail did. Bobby Marks was the perfect hit man, and they didn't even have to pay him."

The instant Heather said "hit man," my mind flashed on the two guys in the silver Lexus. Who were they? What had they wanted? Suddenly, I was very glad I would be spending the night at David Nussbaum's again.

Before I left, Heather gave me the bag of clothes and cosmetics. I don't mean she handed it to me. She *gave* it to me. Free. Wouldn't accept payment no matter how hard I tried. All she said was, "It's not a gift. It's payment in advance."

"But I can't—"

"Just do what you can."

I know I shouldn't have let her buffalo me into accepting a bribe, and I didn't do it because I was eager to have the stuff. Heather was just stronger than me. I could no more refuse her offer than Topanga could escape having her hair brushed. I hate to admit it, but I caved in faster than a dog the size of a guinea pig.

Chapter 13

From Heather's place I drove directly to Michael and Sierra's. I was glad I had warned Michael I might be late for dinner because the freeway was practically at a standstill, and there was an accident on Frank Sinatra Drive. At least no one followed me.

I pulled up in front of the vicarage a little after seven. Even though it was dark, Michael was doing a less than professional job of draping Christmas lights on the fat juniper tree next to the garage.

"Hi, Copper," he called. "Thought I better put up a few lights for Mom and Dad. How are things with you?"

He plugged the end of the light string into an extension cord and the little tree lit up.

"Damn," Michael said. "I could have sworn I bought the non-flashing kind."

"You did," I said. "There's one bulb in there that makes all of them flash. You just have to replace it with a plain one."

"Oh," Michael said. He is one of the least mechanically gifted people I know. "Well, maybe later. Sierra's got dinner ready. She made moussaka."

I love it when Sierra feels her Greek roots. She really is a good cook.

In fact, Sierra had made enough moussakas to feed the Greek army, along with a mountain of Greek Christmas cookies. Every inch of kitchen counter was covered with cups, spoons, pots, cutting boards, powdered sugar, cookie sheets, tin foil, and parchment paper. Sierra was wearing her ratty bathrobe with an apron over it. Her hair was twisted up in one of those big plastic butterfly clips, and she had flour on her nose.

"Wow," I said.

Sierra looked at me, and I instantly realized I was on very thin ice.

"You've been busy."

"What do you expect?" Sierra said with a hefty overtone of exasperation. She wiped her hands on her apron. "Your parents get here day after tomorrow."

Michael shot me a desperate, pleading look.

"Is there anything I can do to help?" I said, thinking I could change the sheets in the guest room or something.

"Actually," Michael said, "There is."

So suddenly I was roped into spending my lunch hour the next day at Sierra's real estate office doing some PR for the Alliance for the Homeless. Michael volunteered me to update the Alliance's website and send out an email newsletter to all the donors and supporters. Ordinarily, Julia Saxon would have done it, but she was busy trying to close the land deal and her assistant, Rachel, was off skiing in Utah. I'd have said no, but Michael said it was vital for everyone to know what was really going on with the service center project, not just what they might have read in the newspaper. The Alliance needed all the money and friends it could get right now.

❖ ❖ ❖

David wasn't home when I got to his house. I let myself in and also helped myself to a glass of Chianti before climbing into the fold-out sofa bed in his wife's study. I sipped my wine while reading *Your Husband and Your Orgasm*, one of a number of books on similar topics from the shelf over the desk. I must have dozed off, because when David knocked on my door, I almost had a heart attack.

"Sorry," he said. "I didn't mean to scare you."

"It's okay," I said. "It's just that I kept hearing what I thought was the garage door opening. I didn't think you could sneak up on me."

"Oh, yeah, that," David said. "It's my poltergeist. Also known as the furnace. It makes a real racket when it kicks on. Probably needs maintenance."

In the living room, David flopped down on the sofa and kicked off his loafers.

"I am beat," he said.

"I think I know who killed Victoria," I said.

"Oh, really?" David said. He still sounded tired, but there was undeniable curiosity in his voice. "Do tell."

He jumped up. "No, wait," he said. "I'll be right back."

He returned with two glasses of Chianti, making me glad I had left enough in the bottle.

"Somehow I feel like I need some fortification," he said, handing me one glass, setting the other on the coffee table, and sitting back down on the couch. He stretched, then reached for his glass. "Okay. Talk to me."

So I did. As entertainingly as possible, I described my field trip to the Silverado RV Resort.

"That's hardly proof, Copper," David said when I'd finished telling him about Victoria's window-breaking encounter with Bobby Marks. "And the only reason I can think of that Heather told you instead of the police is that she's hoping to make Marks look guilty when there isn't any solid evidence. One news item suggesting Bobby Marks might have murdered Victoria is all it would take for the public to convict him without a trial. He's pretty much generally despised around here, and nobody would be sorry to see him locked up for good."

"Why, because he likes looking at pictures of young girls?" I asked, thinking back to the clipping I'd found in Victoria's calendar.

"Yes, but he also has a long and sordid history of using and dealing drugs under his brother's protection. He killed a kid at a bus stop while driving stoned a few years ago and walked away with nothing more than a slap on the wrist. That's not the sort of activity that brings you public adulation."

"Well, what he did to Victoria can be checked out," I said. "I myself saw a glass repair truck at the Beavertail, just after—"

"When were you at the Beavertail?"

"Oops."

"You idiot!"

But he was smiling. I even got the impression David was mildly impressed that I'd tried to interview Bernice Broyhill.

Even so, he continued to discount everything I said, and he refused—or pretended to refuse—to take any of my evidence seriously.

"You're calling Heather a liar because she's a prostitute," I finally said. "You're as bad as the police. You're as bad as all men."

David didn't say anything. He just stood up and headed for the stairs.

"Good night, Copper," he said without turning around. "I'll be leaving around eight tomorrow morning. Just so you know."

"Wait," I said. "There's something else."

David turned to look at me from the landing.

"Two guys followed me when I left work today. They rear-ended me down near the Silverado."

David came back downstairs and made me tell him the whole story.

"Copper," he said when I had finished, "You've gotta stop playing sleuth. You still don't know who trashed your apartment, and the Beavertail's madam took your license. She knows way too much about you. You have to assume that whatever she knows, Marks knows, too."

"Okay, okay," I said. "If you wanted to scare me, you've succeeded."

"You don't want a Marks as an enemy. They don't negotiate with people they see as threats. They eliminate them."

"I thought the mob days were over in Las Vegas."

"Copper, I'm not joking."

I knew he wasn't joking. I was just saying something to drown out the hammering in my chest.

"The police aren't incompetent, you know," he said. "Give them a chance to do their job."

❖❖❖

Wednesday, December 21

The day felt backward from the beginning, because I started out by going to the movie I had to review.

Toto Too was a mess. *Benji Meets the Blair Witch Project* would have been a more appropriate title, but that makes it sound more appealing than it was. The whole thing was a jumble of sepia-tone doggy action shot with a hand-held camera. It was so jerky, I almost needed a barf bag, and I never did figure out the story.

There were only four people in the audience, and I was the only female. After the show, a shaggy guy in a thick turtleneck sweater introduced himself as a movie reviewer for a website called "Fair

Dinkum Flicks." He was Australian, but he'd been living in Las Vegas for over ten years. He thought the movie was "brilliant," and he liked to talk. So I let him. Afterward I could pretend I understood that the movie was a metaphor for the vicious cycle of poverty in the American South. But really, all I saw was a scruffy-looking mongrel trying to get away from the fakest-looking tornado in movie history.

"It's *supposed* to look artificial," Jake the Australian tried to convince me. "It's not a natural disaster, don't you see? It's only masquerading as one. That's the whole point. Brilliant. *Brilliant!*"

Maybe it was, but I still felt baffled. I was worried, too, because I had less than twenty-four hours to come up with five hundred intelligent-sounding words about it.

From the movie theater, I drove directly to Accolade Realty on Maryland Parkway, where Sierra worked. I'd never been inside, even though I'd driven by it many times. Sierra used to be a real estate agent, but she got tired of having to work evenings and weekends, even though she was supposedly good at it and made a lot of money. Her current job was "marketing coordinator," which meant she managed the ads in newspapers and magazines, wrote newsletters, and updated the company's website. She shouldn't have needed my help coming up with a letter for the Alliance, but the holidays were obviously turning her into a neurotic mess, so I figured I'd give her an hour. If nothing else, I hoped it would make my brother happy.

A life-size animated Santa Claus greeted me inside the door of Accolade Realty. Next to him was a ten-foot Christmas tree so covered in ribbon, tinsel, twinkling lights, and glittery ornaments that I couldn't tell if it was real or fake. A jazzy version of "Winter Wonderland" was playing softly, and the whole room smelled like gingerbread.

A chubby woman with overly pink cheeks and way too much red lipstick was sitting at the reception desk. She had a headset clipped on over a fuzzy Santa hat, and her sweater had a reindeer with a flashing red nose on the front. Two candles were burning on her desk next to a couple of plates of cookies, a bowl of ribbon candy, a gumdrop tree, and a snowman made of marshmallows.

"Happy holidays!" the woman said. Her phone buzzed. "One moment, please!" She punched a button.

In between a few more phone calls, I managed to sneak in my request to see Sierra. A few minutes and several more calls later, my sister-in-law emerged from behind the Christmas tree.

"Hi, Copper," she said. "Come on back."

She led me behind a partition where it took my eyes a second to adjust to the bright fluorescent lights illuminating dozens of desks. Most were deserted, but a few were occupied by harried-looking agents wearing headsets. The ones who weren't actually talking were typing madly at computer terminals. Sierra guided me through the warren to a doorway on the far side.

Inside was a row of cubicles. I followed Sierra to hers, which was equipped with an L-shaped desk with a huge flat-screen computer monitor on it. The only other thing on the desk was a framed wedding picture. Michael and Sierra had gotten married at St. Andrew's mission, even though my parents had offered to pay for a major blowout in Connecticut. Sierra had her own ideas, though, and they included a reception at the Italian-American Club.

The wedding was the reason for my first trip to Las Vegas, but I never got the chance to visit the Strip. All I saw were the red-checkered tablecloths, plastic grapevines, and plaster replicas of Michelangelo statues that the Italian-American Club used to decorate its cinder-block headquarters in an asphalt parking lot on East Sahara.

"That's where my father would have wanted to have the party," Sierra said. "And he's our invisible host." She insisted on paying for the whole thing, which included a sit-down lasagna dinner, dance music provided by a deejay she'd gone to high school with, and a strolling bouzouki player. I have to admit, it was the most enjoyable wedding I've ever attended. Even my parents finally broke down and partied, and my aunt got drunk enough to do the Macarena with a Cuban dude in a sequined tux.

My only other Vegas experience that time was a trip to the Liberace Museum. My dad wanted to make a pilgrimage because he felt like he'd grown up with the guy. His mother, my Grandma Mary, who died when I was ten, had been an avid lifelong fan.

"You were too little to remember how much she suffered when Liberace died," my father said. "Mom really believed the press hounded him to an early grave—never could accept the fact that he was gay. No one could ever convince her that Lee Liberace wasn't the innocent victim of a crash watermelon diet."

"But didn't Liberace himself admit that AIDS got him?" I'd asked.

"I don't think so, but it wouldn't have mattered if he had," my dad said. "For my mother, being homosexual was simply not an option."

The thing I'd liked best about the museum was the costume room. I can't say I swooned over the framed photograph of an aging male exhibitionist prancing in a pair of Yankee Doodle hot pants, but the outfits on display were undeniably fantastic. Never have so many feathers and sequins been individually attached to so many furlongs of sumptuous fabric, and I haven't even mentioned the rhinestones. I almost liked the guy when I read that he used to flash his megawatt grin at his audience and say, "Pardon me while I slip into something more spectacular."

When I heard that Michael and Sierra's neighbors Hans and Dustin had a collection of Liberace memorabilia, I wasn't in the least surprised. I wouldn't want that kind of kitsch myself, but there's no better status symbol for a gay Vegas couple of a certain age. And now that I knew firsthand what it felt like to have your private space looted, I sincerely hoped they'd get their treasures back someday. I also hoped their poor macaw was still squawking somewhere.

❖ ❖ ❖

"Am I really going to be able to help you?" I asked Sierra. "I don't know much about the Alliance."

"I can tell you what you need to know, and it would be a huge help if you could write the letter. The office may look quiet, but I'm swamped with end-of-the-year deadlines." Sierra turned her screen so I could see it. "I'm getting a web page set up, with pictures from the gala and the new property—"

"New property?"

"Yeah. The deal on Willow Lake—the property next to the sewage plant—can't close in time to save our funding, but Julia has found another piece of land we can close on by December 31st. It's actually better than Willow Lake in a lot of ways. It's bigger, and it has a motel and two houses on it. Not to mention it doesn't smell like a toilet whenever there's a breeze."

"Where is it?" I asked.

"North Las Vegas. Probably not quite as good a location as the other one, but more potential. It's nearly twice the acreage." Sierra opened another page on her screen that had pictures of an old blue-stucco one-story building with a faded sign proclaiming it to be the Bluebird

Motel, and another sign that said "Daily-Weekly-Monthly." At least it didn't say "Hourly."

"What's even better is that Julia has gotten the sellers of the new property to throw in a $300,000 donation to the Alliance to seal the deal," Sierra continued. "With that money and the existing buildings, we'll be open for business at least a year sooner than we would have at Willow Lake. She's really been amazing."

Sierra gave me a few other details, and while she worked on the page layout, I banged out a letter on my laptop that I hoped would convince the Alliance's friends and donors that the new arrangement was a gift from God. Fortunately, Sierra was happy with my work.

"That's perfect, Copper," she said after she read it. "Thank you."

"Let me know if there's anything else I can do," I said, hoping desperately that there wasn't. It was already one o'clock, and Chris had to be wondering where I was.

"I can take care of the rest," Sierra said. "Thanks for saving my afternoon. What are you doing for dinner?"

Dinner. I hadn't given it a thought.

"Don't count on me," I said. "I'm going to have to work late."

"We miss you, you know," Sierra said, and she actually sounded almost sincere.

"Uh, I miss you, too," I said, sounding far less so. "Everything will be a lot easier after the holidays."

Sierra sighed. "I don't even have a Christmas tree yet. I've never waited this long, and I just don't know when—"

"I'll get one," I said.

"Really? That would be great."

"Yeah," I said, already regretting it. "I'll do it tonight, but I don't know when I'll get there."

"Anytime's okay," Sierra said. "And I made eggnog." She kind of almost put her arm around me. "And thanks again for your help."

As I wended my way back through the warren of desks in the big room, I thought about what it must be like to have my parents as in-laws. Not wonderful, I was thinking as I bade the lady at the front desk farewell in between "One moment, pleases." My mother is too nosy, and my father is not particularly good at two-way conversation. A bloodhound and a sermonizer. Suddenly I was almost glad my apartment was still a mess. My mother would probably stay away, and I wouldn't have to hide the items in my medicine cabinet that suggest I'm not a virgin.

For no obvious reason, traffic was terrible. I was about to turn on my radio when I realized I could extract Victoria's tape recorder from my shoulder bag on the passenger seat. Thinking I might glean something new from her conversation with the American Beauty dudes after talking to Heather, I switched it on.

It took a second for me to remember that I hadn't rewound the tape since I'd first listened to it, but before I could reach the switch, a new set of voices cut in.

"… not sure about—" a man's voice said.

"We're golden, Jaz," a woman's voice interrupted. "The Alliance will go for the Bluebird property to save their funding, and we can close it by the end of the year. There's nothing to keep us from closing on the Willow Lake site in January. No problem. It's all clean."

The voice sounded familiar, but I didn't place it until a man's voice said, "Okay, Julie. But that reverend still seems like a loose cannon to me."

Julie! No wonder the voice was familiar. It belonged to Julia Saxon.

"He's taken care of," Julia said, and she laughed. "Isn't it great to have God on our side?" She laughed again, and I could hear two men laughing along with her.

"Oh, and Johnny—"Julia said.

The tape ran out, and the recorder clicked off. I sat there at the corner of Maryland Parkway and Sahara, waiting for the light to change and trying to decipher the conversation I had just heard. Whatever it was, it didn't sound good. And what was it doing on Victoria's recorder? Then I remembered. Julia had loaned the recorder to Victoria. Victoria must have recorded over a tape Julia had used before, but a little bit of Julia's conversation was still there.

I played the tape three more times on my way to *The Light*. By the time I pulled into the parking lot, I figured I knew these facts for sure: Julia Saxon had talked to two men named Jaz and Johnny about the Alliance's real estate deal, and my brother had been "taken care of," whatever that meant.

Maybe it meant nothing. I wanted it to mean nothing, if only because I had work to do, a movie review to write, and now a freaking Christmas tree to buy. Not to mention parents and boyfriend arriving. *Damn!* How much more could happen before I melted, vaporized, or exploded?

Fortunately, when I got to *The Light*, Chris was still out for lunch. He'd left me a note with a list of calls about New Year's Eve parties to make before five but otherwise, I was relieved to find, I could work on my movie review.

All I really wanted to say about *Toto Too* was "It's awful," but somehow I managed to crank out five hundred words of semi-praise by relying heavily on the exegesis Jake the Australian had provided. I gave the thing three boxes of popcorn—Dazzle's cute rating symbol—and shot the review off to Chris. He had stopped in to say hello on his way back to his office, and I was pretty sure his long lunch had been lubricated with something a little more potent than Diet Coke. His cheeks were usually pink, but this afternoon they were downright rosy.

I was in the middle of my last call when Chris materialized once again in front of my desk. He wasn't smiling.

"Copper," he said. "Did you like the movie?"

"I don't know," I said.

"What do you mean, you don't know? Did you watch it?"

"Yes."

"Well?"

"It sucked."

"So what's with your review?"

"I thought I might be wrong. I thought maybe I didn't understand it. This other guy was saying—"

"Copper."

"Yeah?"

"If it sucked, you have a professional obligation to say so."

I looked at Chris.

"Rewrite," he said. "And this time, the emperor is naked, okay?"

The last thing I needed was to write another five hundred words, but it was my own fault. It was also a lot easier to fill a page when I was telling the truth, and I used Chris's own reference to the emperor's new clothes to make my point. I was taken in for a while, I said, but after an hour, it was impossible to keep imagining a velvet robe when you were staring at a big bare pockmarked butt. I reduced my rating to one bag of popcorn. I could have gone for the turkey award, reserved for the worst of the worst, but I decided I kind of enjoyed the scene where the tornado ripped a bouncy house out from under a backyard birthday party.

The building cleared out a lot at five, and by the time I finished writing it was nearly seven. Unless there was a major media event, the whole place was usually deserted by then except for security dudes and the cleaning brigade. I'd only stayed that late a couple of times since I started working at *The Light*. I didn't like it much. The lights were half off, the temperature was ten degrees cooler, and I couldn't shake the feeling that I was being watched.

Maybe it was because I *was* being watched. I'd been surfing the Web trying to figure out where to buy a Christmas tree when I looked up to see Ed Bramlett. The bastard had sneaked up on me.

"What do you want?" I asked. I knew I sounded rude, but I was justified.

"Your brother's involved with that land deal, isn't he?" Ed said.

"Yeah," I said cautiously. "If you mean the property the Alliance for the Homeless is buying."

"That's the one." Ed said. "He should watch his ass."

I stared at him. I didn't know what to say.

"Good old Julie's chowing down again," Ed said.

"Julie?"

"Julie Saxon."

Julie. That's what they called her on the tape.

"She goes by Julia."

Ed laughed, then started coughing. He kept coughing. He doubled over and coughed some more. It got so bad I finally got up and offered him my chair. He refused in between coughs so wracking I was afraid he might eject a piece of lung onto the carpet. When the paroxysms finally subsided, I sat back down.

"Are you okay?" I asked, but it was obvious he wasn't. His face was gray, and as I looked at him, I realized he had shrunk since I first met him back in the spring. He was almost skeletal.

"Oh, yeah. Julia. To those who didn't know her when." He hacked a few more times.

"How long have you known her?"

"Long enough to call her Julie Big-Below. Her last name was Bigelow until she landed her first husband."

"Look, I have work to do—"

"Just tell your brother to watch his backside," Ed said. "He's swimming with some great whites."

Coughing and hacking, Ed moved off down the hall.

That was creepy enough to make me leave. I didn't like getting a second indication that Julia Saxon might be bad news, and I didn't like hearing about it from a gross old pervert like Ed Bramlett. And I really didn't like having him cough near me. He looked sick enough to have SARS. And what was he doing hanging around so late at *The Light*? If I had been feeling paranoid, I might have thought he was stalking me. Since I wasn't, I figured he just didn't have another life.

Chapter 14

I was cruising along Eastern Avenue munching on chicken nuggets and looking for a Christmas tree lot when my cell phone rang.

"Have you gotten a tree yet, Copper?" Sierra said.

"No, but I'm about to."

"Don't bother," she said. "Michael came home with something."

"*Something?*"

"Yes. Come on over."

Michael was dragging the something in at the front door when I pulled up.

"Hi, Copper," he said. "You're just in time to help decorate."

I helped him drag the thing into the living room, where Sierra was arranging a sheet of plastic on the carpet in front of the window.

"Where'd you get this?" I asked.

"Some dude," Sierra said. "He gets everything from some dude."

I looked at Michael, who was smiling sheepishly.

"I actually am kind of a soft touch." he said, "Especially when people come to the church selling something, not just asking for a handout."

"Soft touch doesn't even come close," Sierra said. "He's a complete and total pushover."

"Tree" didn't come close to describing the skeletal object my brother had spent good money on. It was completely devoid of branches on one side, and it wasn't much better endowed on the other. What needles it had were falling off by the handful.

"Not only hideous, but totally dry, too," Sierra said. "I won't even ask how much you paid for it."

"It wasn't too bad," Michael said.

"Let's just hope it wasn't stolen," Sierra said. "I can't stand the thought of some old lady going out to pick up her newspaper and finding a stump in her front yard."

Decorating Michael's contribution to charity was a challenge, but a few hundred feet of wired ribbon and loads of tinsel—not to mention several glasses of well-spiked eggnog—transformed it from a beaten-up TV antenna into a thing of Yuletide beauty.

"Even Mom is going to ooh and aah," I said when we plugged in the lights. Sierra shot me a look, and I hoped I hadn't given her one more thing to worry about. We sat down on the sofa to admire our handiwork and finish our eggnog. Sierra passed around a plate of Greek Christmas cookies.

"What time do they get here tomorrow?" I asked.

"Noon," Sierra and Michael answered in unison. I had the feeling they could have told me how many minutes of freedom remained.

"I hope you'll be here for dinner," Michael added.

"Wouldn't miss it," I said. "Want me to bring some wine?"

"Sure," Sierra said. "We're having moussaka."

"One box of rotgut red should do the trick," I said, and Sierra glared at me.

"Sorry," I said. "Just joking."

Sierra takes her role as hostess very seriously, with starched linen napkins, hand-lettered place cards, and those big "charger" plates. We were all going to be doing lots of dishes in the next few days, and I knew my life would be much easier if I brought a couple of bottles with real corks and years on the label.

"Michael," I said, mostly to change the subject. "Is Julia Saxon really someone you can trust?"

It was Sierra who replied.

"Who's been telling you stories?"

"No one," I said. "I just—"

Sierra jumped up.

"Whatever you've heard, it's a big lie." She walked over to the Christmas tree, rearranged a couple of gold balls, and turned back. "I'm sorry. I just think it's unfair that Julia has to keep paying for what her father did. People are just jealous of her. And they don't want a woman to get ahead."

Baffled, I turned to Michael.

"Julia's father was an attorney, too, Copper—"

"He was convicted of taking bribes while he was on the City Council a few years ago," Sierra said. "Lost his seat, lost his career. Julia had nothing to do with it. It was all that bottom-feeder Johnny Kusick."

Johnny. Another of the names on the tape.

"The important thing," Michael said, switching to his priestly voice, "is not to judge her by the actions of others. Julia has been a godsend for the Alliance. Without her, we wouldn't be anywhere near this far along with our plans for the new service center."

"The only thing she's done wrong is to donate her time, money, and influence to help the homeless," Sierra said. "Helping the homeless is not a politically correct thing to do in Las Vegas. This city just wants homeless people to disappear. Do you know what the most successful program has been up to now? Give them a free bus ticket to somewhere else. Do you know what the mayor's latest suggestion is? Truck them all to an old women's prison in the middle of nowhere."

"I don't know what you've heard, Copper, and I don't really want to know," Michael said. "It's gossip of the worst kind."

I looked from Michael to Sierra and back again. Well, at least I asked, I thought, and I got an answer. They both trusted Julia and they seemed to know what they were doing. The tape still bothered me, but I hadn't heard enough of the conversation to know for sure what it meant.

"I guess we have other things to worry about, anyway," I said. "Like how to show Mom and Dad a good ol' Vegas time."

Just then, something darted out of the kitchen, streaked across the carpet, and jumped into the Christmas tree. The branches shook, and a couple more bushels of dry needles fell to the floor.

"I knew it wouldn't take her long to notice!" Sierra said.

Damn. It looked like I didn't have to worry about Sekhmet anymore.

"She's been coming around looking for you," Sierra said.

The cat burst out of the tree, ran across the room, and jumped into Sierra's lap. She settled in, purring and kneading Sierra's thigh.

"I can see she really misses me," I said.

"She does, Copper!" Sierra insisted. "She's brought something to your apartment every day you've been gone. Yesterday, it was most of a dead chipmunk, but today it was a cinnamon roll. It wasn't even in very bad shape."

"What?"

"I'm not kidding. I've been going up there every day to make sure nobody else has broken in, and there it was on the doormat, in the same spot where she always leaves body parts. Who else could have done it?"

"I have no idea, but it gives me the creeps," I said.

"I think it's sweet. She loves you." Sierra was petting the cat now, and Sekhmet was doing all that feline affection stuff, like stretching her neck out and purring even louder.

I sighed. With so many other things to worry about, I wasn't going to argue with Sierra about whether cats hunt cinnamon rolls. In fact, I was glad Sierra thought the cat had brought it instead of what had to be the truth—someone had been hanging around eating breakfast at my front door. I was also glad that Sekhmet—or Delilah—had found someone who could take care of her properly. Sierra is a much better kitty mother than I will ever be.

"I better get going," I said. "Unless there's something else I can do to help you get ready for Mom and Dad."

"Bed's made," Michael said. "The right brands of booze are in the liquor cabinet. We're set, now that we've got a Christmas tree."

Sierra rolled her eyes at Michael's summation, which had failed to include any of the ironing, window washing, toilet detailing, and doily arranging she'd been perspiring over for the last two weeks. Not to mention five thousand moussakas and three billion cookies.

❖❖❖

It was nearly ten when I got to David's house, and he wasn't there. I had just set my stuff down on the bed in the guest room when the phone rang. Without thinking, I answered it.

"Nussbaum residence," I said, dredging up a phrase my mother had drummed into my head as a kid.

"Who is this?" a woman's voice said.

"Um, Copper Black," I said. "A houseguest."

"A houseguest?"

"Yes," I said. "May I take a message?"

"A *houseguest?*"

"That's right," I said. "Who may I say called?"

"Rebecca Nussbaum," she replied in a tone so icy it practically froze my ear. "Have David call me."

She hung up with a crash.

Damn! I don't know why I was so quick to answer the phone. David had an answering machine, and if he wanted to reach me, he'd call me on my cell phone.

Two minutes later, he walked in through the door from the garage. He was setting a grocery bag on the table in the kitchen when I met him at the doorway to the dining room.

"Hi, Copper," he said, walking with me into the living room. He dumped his backpack and a pile of mail onto the sofa.

"Your—um—wife called," I said. "Just a couple minutes ago."

"You talked to her?"

"Yeah. Sorry."

"Hell, I don't care," he said, and I could swear he was having trouble concealing a smile.

"She wants you to call her back."

"Yeah, well, okay," David said, sitting down. "Message received. Thanks."

He started looking through his mail.

"Anyway, you'll have your house to yourself again after tomorrow night. I'm really sorry I answered your phone. I certainly don't want to create any problems—"

"Copper, it's *fine.*" He slipped his shoes off and started flipping through a new *Atlantic Monthly.*

"Do you know anything about somebody named Johnny Kusick?" I asked, mostly to keep the conversation going.

"He's a real estate developer," David said, putting his feet on the coffee table and stretching. "Had some press a while back for a land acquisition scam. Other things, too. Tried to build houses on property he didn't really own. 'Wheeler-dealer' is the nicest thing I can think to call him. 'Criminal with connections' is probably more accurate. Why?"

"Oh, I just heard the name and was wondering," I said.

"Speaking of people with connections," David said, "I heard today that the police are looking at Bobby Marks in connection with Victoria McKimber's death."

"Really?" I said. "Are you writing a story about it? What else do you know?"

"No. And not much," David said. "So far, it's only a rumor. The cops are keeping it under the radar, which probably makes sense. A guy with that much juice can be pretty slippery. They'll need all their ducks in a perfect row if they ever hope to build a good case."

"Well, let me know if you hear anything more," I said.

"You know I will," David said. "If the cops arrest him, it'll be big news."

He went back to reading his magazine.

"David?"

"Yeah?"

"Thanks for letting me stay here. It's been a huge help."

I told him about the cinnamon roll. David put down his magazine and looked me square in the face.

"Have you figured out what you have that somebody wants, Copper?"

"No," I said. "I can't think of anything."

"I hate to ask, but—" David sounded almost shy. "Is any of your underwear missing?"

"Not that I noticed," I said.

"Check again," David said. "It could be a peeper who wanted a souvenir."

"Okay, sir," I said, saluting him. "Next time I'm there, I'll count my underpants."

"Want a beer?" David asked, standing up. "I got some pale ale."

"Sure," I said. "That's my current favorite."

"I was hoping you'd like it," David said. "Oh, and would you like to have dinner here tomorrow night? I haven't cooked in a couple of eons, and I got all the stuff to make meat loaf."

Meat loaf!

"David, you're full of surprises," I said. "But I can't. Command performance at my brother's house. My parents arrive tomorrow."

"Oh, okay."

"Want to come?"

Really, I don't know why I said that. Maybe it was because I was positive he'd say no.

"Sure!" David said, and there was nothing I could do but give him directions.

One beer led to three, along with a half a dozen games of backgammon, most of which David won. It was way past midnight when I finally went to bed, and I had to be at work by eight thirty. I lay there staring at Rebecca Nussbaum's sewing machine thinking about how much Christmas shopping I still had to do. And I'd have to call Sierra and tell her about the extra guest for dinner. I decided to bring her a bottle of apple schnapps and some expensive vodka along with the wine to soften her up. I knew how she loved those stupid sweet girlie martinis.

Instead of sheep, I fell asleep counting panties.

❖❖❖

Thursday, December 22

I can't survive on three hours of sleep, and three shots of espresso were no match for three late-night beers. But I made it to work in time to beat Chris, and he looked like he needed his Starbucks even more than I did. I could have sworn he was wearing the same clothes as the day before, too, which made me wonder once again about his private life. I always thought I could tell whether a guy was gay or not, but Chris Farr was a mystery to me. I was leaning toward gay—not that it was any of my business. I just couldn't help being curious.

Anyway, this was the big day. Michael was collecting the parental duo at McCarran Airport at noon. Sierra wouldn't get home until four, and I'd promised I'd get there no later than six. I still had to buy the required alcohol, and I was also hoping to get my Christmas shopping done. If there is a place in the universe where you can get all your Christmas shopping done in one lunch hour, it's got to be Las Vegas. And I guess I had nasty old Ed Bramlett to thank for the extra hour Chris was allowing me for lunch. It just proved there's an upside to everything, even randy old geezers with bad coughs.

I couldn't quite believe that Daniel was arriving the next day. With everything that had been going on, I'd barely had time to email him. He'd been busy, too, though. He was trying to finish a report he had to write to get his fellowship funded for the second half of the year, and he was also applying to graduate school. He was acting like it was the end of the world, but I knew he'd get it done. Daniel was a down-to-the-wire kind of guy. He'd probably have to run to catch his plane, but he wouldn't miss it.

I needed to focus on work and get a serious amount done. I had made a deal with Chris about the following week. I had been planning to take the whole week off, but he told me if I'd come in Monday,

Wednesday, and Friday, I could have Tuesday and Thursday off, and he wouldn't count them against my vacation time. Two free days was too good a deal to pass up, and I convinced Daniel it was a good idea, too. He'd be in town the whole week, but he wanted to play poker. If I had to go to work, he wouldn't have to feel guilty about deserting me. But in the meantime, I had about four thousand phone calls to make. I was still getting final details for the calendar about New Year's Eve parties.

My salvation was the bookshop at the Monaco, a big megaresort on the Strip. Not only did I find something more or less appropriate for everyone on my Christmas list, the store provided gift wrapping at no extra charge. All I had to do was stop by the next day and pick everything up, which I could do on my way to the airport to meet Daniel. I still couldn't believe there was a bookstore in a casino, much less a well-stocked one with knowledgeable clerks who wrapped things up for free. One more thing my Connecticut friends would never believe about Vegas.

I also bought a leather jacket for Daniel in a fancy men's boutique in the shopping mall at the Bellagio. It cost more than a week at the Golden Nugget, but I figured, what the heck? It's fun to spend money on people you love, especially ones who also happen to make you quiver. Tomorrow, I kept thinking. *Tomorrow!*

❖❖❖

I had started making calls again when Ed Bramlett appeared in front of my desk. I braced myself for the worst, but he just handed me a manila folder. He left without even coughing much. I looked inside and found a few xeroxed pages that all seemed to be about Julia

Saxon. But my phone rang, and I still had a meeting with Chris Farr scheduled. The contents of Ed's folder would have to wait.

It was Heather on the phone, wanting to know what I'd done about Victoria. As if I'd had time to do anything. *Damn!* I wished I'd never let her talk me into accepting that stupid dress. On the other hand, I couldn't wait to wear it for Daniel. Heather would just have to be patient. Victoria was dead. She wasn't an emergency.

I was trying madly to make all my calls before five, but then Heather called me again, worrying now about Victoria's husband and kid. I agreed they were probably in for a pretty sad Christmas, but what was I supposed to do about it? Once again, Heather out-muscled me. I agreed to meet her on Saturday to talk things over. I kicked myself after I hung up. All I wanted was one measly uninterrupted week with Daniel, but now that was looking like a pipe dream. I wished I had gone to Costa Rica after all. How could I have ever thought that spending New Year's in Vegas was better than basking on a tropical beach?

I was never going to make it to my brother's house by six. I hadn't even bought the booze. I decided to call David and tell him to wait until six thirty to arrive. Somehow, I didn't think it was a good idea for him to meet Sierra and my parents unless I was there to run interference. David's volume knob was cranked up a couple notches past reasonable, and I wanted to make sure my mother knew he went to Princeton before she labeled him a boor.

Chapter 15

Actually, the evening didn't start out too badly, even though David got there before me. I tried my best to reach him, but he didn't answer any of his phones. When I finally arrived with my bag of liquor at seven or so, he had already engaged my mother in a deep conversation about shrimp farming in the Mojave Desert. She paused long enough to hug me, kiss me, and offer to trim my bangs, but David really had her captivated with stories about a guy who wants to grow seafood in man-made ponds somewhere out near Mesquite.

Sierra didn't seem to mind at all that I'd added David to the party. In fact, I had the feeling she appreciated the fact that he was keeping Mom out of the kitchen. My dad was in there, though, drinking bourbon and petting the cat formerly known as Sekhmet. He greeted me with his usual bear hug and "Love you, sweetheart."

"Whoa! A mustache!" I said. He was sporting a neatly groomed brush on his upper lip, and it only had a few gray hairs mixed in with the reddish-blonde ones.

"Looks hip," I said.

"I needed a change," Dad said, "and it's a lot easier to grow facial hair than lose twenty pounds."

"You're not fat," I said, and he wasn't. He looked fitter than I'd seen him in quite a while, and even kind of tan. "You look great, Dad."

"So do you, sweetheart," he said. "Sin City must agree with you."

I heard Sierra emit a huff when Dad said "Sin City." She hates the nickname, especially when applied by outsiders.

"It's just so wrong," she would always say. "Las Vegas is no more sinful than anywhere else. It's just more honest."

"Let me help you," I said to Sierra. I unloaded my bottles and presented her with the martini makings.

"Wow!" she said. "Thanks!"

A "wow" *and* a "thanks"! I washed my hands and started cutting up tomatoes, pleased that the evening had begun well.

At dinner I was even happier that David was there. He talked more loudly than the rest of us, but he also had a lot of interesting stuff to say. After crustacean ranching, he told us all about the Las Vegas jewelry business, some scary stuff about how the Stratosphere Tower was built, and the odd tale of an eccentric Norwegian casino owner who used to hold parties to celebrate Hitler's birthday. If I had told those same stories, my parents would have interjected rude comments about Las Vegas the whole time, but since it was David doing the talking, they just said things like "Really?" and "That's fascinating!"

By the time we were digging into Sierra's signature baklava, I was feeling pretty proud of myself for contributing David Nussbaum to the evening. His presence even made my mother compliment Sierra on her Greek coffee. My mother hates Greek coffee, but she hates appearing unsophisticated even more. We had retired to the living room, where Sierra brought us our cute little demitasses. Unfortunately, David left as soon as we had sipped our way down to the sludge.

"I hate to eat and run," he said, "but I've got an early call in the morning. A press conference with the mayor. He's announcing an endorsement deal he's doing with Black Opal gin. He's getting fifty grand to say it's his favorite kind."

"That sounds fascinating," my mother said.

"I think it's inappropriate," I couldn't help saying. "He drinks too much, and he tries to make it seem charming."

"Oh, Ozzie's okay," David said. "He just enjoys ruffling feathers and being colorful. And he's giving the money to a worthy cause. That's what we're supposed to be finding out in the morning."

"This city is so fascinating," my mother said again, and I'm not sure I was very subtle about rolling my eyes.

"Copper, he's very nice," my mother said as soon as the door closed. "And it's so nice that you have Princeton in common."

"He's just a coworker," I said. "Not a boyfriend."

"You're staying with him, aren't you?"

"Yeah," I said. "But he's married. I invited him tonight because his wife's out of town." I felt a little guilty saying that, but it was true. And it seemed to satisfy Mom.

"Copper, show me your apartment," she said. "I'm so sorry about what happened. Maybe I can help you put it back together."

"Oh, it's okay," I said, but Mom insisted. Together we climbed the stairs, and I unlocked the door.

"Good heavens!" Mom said when I flipped on the light. "I'd better take you shopping."

The place did look pretty terrible. I'd done some picking up, but it still looked like a crime scene.

"Copper, may I use your computer?" my mom said suddenly.

"What for?" I said. "I mean sure, but—"

"I need to send some email," Mom said. "Where is it?"

"Oh, it's back in the house," I said. "My laptop. It's in my backpack."

I looked at Mom. She's often hard to read, but I had the fleeting impression that she might start to cry.

"Can you get it?" she asked.

"Sure," I said. "But you could use Michael's in the house—"

"Could you just get it?" Mom said. Now she sounded desperate.

"Okay," I said, not really wanting to leave her alone in my apartment. But Mom had already shifted some magazines and sat down on the end of my sofa, so I had no choice.

"What are you doing?" Sierra asked when I went into the living room and picked up my backpack. "Where's Jackie?"

Sierra and Michael always called my parents by their first names. I kind of wanted to do the same, but it felt too weird.

"Michael and I have an announcement to make," Sierra said.

My dad and my brother were nowhere to be seen.

"An announcement?"

"Yes. An important one."

"Mom's having a cow in my apartment." I said. "She says she absolutely has to send some email. I tried to get her to come back in here and do it, but she won't." I slung my backpack over my shoulder. "You know how she gets. I'll get her down here as soon as I can."

"Shit," I heard Sierra mutter under her breath as I left her standing in an empty living room holding a tray full of dirty coffee cups.

"Shit," I said myself as I climbed back up my stairs. "Should've gone to Costa Rica."

My mother was sitting in the same spot on the sofa when I opened my door, but the bathroom door was now open, and the light was on. I was right. She'd checked out my medicine cabinet. Did she really think she was fooling anybody? But I didn't say anything. I just felt relieved that I had transferred my personal lubricant to an unmarked container. I set my laptop on the desk, hooked it up to my cable modem, and turned it on.

"Who're you writing email to?" I asked.

"Oh—a friend," Mom said quickly. "Someone in my ceramics class."

My mother had been exploring her inner artist by learning how to throw pots at an upscale studio in Stamford.

I made sure my Internet connection was live, but Mom didn't seem to need any help beyond that. I had just finished straightening up my bed when she announced she was finished.

"Thanks, Copper," she said, all smiles.

"It worked okay?" I said.

"Message sent," Mom said. She seemed almost giddy. "I don't know what we did before email."

❖ ❖ ❖

Back in the house, Michael and my dad had reappeared, and a dusty bag of golf clubs was leaning against the wall next to the front door. I had seen those clubs before. They had belonged to my grandfather, and Michael had appropriated them in high school, when he had a brief and unsatisfactory career as the captain of the golf team.

My dad saw me looking at them.

"Las Vegas is a golfer's heaven, isn't it, Copper?" he said. "Thought I might hit the links."

"I had no idea you played golf," I said.

"Well, I haven't since before you came along," he said. "But I was the captain of the golf team in high school."

"Hey! Just like Michael!" I said, knowing it would bug him. Unlike Michael, my dad is actually coordinated.

"Well—"

"Michael!" Sierra called from the kitchen. He rushed off, and a second later they both emerged, Sierra with a silver tray full of champagne glasses, and Michael with an ice bucket.

"Ooh, must be something big," my mother said.

"It is, Jackie," Michael said. He popped the cork on a bottle of Veuve Clicquot and filled the flutes. Sierra passed them around.

"You want to?" Michael said, looking at Sierra. "Or should I?"

"Go ahead," she said.

"Jackie, Ted, Copper," Michael said, looking at each of us in turn, "I'd like to propose a toast."

We all raised our glasses and waited.

"To the newest member of our family, though he's not quite here yet."

My parents were still looking stunned when I filled the silence.

"You're having a baby? That's great!"

My dad came up with the next line. "Congratulations, son."

Sierra took a huge gulp of champagne.

"Should you be drinking in your condition, dear?" my mother said.

Sierra looked stricken, and for a second I thought she might start bawling. Instead, she turned and walked into the kitchen.

"Sierra's not pregnant," Michael said. "We're adopting."

"Oh," my mother said. "I'm so sorry."

I couldn't tell whether she was apologizing for what she had said or was sorry that some kid with alien DNA was going to be calling her Grandma. Either way, I didn't want to hear any more. I headed for the kitchen, where I found Sierra rinsing dishes while tears streamed down her face.

"That was really terrible," I said. "I think it's wonderful news. I can't wait to be an aunt."

"Go away," Sierra said. "Just leave me alone."

What I really wanted to do was to drive away, but I was still feeling the effects of three glasses of wine and the glass of champagne. The kitchen door provided an inconvenient route to my apartment, especially at night. Even so, a detour through the backyard beat having to talk to my parents again. I navigated the trash cans and managed to unlatch the gate next to the garage by feel.

When I got to my front door, I stepped on something. I looked down, but couldn't make out what it was until I'd opened my door and flipped on a light.

It was something white. I snagged it with my index finger, and as I lifted it up, I gradually came to the realization that it was a huge pair of men's knit underpants. Unable to stifle an "Ew!", I dropped them back onto my doormat. Those things definitely hadn't been there earlier, which meant that while we were drinking champagne, some fat dude had dropped his trousers and removed his briefs at my front door. David was on the right track, but he had it backward. Instead of stealing my panties, the pervert was leaving his own.

Relying on the vast amount of information I'd gathered from watching TV shows about crime scene investigations, I proceeded to "preserve the evidence." Rummaging around in the disaster area that used to be my kitchen, I found a large ziplock bag and a pair of spaghetti tongs. After bagging up the briefs, I washed the tongs, but I was still grossed out by what I had used them for. I couldn't find any bleach, so I rinsed them off in some mouthwash and left them to dry in the sink. Then I boiled some water, found my one intact mug, and made myself a cup of tea.

I sat down at my computer and thought about the scene at the vicarage, wishing David had stuck around long enough to ensure civility when Michael made the announcement about my new nephew. Thank God Daniel was arriving soon. I not only wanted him, I needed him.

My laptop was still set up from when my mom used it, so I decided to log on. I knew I wouldn't find Daniel online because, unless he missed his plane, he was already on a red-eye to Mexico City. But maybe he'd sent me a message.

My inbox was practically overflowing with messages. Most of them were advertising miracle tonics for insecure men, but near the top was a message with this subject line:

SENDING YOU ALL MY LOVE

Great, I thought. Daniel must really miss me. He's usually far more reserved in his declarations of love, and he never uses all caps. I clicked the message open.

I MISS YOU MY DARLING & LOVE YOU. HOPE YOU'RE DOING WELL THERE. XXXXXXXXOOOOOOOOO & LOVE & MORE LOVE & MORE LOVE & YOU'RE IN MY HEART & MORE LOVE, P

Well, that kind of prose was definitely not Daniel's style, and I didn't know anybody named "P" whose heart I inhabited. I was about to delete the message when a thought occurred to me. I clicked over to my "Messages Sent" file.

Damn! I was right! My mother had used my email account! She had seemed so confident on the computer that I assumed she had gone to some Internet site to send her message. I'm sure she had no idea that if she sent an email from my account, any replies would come straight to me. I'm also positive she had no idea that a copy of her original message would be automatically saved on my machine.

Dearest Patrick,

I made it to Las Vegas fine, and everything's going as well as can be expected. I just wish we could be enjoying "Sin City" together … we'd justify its reputation, don't you think? I can't wait until I'm in your arms again. That's when all's right with the world. Soon …

I love you, J.

I sat staring at my screen for I don't know how long. My mother! *Having an affair!* I really couldn't get my head around it. I mean, she was my mom! I had a hard time imagining her in the missionary position with my dad, much less doing acrobatics with a dude named Patrick who didn't know how to turn off a caps lock. "Someone in my ceramic class," she had said. I pictured a long-haired guy in torn jeans and a Greenpeace T-shirt. And somehow, in my imagination he was my age! *Gross!* I shook the image out of my head and turned off my computer without even checking for a message from Daniel.

I just sat there for a while. My head was like Grand Central Station with new thoughts pulling in every few seconds. Does my dad know? Should I tell him? Should I tell Michael? Should I pretend nothing happened? Mom will probably want to use my computer again, and I can find out even more stuff I don't want to know. Or, hey! Maybe I should write to Patrick. I have his email address, after all.

The one good effect of this fiasco was that I immediately felt stone-cold sober. I could drive, and David Nussbaum's house was looking pretty damned appealing. I could have left without going back inside the house, but it seemed rude to just sneak away. Anyway, I had to find out what delightful family activities might be planned for the next day. Why in hell I didn't go to Costa Rica, I'll never know. Relaxing under a palm tree on a black-sand beach was infinitely more appealing than dodging thoughts of my mother getting naked with a horny potter who called her "DARLING."

The front door was locked, but I had my key in my pocket. The living room was dark, even the Christmas tree. There was a light on in the kitchen, but when I got there, it was deserted. A half-full glass sitting next to the fancy bourbon bottle suggested somebody was still up, though, so I waited. Pretty soon, I heard the toilet flush in the hall bathroom, and Michael appeared.

"Everybody's in bed," he said, sitting down at the table. He looked pretty dejected.

"I think it's great about the baby," I said.

"It's overwhelming," Michael said. "But most of the time, I think it's great, too."

"It's a boy?" I said.

"Yeah," Michael said. "Nicholas Edward. Nicholas after Sierra's father, Edward after ours."

"Do you think they'll be okay about it?" I asked. "Our parents, I mean?"

"Yeah." He didn't sound absolutely sure. "I think they're already starting to come around."

"So when do you get him? When do we get to meet him?"

"He's in the hospital. Do you remember the baby that was abandoned at the church?"

"The one in the shopping cart after Thanksgiving?"

"Yes. He's our new son. Or he will be soon, anyway. We still have quite a few hoops to jump through. The police found his mother."

I listened to the rest of Michael's story, and I can't say I entirely blamed my parents for having doubts about the arrangement. Baby Nicholas had a large Filipino family, most of whom lived in a slum in Manila. Mariela, the baby's mother, was only fifteen. She came to the U.S. with her uncle and got pregnant almost as soon as she enrolled at Desert Pines High. The baby's father was a 32-year-old go-kart mechanic, and he was eager to pretend none of this had ever happened.

The family had tried to care for the baby, but he had medical problems that they couldn't handle. That's why he ended up in a shopping cart on the doorstep of St. Andrew's. Now he was in the hospital, where he'd have surgery to close a hole in his heart as soon as he was strong enough.

"But he's not a crack baby," Michael said. "That's something to be thankful for."

"Well, I can't wait to meet him," I said, hoping I sounded sincere. One look at Michael was all it took for me to decide not to tell him Mom's little secret. He had enough on his mind.

"What's on for tomorrow?" I asked.

"We left everything up in the air," Michael said. "Dinner, though, for sure. Okay?"

"Yeah," I said. "Wouldn't miss it for the world."

❖❖❖

As I covered the miles to David's house, I found myself hoping he'd still be up. I was dying to know what he thought of my family. As I made my way along Warm Springs Road, a flashing arrow sign caught my eye. Lou's Discount Liquor was still open, and on impulse, I pulled into the parking lot. I figured I owed David at least one bottle of Chianti.

The spaces in front of the store were taken, so I pulled around to the side. There were no other cars parked there, and it was dark. In some Las Vegas neighborhoods, I might have found this scary, but not here. This was Green Valley, the kind of community that advertises its family values.

Inside the store, it didn't take me long to pick out a bottle of red wine and pay for it. I had just reached the Max when I heard heavy footsteps behind me. Surprised, I turned to look.

All I saw was a ski mask before I was spun around and slammed against my car. The brown paper bag in my arms fell to the ground and the wine bottle smashed as my assailant wrenched my right arm and twisted it against my back. His forearm crushed my throat, pressing so hard I couldn't breathe.

"Don't make any noise, bitch," he said. "I've got a knife."

He wrenched my arm even harder, and I caught sight of the glint of metal. He moved the blade under my jaw, letting up on my neck.

"Please," I tried to say, but all that came out was a croak.

"Shut up," he said, twisting my arm until I felt my shoulder pop. I stifled a scream. "You don't want me to slip."

Just then a door on the side of the building opened. A man carrying boxes emerged, silhouetted by a flood of light.

"Shit!" my captor hissed. He released me, and I turned in time to see him sprinting away. He disappeared into his car and sped out of the parking lot.

I slumped against my car, struggling for breath. The liquor store man had seen everything, I told myself. But as I tested my arm and decided it wasn't broken, the man threw his boxes into the dumpster. He walked back into the store and shut the door.

As soon as I could manage it, I climbed into the Max. Pain shot through my shoulder and arm, and my neck felt bruised. With my

good arm, I pulled down the visor and checked my face in the mirror.
That's when I saw the blood.

Blood! There it was, spreading on my white sweater. The guy had cut
me, and I hadn't even felt it! I pulled my turtleneck down. There was
blood all over my neck, but I could see the source. It was a cut on my
jaw about an inch from my earlobe. God, if it had been a little lower …

I squeezed my sweater against the cut. I could feel it now, but the
flow of blood was definitely diminishing. *Damn!* I'd just been mugged,
and the guy could have killed me! I thought of all the times I'd walked
around New York City after dark, and no one had ever bothered me.
Now, here in Henderson, Nevada, "a great place to call home," a man
in a ski mask had attacked me with a knife. And it was apparently
such an everyday occurrence that the liquor store guy didn't even care.

Or maybe he didn't see it happen, I thought as I looked again at
the store. The light was behind him when he stepped outside, and
he'd had a stack of boxes in his arms. He probably hadn't even realized
something was going on. There wasn't much noise, and it had all
happened so fast. I looked again at the store, wondering if I should
go back inside and get help. I thought about calling the police, but
I realized I didn't even know what kind of car my attacker had been
driving. If it weren't for the smashed bottle of wine and the blood on
my sweater, I might have wondered if it really happened. I rubbed
my shoulder. It had happened, all right.

I decided the best thing to do was to go to David's house. It was
less than three miles away, and I'd be able to collect myself and wash
the blood out of my sweater. It was too bad the Chianti was gone, I
thought as I backed out of my parking space, but that seemed to be
the only real casualty. The cut on my neck had almost stopped bleeding,
which meant it probably wasn't be too serious.

I kept repeating "It's not too serious" to myself like a mantra as I drove to David's house. Even so, by the time I pulled into his driveway, I couldn't grip the steering wheel tight enough to keep my hands from shaking. I was shivering all over when I pressed the doorbell, and it was only after I had already rung it that I remembered I had a key.

I was fumbling in my backpack when David opened the door in his bathrobe.

"Copper!" he said. "I know I gave you a—good God! What's wrong?"

He pulled me through the door and held me by the shoulders at arm's length.

"What happened? You're bleeding! Are you all right?"

I was shaking all over. I stared at him as tears formed in my eyes. David wrapped his arms around me, and I couldn't hold them back.

"I'll—get—blood—on—your—robe," I wailed.

"Hey, hey," he said, stroking my hair and hugging me. "It's okay. It's okay."

The shaking had mostly subsided when David finally got me settled in his recliner and tucked a fuzzy plaid blanket around me. He pulled up a footstool and held my hand.

"What happened, Copper?"

As my story emerged, David grew more and more insistent that we call the police.

"You need to make a report, if nothing else," he said. "The guy could try it again."

"I'm not *ever* going to that store again," I said.

"What if he's not an ordinary mugger?" David said. "What if he works for Bobby Marks? You've got to consider the possibility that you're making some people nervous."

I pulled the blanket around myself more tightly. I was shaking again.

"I didn't see him. He was wearing a ski mask."

"You don't remember anything else? Even your impressions could be important."

I closed my eyes.

"He was about my height," I said. "And not fat. Oh, and the ski mask was dark green, I think." Somehow, thinking about the attacker was actually calming me down, and I was beginning to remember more details.

"Good work," David said. "Do you remember what else he was wearing?"

"Maybe something dark," I said. "Oh! And running shoes! He was wearing white sneakers!"

"How about his car?"

"I think it was a sedan, but I don't know what color," I said. "And I didn't see the license plate."

"What color was he?" David asked.

"What?"

"The guy. Was he white? Black?"

"Oh. I don't know," I said. "No, wait! I saw his arm. He was white, and his voice sounded old. Not ancient—maybe my dad's age."

"See, you really know quite a bit. More than enough to make it sensible to call the police."

"No," I said.

"Copper, can you give me one good reason why not?"

"I don't want to call them. It won't help," I said. "Look how much good it did after my apartment got ransacked."

"It can take time," David said.

"It would be all over the newsroom tomorrow," I said. "I can't face Ed Bramlett." And a police investigation would definitely spoil my time with Daniel. There was no way I was going to let that happen.

"This is more important than what people think," David said. "Copper, you could have been killed."

"Calling the police doesn't change that."

David sighed heavily. "You should change your clothes at least," he said.

I couldn't argue with that. I was still wearing my bloody sweater.

My arm and shoulder were getting stiffer by the minute, but after I cleaned the wound, put on some sweats, and left my sweater soaking in the bathroom sink, I felt much better. I found David in the kitchen eating chocolate ice cream out of a half-gallon carton.

He had changed clothes, too. He was wearing a pair of dark blue sweatpants and no shirt. I couldn't help noticing that he looked pretty good without a shirt—not nearly as hairy as I would have guessed, and his chest muscles were nicely defined in a way that didn't look too locker-room macho.

"Did I get blood on your robe?" I asked.

"Not enough to matter," David said.

"Good," I said. "And thanks."

"What for?"

"For putting me back together," I said.

"Feeling better?"

"Much," I said. "My arm's going to be stiff for a while, and the cut still hurts, but I'll live." I tilted my chin up to show David the scab that was forming on my jaw.

"You need ice cream," David said. "It's very restorative."

He got up, retrieved a spoon from the dishwasher, and handed it to me.

"I don't do bowls after midnight," he said, holding the carton out to me. I loaded up my spoon.

"Your family's a trip," David said. "A real adventure in WASP land."

"What makes you say that?" I asked. "I mean, I know we're pretty much the Anglo-Saxon stereotype, but—"

"Very nice, very polite Mount Rainier kind of folks."

"What are you talking about?"

"Everybody's cool as a snow-capped peak on the outside, but lots of geothermal activity deep down. You know, secretly ready to blow up without notice and destroy Seattle."

"You think we're that bad?"

"It's not bad. It's just different from my family. We're more Mount Etna. No buildups. Lots of little eruptions all the time. And a whole lot of venting steam."

"We've never talked much about how we're feeling."

"We've always talked too much about how we're feeling. Or maybe I should say 'yelled.' Which reminds me, I've got news." He scooped another spoonful of ice cream out of the carton. "Rebecca wants to go through with the divorce."

"Oh," I said. "I'm sorry if I—"

I couldn't help thinking that I had pushed things along by answering the phone earlier.

"You had nothing to do with it," David said. "I told you I wasn't very married. This is just proof."

I licked my spoon.

"I've got some news, too," I said. "After you left tonight, Michael and Sierra announced that they're adopting an abandoned baby. My parents aren't too happy about it, and—they're having their own problems, as well. Seattle just might be in serious danger."

David chuckled and dug into the ice cream again.

"You know," he said, "there's a big upside to your family reunion."

"Right," I said.

"There is! You have much less time to worry about Victoria McKimber."

I groaned, but he was right. A few days ago she was all I could think about. Now, in the cargo van of my life, she was taking the way back seat to Mom, Dad, brother, sister-in-law, nephew-to-be, and approaching boyfriend.

Except, *damn*! I still had to meet Heather on Saturday.

Chapter 16

Friday, December 23

The alarm on my cell phone went off at seven. I must have fallen asleep, because it woke me up. But I couldn't have slept for more than three hours, because David and I stayed up until after three playing backgammon, and I was still wide awake when I went to bed. My arm still hurt, and my brain refused to slow down.

I dragged myself to the bathroom. One look in the mirror told me there was no way I was going to work. The scab on my jaw was far too noticeable, and I had huge dark circles under puffy eyes. A constellation of purple bruises had appeared on my right arm, and my shoulder ached.

I called Chris Farr, got his voice mail, and left a message saying I was sick. It wasn't quite true, but it didn't matter. I had to look at least halfway presentable when I picked up Daniel, and that was going to take coffee, Advil, dark circle concealer, and time.

David had left early, and I was happy to have a whole peaceful house to myself for a couple of hours. I turned on some Mozart and took a leisurely bath improved with what I assumed was Rebecca Nussbaum's ylang-ylang bubbling bath oil. The phone rang while I was in the tub, but this time I wasn't even tempted to answer it.

The hot bath made my shoulder feel much better, and afterward I made coffee and sat down at David's kitchen table in my sweats. Thank God for David, I thought, and I wondered how I could ever thank him enough for letting me stay at his house and for taking care of me after my awful experience. A Christmas present didn't seem quite right, even if I called it a Hanukkah gift. I finally decided I'd get him something nice for New Year's. Something to wish him a happy new life, since it looked like his marriage really was on the road to nevermore.

But mostly, as I sat there in David's kitchen, I was thinking about Daniel. Even with my cut and bruises, I still felt that kind of anticipation you only feel when someone you've been longing for is about to arrive. While I was in the bath, I had let that delicious, tingly feeling take hold of my belly and spread out all over my body. It stayed with me while I dried off, and it didn't go away when I put on my clothes. As I sat imagining our reunion, it grew even more intense. I'd often gotten pretty excited when Daniel and I were online, but there was nothing like the real thing—real bodies, real contact.

By the time I left to pick up my Christmas gifts and go to the airport, I felt almost completely normal. Except for the cut on my chin, my face looked pretty good, and I was glad it was long-sleeves weather. None of my bruises would show until I took my sweater off.

❖ ❖ ❖

I love McCarran Airport. If I ever get really depressed, my cure will be to go there and hang around the escalators all the arriving passengers come down. College buddies, party girls, Asian families, brides-to-be—they're all exploding with excitement because they're finally setting foot in—ooh, ooh, *ooh!*—Las Vegas. The anticipation is so intense that if you inhaled it, you'd probably get high. But when I arrived to meet Daniel, all that euphoria was no match for my own. I hadn't seen him since August. That was nearly four months. In four months, a rabbit attains adulthood! In four months, entire insect civilizations rise and fall! It's a freaking eternity!

But now, it was about to end. Daniel's plane was on time—hallelujah, praise the Lord, and thank you, Jesus!—and I knew he was on it because he sent me a text message from L.A.

I'm about to board! See you in an hour or so, babe!

He sounded as excited as I felt.

I waited behind the security checkpoint, where I could see arriving passengers walking from the gates. Daniel was easy to identify from a distance. He is tall, and I would recognize his sweetly gangly lope anywhere. He had a curly mop of sun-streaked hair, and I could swear his smile was electrically enhanced. If a fairy turned a golden retriever into a man, the result would be Daniel Garside. A shiver ran through my body as I watched his approach. He was here at last!

I kept my eyes glued on him, but he didn't make especially rapid progress. He was talking to a woman while he walked. They were laughing and using their hands, and then she dropped her shoulder bag. A bunch of stuff spilled out of it, and Daniel helped her pick everything up. *Damn.* I wouldn't have paid much attention if she'd been an old lady or a mom with three kids, but this chick was Vegas perfect. She had the mile-long legs, huge yet mysteriously perky breasts, and a lion's mane of blonde hair. I watched as she touched Daniel's arm, and they both laughed. Then, all of a sudden, something seemed to be wrong with her shoe. Needless to say, it was of the stiletto-heel variety, and she leaned on Daniel while she adjusted it.

I suppose I shouldn't have been surprised. Daniel really did have the irresistible charm of a beautiful, friendly dog. Women and children always found him instantly appealing. I couldn't begin to imagine what it was like to have dental hygienists, postal clerks, and Denny's waitresses all immediately ready to climb into bed with you, but that was the story of Daniel's life. The amazing thing was that men liked him, too. My father thought he was "a wonderful guy," and Michael had told me that he was really glad he was joining the family for Christmas because "he's a lot of fun and so obviously right for you, Copper."

What they also meant was that Daniel was the sort of guy who could pull in a reasonable paycheck and maintain the family baby in the style to which she was accustomed. I could live with that. It kept them from asking too many questions about other aspects of our relationship, like the ones we were going to be enjoying between the Golden Nugget's sheets. I had friends in college who could talk openly with their families about sex, but there's pretty much a blanket taboo against it in mine.

I was beginning to wonder how Daniel was going to handle introductions when he and the babe moved past the security checkpoint. But I needn't have worried, because as soon as he saw me, Daniel stopped talking midsentence, broke into a huge smile, and sprinted toward me. He gathered me into his arms, and lifted me off my feet. Right there in the airport, we kissed again and again and again.

"Oh, God, I missed you," he said, crushing me close. "I love you. I love you. I love you."

Before I could say a word, he kissed me again—long, deep, and hard. Then again. And again. Finally, he pulled back a little, and I tried to speak.

"I love y—"

"What happened to your face?"

"Oh—nothing. Cut myself shaving. Daniel—"

"Yeah?" he said, kissing me again.

"Let's get out of here."

Fortunately, the only luggage Daniel had brought was on his back, and we didn't have to waste any time at the luggage carousels.

"Okay," I said after Daniel's backpack was stowed in the back of the Max and we had finished hugging and kissing each other some more in the parking garage. "We can cruise the Strip, or we can take the freeway. The Strip will take an hour. The freeway will take half."

"Where are we going?" Daniel asked.

"Hotel," I said.

"Freeway," Daniel said.

❖❖❖

I had thought we would have dinner at Michael and Sierra's—I know that's what Sierra had planned—but that's not what happened. My cell phone rang at five o'clock. By the time I had unwillingly extricated myself from a complicated embrace, crossed the room, and rummaged through my backpack, the ringing had stopped. Michael had left a voice message.

"What was that?" Daniel asked as I slid back into bed and snuggled up next to him.

"Change of plans," I said. "I have no idea why, but we're having dinner on the Strip instead of at my brother's house. At Mondrian. It's a 400-star restaurant at the Bellagio. You know, the kind where the chef owns his own jet."

I kissed him, and fifteen minutes went by before we took the time to breathe again.

"It's weird," I said. "Sierra made *pastitsio* for tonight."

"Maybe she's saving it for tomorrow."

"Nope. She has a crown roast for Christmas Eve. Something's definitely up."

Daniel rolled over on top of me, pinned my arms down and kissed me.

"How's your shoulder doing?" he asked. "Better?"

"All of me's better, now that you're here," I said.

Daniel kissed the bruises on my arm.

"You won't need a stepladder as long as I'm around," he said.

So, okay, I lied to him about my injuries. I just couldn't bring myself to ruin our reunion by telling him about all my problems. I'd tell him when the time was right. I'd tell him when I could make him understand the whole picture.

"Whatever's going on with your family, we can handle it," Daniel said.

"What makes you so confident?"

"I'm great with other people's parents," Daniel said matter-of-factly.

"And sisters-in-law?"

"I like Sierra," Daniel said. "She's feisty."

"She's about to become a mother," I said, and I told him about my soon-to-be-nephew.

"Really, Copper, it'll be okay. We can't let a little family drama mess up what little time we have together."

My family's theatrics seemed a lot more like a major Broadway production, and that was nothing compared to the other drama going on in my life. But Daniel managed to take my mind off it all with a kiss I felt all the way to my toes.

"So how do we dress for dinner on the Strip?" he asked during a lull in the action. "I've been living in cargo shorts for months, but I did bring some long pants."

"Oh!" I said. "That reminds me!" Slithering out from under Daniel and crossing the room to the closet, I pulled the strapless minidress Heather had given me from my garment bag.

"What do you think?" I said, slipping into the dress and holding it around me.

"Damn!" Daniel said, a huge grin spreading across his face. "You really have gone native!"

But I didn't wear the dress to dinner. Despite Daniel's best efforts to talk me into it, I chickened out and put on my demure little black dress. I wasn't as ready as I thought I was to shock my family.

We took a taxi to the Bellagio, though I could have driven the Max. I figured that if the evening got intense, I wouldn't want to restrict my alcohol intake. Daniel didn't feel like driving, either.

"I have all sorts of fantasies involving the backseat of a Vegas cab," he said.

"They have cameras now, you know," I said.

"Ooh. Better yet."

We arrived at the Bellagio about half an hour early, which gave us time to gawk at the glass-flower ceiling in the lobby, check out the oversize Christmas tree and four trillion poinsettias in the conservatory, and gasp at the price of beluga at the piano 'n' caviar bar.

We were still early, and the slim blonde at the desk suggested that we wait in the bar. Daniel ordered a beer, but when the bartender asked me what I wanted, I couldn't resist ordering a dirty martini. I've always found those girlie, fruity martini drinks easy to resist, but the flavor of expensive vodka and olives is something else entirely. Dirty martinis are my tragic weakness.

"Want a double?" Daniel asked. "You're not driving."

Unfortunately, I said yes.

Well, maybe it wasn't so unfortunate. I didn't get drunk. And it was probably good that I was a little anesthetized when my beloved family members began to darken the doorway.

My mother showed up first. She was alone, and at first I didn't recognize her. The light was dim, but that was only part of the reason. Her hair was different. It was blonder and fluffier. In addition, she had on a black, V-necked top I'd never seen before. It wasn't super racy, but it was definitely clingier and lower cut than anything I'd ever seen her in. This was a lady who usually wore big bulky sweaters, the kind knitted from fat yarn on needles the size of rolling pins.

I looked at her again, and there was no doubt about it. She'd lost weight. She had never been hugely heavy, but now she qualified as almost slim. I hadn't noticed yesterday because she was wearing a big Christmas sweater and roomy slacks. Tonight she was wearing snug black capris and high-heeled sandals.

"Hi, Mom!" I said as soon as my vocal chords would obey.

"Darling!" she said. "And Daniel! Merry Christmas!"

She did the hugs and kisses thing, and I noticed that her perfume was different, too. "Makeover" was the word that kept popping into my head. I didn't think she'd gone under the knife, but she'd definitely had a noninvasive remodel.

Daniel asked her what she wanted to drink.

"Campari, thanks," she said. "Oh, and soda." She turned to me while Daniel relayed her wishes to the bartender.

"Darling," she said, reaching her hand out to touch my jaw. "What happened here?"

"Oh," I said, "just a stupid little cut. I ran into something in the dark."

She peered at my face again in the dim light, but my answer seemed to satisfy her.

"Daniel's wonderful, Copper," she said. "We're all so happy for you."

"Thanks, Mom," I said, wishing I'd had enough vodka to add, "And I'm so thrilled about you and Patrick." But instead I said, "Where's everybody else?"

"Oh, they'll be here any minute, I'm sure," she said, looking at her watch. "What do you think of my hair? I went to the salon here at the Bellagio this afternoon."

"It's great, Mom," I said. "What does Dad think?"

She didn't answer, and I was still wondering how she had managed to arrive on her own when Michael appeared. He was wearing a white turtleneck sweater under a sport coat, which looked kind of clerical if you already knew he was a priest, but ordinary if you didn't.

"Where's Sierra?" I said. "And Dad?"

"Sierra's here," he said. "She just stopped at the restroom."

That didn't answer my question about my dad, but he showed up before Sierra did. He looked pretty sharp in a camel hair jacket and white shirt, and it was the first time I'd ever seen him in designer jeans. They were even the kind with a few tiny artful rips and artificially faded spots.

We were just about to follow the slim blonde hostess to our table when Sierra joined us. If I had been startled by my mother's enhanced appearance and my father's updated wardrobe, I was nothing less than stunned by Sierra's ensemble.

She was wearing a dress, and the last time I had seen her in a dress was on her wedding day. This, however, was no virginal billowing of white tulle. It was fire engine red. Strapless, it ended midthigh, and the fabric was something that looked stretchy, slick, and wet. The dress was enough to cause instant eye fixation, but I did manage to notice the fishnet hose and high-heeled gold sandals. She'd also fluffed her hair up into a sex kitten 'do. I used to wonder how Sierra had made it as an exotic dancer, but now I realized I had things backward. The real question was how she'd managed to hide her headlights under a bushel well enough to masquerade as a preacher's wife.

As we walked to our table, my parents seemed as stunned as I was by Sierra's entrance. They kept sneaking glances at her and looking shocked. What was going on? I wondered. Hadn't they seen her at home? Then I looked at Daniel. He was smiling a little too happily. I poked him in the ribs.

"I told you to wear that dress," he whispered.

Damn! He was right! I'd missed my chance to make a splash, and I'd never have another one. If I wore that dress tomorrow, it would only look like I was trying to catch up.

"I don't like being the center of attention," I snapped back.

"Right," Daniel said. "I'll keep that in mind."

We all sat down, everybody sticking with their partners. That was fine with me because I've always enjoyed the exciting secret games you can play under a tablecloth. The hostess handed my dad an electronic tablet and told him it was the wine list.

"Just touch each selection with the stylus for more information," she said in a well-rehearsed soliloquy. "We have over three thousand fine bottles to choose from, and our wine steward will be with you in a moment to answer any questions you may have."

And probably run a credit check, I thought to myself. This was the kind of place with plenty of four-digit prices on the wine list.

As we sat there in the silence following her departure, I looked around the table. "Why are you all dressed like fashionistas?" I wanted to shout. "And how come you didn't arrive together?" Suddenly, I was jealous of David Nussbaum. In his family, it would probably be fine to blurt out whatever question was on your mind. But in the Black household, rule number one is: Never ask the obvious question, especially if you're dying to know the answer.

The silence continued until I said, "How did you manage to get reservations here at the last minute?" I looked at Michael when I said it, but I realized I had no idea who was responsible. Mom? Dad? Sierra?

"Julia Saxon got them for us," Michael said. "One more reason I'm glad she's on my team."

Just then, the wine steward showed up. Right behind him was a stylish young sidekick carrying an ice bucket already holding a champagne bottle.

"A friend thought you might like to start with a bit of Cristal," the steward said in one of those generic European accents that might be French, might be Italian, and might have been learned in wine steward school. He handed Michael an envelope, popped the cork, and filled six flutes.

"À *votre santé*," he said before he vanished.

Michael opened the envelope and slid out a card. "Oh, how nice!" he said, and he read the message aloud. "*I understand you have something to celebrate—I hope this helps! Merry Christmas to the Black family. Julia.*"

"That is so lovely!" Mom said. "Merry Christmas to all!"

We all drank and pretended to smile, but nobody said anything more, even though I was positive Julia meant us to celebrate Michael and Sierra's new baby, not Christmas. Damn. It was going to be a long, weird evening, so I practically emptied my glass on that first swallow.

"So how's life in Costa Rica?" Dad asked suddenly. Black family rule number two: When the going gets tough, change the subject.

"Damp," Daniel said. "Green."

"Tell us all about it," Mom urged, leaning forward on her elbows. "I'm sure it's fascinating."

But just then the waiter showed up and recited the evening's epic poem about what the chef was concocting in the kitchen. After we had all decided which free-ranging creature and prepubescent vegetable we preferred, I excused myself to find the restroom. I didn't really need to go. I just wanted a break.

I had almost reached the door when Michael stopped me.

"They moved out," he said.

"What are you talking about?"

"The parents. They're staying here now."

"You mean here—at the Bellagio? Why?"

"Hell, I don't know."

Michael was upset. He never says "hell" otherwise.

"No idea?"

"Nope. But Sierra's taking it personally, and I can't say I blame her. She knocked herself out getting the house ready for them, and now it's not good enough."

Unless it's the new grandson who isn't making the grade, I thought. If this was a comment about baby Nicholas, it was despicable.

"It's a horrible thing to do," I said, still not quite believing it. "Except—"

I paused. I still wasn't sure I should tell Michael about Mom's email correspondence.

"Except what?" Michael glanced back in the direction of the table. "Tell me. I've got to get back and keep the peace. If something sets Sierra off—"

"It's just that Mom—well, she's got some things going on."

"Now there's news," Michael said.

"No, new ones," I said. "I think—I think she's having an affair."

Michael laughed. "You're joking," he said. "Right?"

I shook my head, and his smile faded.

"Well, I wish you were," he said, "because that's exactly what I'm beginning to think about Ted."

"Really?" I said. "Why?"

But just then my father appeared. Michael sighed and rolled his eyes at me as the two of them disappeared into the men's room.

"We took a boat over to Cocos Island," Daniel was saying to my mother when I got back to the table. "There are still a lot of people who think there's a fabulous treasure hidden there, but we were just doing plant inventory. The only treasure I found was a perfect conch shell, unless you count all the iguanas and hermit crabs."

"It really does sound intriguing," Mom said. "I've always wanted to visit Central America, but Ted always talks me into Europe."

That was news to me. I'd always thought my father traveled only to please my mother, and she always chose Paris or London. I looked at Dad as he picked up his napkin and sat back down. His mind was at least a light year away. What the hell was going on with them? I wondered. Half listening to Daniel's description of the iguanas and parrots that shared his beachside cottage and half wondering what secrets my parents weren't telling, I polished off another glass of champagne.

About the time the waiter was trying to talk us into an architecturally significant dessert, I heard a familiar voice talking to the blonde at the check-in desk.

"The Black family," it said. "They had an eight o'clock reservation."

It was Julia Saxon, all smiles in a sparkly green cocktail dress that made me wish once again that I had worn my bronze satin number. A man in a tux was with her, but he hung back. I tried to get a good look at him, but all I could see was curly gray-brown hair ringing a bald spot, a hawk's beak of a nose sticking out from under black-rimmed glasses, and a cell phone earpiece the size of a TV remote stuck to the side of his face.

"Michael!" Julia practically gushed. "I'm so glad everything worked out!"

Michael introduced her around, and we all thanked her for the surprise champagne.

"Congratulations to all of you," she gushed again. "I'm so happy for you, Sierra, and I can't wait to meet little Nicky."

Sierra was trying to respond when Julia abruptly turned again to Michael.

"Can you meet tomorrow?" she asked, suddenly all business. "I've got a few things we need to go over."

Michael was caught off guard.

"Uh, sure," he said.

"My office. Eleven o'clock." Then she turned to me.

"Copper," she said, too fiercely to be friendly. "Have you found the tape recorder I loaned to Victoria? Or any cassettes? Richard McKimber doesn't have them."

I gaped at her.

"Copper, they could be very important to her case against American Beauty."

"I haven't seen anything like that so far, but I'll keep looking," I said, "I still have quite a bit of material to go through."

Julia stared at me, and I couldn't squelch the feeling that she thought I was lying. "Do it tonight," she said at last. "Call me tomorrow. Have you got my cell number?"

As soon as I punched her number into my phone, Julia pasted another big smile on her face, wished us all another "Happy holidays," and swept away on the arm of her tuxedoed escort. As they disappeared, I saw the guy was wearing white running shoes. They couldn't have stood out more against his black suit if they'd been wired with Christmas lights. Just like the creep last night, I thought. What an odd coincidence.

❖❖❖

I mentioned my parents' change of address to Daniel on our way back to the Golden Nugget.

"I'm sure that's why Sierra was dressed like that," I said. "She's always tried to come across as the demure daughter-in-law, but now I think her attitude has pretty much changed to 'Go to hell.'"

"I don't think it's Sierra's housekeeping that made your folks move out," Daniel said. "I think they're splitting up."

"Mom and Dad? Never. They still hold hands at the movies. They still pinch each other's bottoms."

"They're staying in separate rooms."

"No they aren't!"

"You didn't notice when we were leaving?"

"Notice what?"

"Your mom said, 'Ted, I've got your reading glasses, in case you need them.'"

"So what?" I said. "She probably meant they were in her purse. She keeps a fully stocked drugstore in there, among other things."

"Your dad said, 'I'll stop by later and get them.'"

"He said that?"

"Yup."

"You must have misunderstood."

But I can't say I really believed that as we walked toward the hotel. My parents are sometimes clueless, but I've never known them to be rude. Was it possible they had moved to the Bellagio because they couldn't handle sharing a double bed? The four-poster in Sierra's guest room wasn't even a queen. As we walked into the casino, my head was spinning at the thought of my parents ceasing to be a unit. It was as though someone had just told me that all the faces had fallen off Mount Rushmore or the Brooklyn Bridge had collapsed.

I looked at Daniel. His face was wearing a mesmerized half smile, and I suddenly realized that this was the first time we were walking through a casino together without pressure to get to the other side. Earlier, we'd checked in and made a beeline for our room. At the Bellagio, we'd steamed right past the slots and table games to get to the restaurant. But now, the glitz and *ka-ching* were working their magic on Daniel. As I watched him survey the scene, I tried to remember the first time I'd stepped into a Las Vegas casino. It hadn't been all that long ago—less than a year—but it seemed like an eon. God! I was already a jaded old-timer.

"It's still pretty early," Daniel said tentatively when we reached the elevator. "Would you like another dirty martini?"

"Would you like to play poker?" I said.

"Maybe just for a few minutes," Daniel said. "I've been practicing online."

After assuring Daniel that it was perfectly fine with me if he played poker for a while, I went up to our room alone. I'm not sure it was perfectly fine, but it also wasn't horrible. I should be glad he'll be able to entertain himself while I'm at work, I told myself. Really, it's a good thing.

I fell asleep watching *Celebrity Dance Marathon*, and I woke up when a naked man slipped in next to me and kissed me on the ear.

Chapter 17

Saturday, December 24

I had a hard time believing that tonight would be Christmas Eve. I had always spent the day before Christmas hanging around the house, wrapping presents, listening to Nat King Cole croon about chestnuts, and maybe watching *A Christmas Story*. The most strenuous activity was cooking dinner and then trying to stay awake until it was time to go to church for the midnight service.

This just wasn't going to be an ordinary Christmas, although waking up in the arms of a good-looking guy in a friendly mood was a change I'd be happy to incorporate into future Yuletide celebrations. Only now I had to inform said guy that I'd promised to meet a retired prostitute for lunch. I'd been putting it off because I knew Daniel wouldn't like the idea of going to a trailer park to chat with a working girl. Actually, he probably would have liked it if I hadn't been the one to suggest it. I lay in bed wondering how to break the news to him while he went downstairs to buy us a quick breakfast.

When my cell phone rang, I thought it might be Daniel, explaining why it was taking so long to acquire a couple of lattes. But it wasn't. It was Heather. Instead of meeting at her rig, she wanted to meet at a McDonald's inside a Walmart down near where David Nussbaum lives. She said she was buying presents for "lost angels." I wasn't sure what "lost angels" were, but I had once seen a book about Wild West hookers called *Soiled Doves*. Maybe "soiled doves" were called "lost angels" at Christmastime. Anyway, now I not only had Heather to explain to Daniel, but also why we were going to join her for a Happy Meal.

❖❖❖

Daniel finally got back with our lattes and a couple of quite outstanding chocolate-filled croissants. I tried to slip my meeting with Heather into the conversation casually.

"I guess we better force ourselves to put on some clothes," I said, my legs still entwined with Daniel's under the covers.

"I already did that once this morning," he said, locking his ankles around me. "What's the rush?"

"Oh, nothing," I said. "Except—well—Las Vegas."

"This *is* Vegas, baby," Daniel said, sliding his arm around my neck and kissing me in a manner that proved once again that my lips and tongue have a high-speed connection with the bikini triangle.

"Mmmm," I said. "You have a very good point." I sneaked a look at the clock radio. 11:15. I let my hands start sliding, and the next time I caught a glimpse of the clock, it was after noon.

"Oh, my God!"

"What is it, babe?"

"I have an—appointment—at one!" I said. "I'm never going to make it!" I leapt out of bed. Daniel was right behind me.

"On Christmas Eve?" he said, grabbing me from behind and resting his chin on my shoulder. "I thought our only command performance was dinner at your brother's house."

"Well," I said, "I forgot to tell you about Heather."

"Heather?"

As I gave Daniel a brief rundown of my continued inquiries into Victoria's death, the atmosphere in the room grew noticeably chillier.

"So—do you want to stay here or go with me?" I asked, honestly unsure what I hoped his answer might be.

"What choice do I have?" he said. "Somebody has to look out for you."

❖❖❖

On the way down to Walmart, I realized that I had to fill Daniel in on some of the details of my life. He took things pretty well until I explained the scab on my jaw. He just sat there for a moment, staring through the windshield.

"You were knifed?" he finally said. "You were burglarized?"

I nodded.

"You went to a *whorehouse*?"

I almost laughed. He made it sound like my trip to the Beavertail was worse than getting mugged.

"It's not like they're all connected," I said, but I don't know how convincing I sounded. I was still bothered by the white sneakers Julia Saxon's companion had been wearing at dinner. But I shrugged it off. It was hardly solid evidence.

"God, Copper," Daniel said as we pulled off Eastern Avenue into the Walmart shopping center. "God *damn*." He looked at me, and I think I'm reporting accurately when I say I saw genuine concern in his eyes. "This place isn't good for you."

"I like living here," I said. "It's not what I thought it would be."

"It's everything I thought it would be and worse," Daniel said. "You've been injured, terrorized, robbed, and—I don't know—you're not the same. You're—tough."

Tough! I couldn't help smiling. The adjective had never been applied to sweet little Copper Black before. Well, maybe back in second grade when I finally developed enough calluses to go on the monkey bars without getting blisters.

"I'm still me," I said. "I'm just having significant life experiences. Just like you."

"I can't believe you're trying to make a knife wound near your jugular sound like a botany field trip."

"Look, I don't want to fight," I said, pulling into a parking place at least a mile from the store's entrance. It seemed like every car in town was at Walmart. "I just want to have a Big Mac and find out what's eating Heather. Are you coming?"

Daniel joined me in the crowd surging toward the entrance to Walmart, a dark look still clouding his face.

Heather was easy to spot. McDonald's was almost as crowded as the parking lot, but she had managed to stake out a table for four near the entrance with three shopping carts piled high with a remarkable haul of dolls, stuffed animals, games, and toys. She was poring over a computer printout on the table and making checkmarks with a pencil when I said hello.

"Oh, good!" Heather said, without looking up. "I'm glad you're here. Sit down."

"I brought a friend," I said. "This is Daniel."

That got Heather's full attention.

"Oh!" she said, standing up. "How nice to meet you!"

It wasn't what she said that had the effect. It was how she said it and what her body was doing simultaneously. She shook her hair and

shifted her shoulders so her breasts—which were barely encased in
a tight, pale green turtleneck emerged from her leather jacket like
a couple of honeydews. She took Daniel's hand and looked straight
into his eyes, which was easy because they were almost exactly the
same height. She smiled a glossy fuchsia smile.

"Welcome to Las Vegas," she said.

Really, men are so easy. Daniel melted faster than chocolate in
August. He puddled into a chair directly across from Heather, and I
took the one next to him.

"I'm not quite done with my shopping," Heather said. "We have a
bumper crop of lost angels this year."

Lost angels, it turns out, aren't fallen women. They are the
Christmas dreams of orphans. Every year, children who otherwise
would get no presents at all write their fondest wishes on little white
paper angels. The United Christian Charities of Southern Nevada
sets up Christmas trees at malls and shopping centers around the
valley, each one decorated with the paper angels. Passing shoppers
are invited to take an angel, buy the item noted on it, and turn it in
at a table staffed by volunteers.

"The trouble is," Heather explained, "some people take the angels
and never bring back the gifts."

She turned her computer printout around so Daniel and I could
see how many names were on the list.

"Maybe they forget or decide they can't afford the gift after all, but
it's real kids those thoughtless bastards are shafting," she said. "This
year more than ever before. I've bought fifty-eight gifts so far, and
I'm only about two-thirds done. I thought I could get everything here
at Walmart, but it looks like I'll have to hit Toys-R-Us and maybe
even Target to finish up." She sighed. "The big challenge this year is
Go-Go Godfrey. I've got eight, but I need eleven. Personally, I don't

see the appeal of a burping platypus, but that's not the point." Heather looked at her watch. "I'll make this fast," she said. "Do you need food?"

While Daniel was off acquiring burgers, fries, and Cokes, Heather opened her shoulder bag and pulled out a yellow envelope.

"Take a look at these," she said, pulling out some snapshots. "I think you'll understand why I'm concerned."

She spread the pictures on the table in front of me. Two showed the filthiest kitchen I've ever seen, complete with spilled garbage and dirty dishes on the floor. Two more showed a living room that looked worse than my apartment right after it was ransacked.

"The McKimber residence," Heather said.

"What happened?" I asked. I thought back to my own visit to Victoria's house. I hadn't gone inside, but it had certainly looked tidy on the exterior.

"Things are going downhill fast," Heather continued. "Mostly because of Jason. He's bipolar, and when he doesn't take his meds, he turns into Freddy Krueger. I'm sure that's why the house looks so bad. He was on a rampage when I showed up the other night. Richard got a pretty bad gash over his left eye before we managed to calm Jason down. I stopped the bleeding with a butterfly Band-Aid, but he probably could have used a few stitches. But a cut is the least of his problems. Richard's a wreck without Victoria. He used to keep the house immaculate, but now it's like he's paralyzed."

She paused and looked straight at me.

"So, here's the deal. If things continue the way they are, somebody's going to get hurt or arrested or both. Jason needs to go someplace. A school. A camp. A hospital. I don't know. But he needs residential care, and it takes money. I've given Richard all I can. It really ought to be Bobby Marks who coughs up the cash, but that's not happening, so that leaves American Beauty. Those bastards are benefiting from

Victoria's death too much to get off without paying a nickel. They owe her."

Suddenly I remembered Victoria's photographs, the ones from the film I'd had developed. I rummaged in my own shoulder bag and pulled them out.

"Do you know who these guys are?" I asked, showing her the picture of the two men in the dark restaurant.

Heather grabbed the whole stack of pictures out of my hand.

"This guy on the left is Rick Mack," she said. "He works for American Beauty. I've never seen the chubby dude before."

She flipped through the other pictures.

"Hey, I know who this is, too." She turned one of the pictures around. It was one of the close-ups, the one showing teeth.

"I'd recognize that sneer anywhere. It's Jason. He crashed his skateboard a year ago. Broke his arm badly enough to require surgery to set it. He also chipped a tooth, and he likes it. He thinks it looks like a vampire fang." She handed the pictures back to me. "I bet he took that himself," she said. "You know, a selfie."

I looked at the picture again, noticing that Jason had been in a car when it was taken. The headrest and the back window were visible behind him.

"Is there anything we can do?" I asked.

"I've done what I can, Copper. I'm tapped out. It's time for some deep pockets."

I looked at her, wondering whether she had me confused with a cash cow.

"Julia Saxon can strong-arm the right people, but she won't answer my calls. That's why I called you. I need the power of the press."

Daniel arrived back at the table just in time to hear that. As he set the tray of food down, he shot me a quizzical look that almost made me smile. Daniel knew what my job was, but I'm sure he had never thought of me as a member of "the press."

"I guess I could give her a try," I said, deciding not to mention that I had promised to call her anyway. "But I think the reason she's been hard to reach is that she's—well, she's trying to close a big deal before the end of the year."

"Of course she's busy," Heather said. "Everybody's busy when you want to talk about a dead hooker."

I looked at Daniel, but he didn't return my glance. He was too entranced with Heather's chest.

"But it's not impossible to get her to cut the crap and do something," Heather went on. "You just have to be a bigger pain in the ass than everybody else." She took a sip of Coke. "Or maybe drop a hint that you're working on a story about lawyers who drop their pro bono cases when the going gets tough."

By the time we headed back to the Max, I had promised Heather at least a dozen times that I would talk to Julia about putting the squeeze on American Beauty. It seemed unlikely that anything would happen anytime soon, though. It was the holidays, for Christ's sake.

"It's the holidays for Christ's sake," Daniel said as we inched out of the parking lot.

"What do you mean?"

"Can't you take a few days off? I'm beginning to think I should've gone to Austin for Christmas. At least it would have made my mom happy."

Daniel's father is a geology professor at the University of Texas. He met Daniel's mother when they were both doing research in South Africa. He's originally from California, she's originally from Scotland, and even though they'd lived in Austin for decades, neither one seemed very Texan. Neither did Daniel.

"Come on, Daniel," I said. "This isn't ordinary work. Victoria's family is suffering."

"People are suffering all over, Copper."

"These are people I know."

"So am I."

I glanced at him. He was staring straight ahead.

"I love you," I said.

"I love you, too," Daniel said.

"So—what did you think of Heather?"

"Bad role model," he said. "For you anyway. She'd be okay for someone training to be a ballbuster."

"Heather's okay," I said. "You know why she's doing all that shopping?"

I told Daniel about Hayley, her daughter who died of cancer.

"Look, Copper," Daniel said when I had finished. "I think it's wonderful that a—person like Heather loved her kid and does charitable works in her memory. I even think it's fine that you want to write a story about Victoria. I'm sure it'll be fascinating. What I don't get is why you have to have a personal relationship with all of them—any of them. Really, I just don't get that part."

"Where are we going?" I said. When I said it, I thought I was asking about our immediate physical destination, but as it hung in the air, it seemed more like a question about our relationship.

"I don't know. This is your town, babe."

It was only two o'clock. I didn't really feel like going to Michael and Sierra's yet, but I didn't have any other brilliant ideas.

"I like Las Vegas," I said. "It's not what I thought it would be."

"So you've told me," Daniel said, doing a great job of making his voice sound like a pout.

Inspiration struck. I got on the freeway heading west. Traffic was still light, and soon we were cruising out Blue Diamond Road. The sky was clear, and the snowcapped summit of Mount Charleston peeked over the red and gold ridges of the Spring Mountains.

The thing that has surprised me the most about Las Vegas is the surrounding countryside. Somehow, when I was here for Michael and Sierra's wedding I didn't notice that the city is ringed with mountains. I left with the same impression I'd arrived with—that Las Vegas is an artificial oasis in a flat, arid expanse, sort of like an outpost in Antarctica or a colony on Mars. That impression is helped along by quite a few people who live here. They act like the city is an island surrounded by deep space. Maybe that's a good thing for those of us who've figured out differently. It keeps places like Red Rock Canyon and Mount Charleston from being as crowded as Walmart.

My first thought was to drive Daniel through the amazing geological formations in Red Rock Canyon, but when we neared the entrance to Spring Mountain Ranch State Park, I changed my mind, paid the entrance fee to the ranger at the gate, and drove up the road to the parking area next to the old ranch house.

"The other side of Vegas," I said, unbuckling my seat belt. "Come on."

"It's cold," Daniel said when he opened his door. "I didn't bring a jacket."

"I should have warned you," I said. "Sorry."

"Brrr," Daniel said as a breeze caught the sleeves of his T-shirt.

"Hey, wait a second!" I said. "I've got something for you!"

I moved around to the side door of the Max, opened it, and rummaged through my bags of presents.

"Merry Christmas Eve," I said, presenting Daniel with a flat box from Electric Canoe. "I'm sorry it isn't wrapped."

Daniel lifted the lid off and pulled the tissue paper aside.

"This looks expensive," he said, running his fingers over the leather. I looked at the garment the suave salesman had helped me select. I could have sworn I had purchased a dark brown jacket, but in the natural light of day, there was no denying it looked like ripe eggplant. And the appliqué insets and tooled details that had seemed so understated next to all the more flamboyant offerings in the store now looked like the sort of accents the cast of *Hombre* might choose. But—well, there it was, proving beyond a doubt that Las Vegas had stripped me of any good taste I might ever have possessed.

I sucked in a breath and steeled myself for whatever Daniel was going to say. But he didn't say anything. Instead, a slightly stunned smile appeared on his face as he slipped the jacket on.

"What do you think?" he asked dubiously, holding his arms out.

Damn! He looked like a hustler in training.

"It'll keep you warm," I said.

Daniel tried to catch a glimpse of himself reflected in the car window. I'm not sure he did, but when he turned back to face me, his smile had stretched into an all-out grin.

"I can keep up with your family now," he said, turning up the collar and striking a male model pose. "How did you know I've always had a secret longing to be a lounge lizard?"

"You'll really wear it?" I said.

"Well, it'll look a lot better after I grow a mullet," he said, "but if you don't mind a nerd in pimp's clothing, sure!"

He zipped the jacket up, and I was glad that I had chosen the right size.

"I actually love it," Daniel said, and he wrapped his purple arms around me. "And I love you."

After that, it was as though we'd never been apart. Hand in hand, we walked the trail in the hills above the ranch house. Quail scattered in front of us, and we heard wild burros hee-hawing in the distance. On our way back to the car, a stag with many-pronged antlers suddenly bounded over a nearby ridge. He stopped when he saw us. We stared at each other for a moment. Then he turned, and his sure-footed hooves danced over the rocks and carried his white tail out of sight.

"I told you Las Vegas isn't what you think," I said as we made our way back down the hill to the Max.

"We aren't in Las Vegas," Daniel said.

"That's like saying you aren't in New York if you go to the Statue of Liberty," I said.

Daniel was quiet for a moment, and we paused to watch a hawk circle overhead. Then he turned to face me.

"You're absolutely right, Copper," he said. "Las Vegas isn't what I expected." He looked down at his jacket. "That's not the surprising thing, though." He stroked a sleeve and shot me the same smile that made me fall in love with him back in college. "The surprising thing is that *you* aren't what I expected."

After our jaunt out to Spring Mountain Ranch, we stopped at the Golden Nugget to take a shower and change clothes. That should have taken thirty minutes tops, but somehow an hour went by before we were ready to leave. Our clothes came off quickly enough, but showering and getting the new ones on was extraordinarily time-consuming. It also left the bed rumpled.

Daniel drove my car to Michael and Sierra's because I don't like mixing cell phone conversations with steering responsibilities, and I wanted to get my call to Julia Saxon out of the way before Heather called to grill me about what progress I'd made.

I figured with a little luck, I'd get her voice mail.

I had no luck. Julia answered on the first ring.

"Copper!" she said when I identified myself. "Thanks for calling! How was the rest of dinner?"

I had to give her credit. She always started with social banter.

"The champagne was the best part," I said. "Thank you. It was really thoughtful of you."

"It's not every day you add a family member," Julia said. "That's so exciting."

"It is! I—"

"Did you find the tape?" So much for social banter.

"No," I said. "But I've talked with Heather Vetra."

There was a pause.

"Tell Heather Victoria's the reason I'm working on Christmas. I'm fully aware of the family's—needs."

"Good," I said. "Because apparently things are going downhill."

"You mean Jason," Julia said. "I know."

I was about to say something more on the subject, but Julia cut me off.

"I'm very interested in getting my hands on any tapes, Copper. I asked Victoria to record her conversations with the American Beauty guys. If she did, it would be very helpful to hear them. It could help her case, and her case could help her family."

I had to admit that made sense, but I still didn't want anyone to know I had pilfered some of Victoria's stuff. I also couldn't help thinking about guys in white sneakers. I had a hard time believing that Julia's sidekick was the thug who attacked me, but the thought kept popping up.

"So keep looking." Again, I got the distinct feeling she thought I was lying. "Call me if you find anything, no matter what time. And I don't care about Christmas."

Wow. Julia was working on Christmas. I was impressed by her apparent dedication to Victoria's case, but I still wondered what I didn't know. After all, I *was* lying about the tape. Maybe Julia was lying, too. Maybe she didn't want it to nail the American Beauty guys; maybe she wanted it for something else entirely. Was she the right person to trust? For that matter, was Heather? Clearly, I needed better perspective, but how I could get it was anyone's guess.

I might as well report what Julia had said to Heather, I decided. She answered her cell phone on the first ring, too.

"It *might* be good news," Heather said after I'd relayed Julia's comments about getting the McKimber family back on track. "But I'll reserve judgment until there's cash on the barrelhead. It's just too easy to say, 'I'm working on it.' 'I'm working on it' doesn't get Jason help. Speaking of which, what are you doing for Richard and Jason for Christmas? I'm taking dinner."

"Oh—um—I've assembled a care package," I said. "I was going to take it over there tomorrow afternoon," I added, improvising as fast as I could. "It's food, mostly. A ham and—cans of stuff. Things you can eat without cooking. Also paper plates, napkins—you know, picnic stuff."

When I hung up, I sensed some serious attitude beaming at me from the driver's seat, but Daniel didn't say anything except, "I turn left here, right?"

"Right," I said, "I mean yes—I mean left, and—" I paused. I had been about to say, "I'm sorry," but I wasn't sorry. I was actually shocked that I hadn't thought of doing something nice for Jason and Richard on my own.

"I'm going to have to go shopping later," I said. "Or tomorrow."

"Tomorrow? What's going to be open on Christmas?"

"Pretty much everything," I said. "It takes more than a holiday for Las Vegas to shut down."

Daniel let out a big, overburdened, long-suffering sigh, but he didn't have time to say anything before we pulled up in front of the vicarage.

Chapter 18

Dinner was better than I thought it would be. Something had gotten straightened out between my parents and Sierra. She was talking again, and she was wearing pants.

My mom looked more like her normal self, too, except for the poofy golden hair. And my dad made a really sweet attempt to be fatherly.

"Want to play backgammon, Copper?" he asked, after he had helped clear the dessert dishes. "It'd be like Christmases past." We used to play backgammon after dinner on Christmas Eve while we waited to go to the midnight service.

"Sure, Daddy," I said before I could stop myself. *Daddy!* It had been a long time. Our eyes met, and I think all four of them twinkled. "So long as we use the doubling cube the way it was intended."

He laughed. "Oh, yeah," he said. "You mean I should never touch it, but if you're winning, and you do, I have to accept?"

"Something like that," I said, smiling. Really, my dad can be so sweet.

And so can Daniel. He took on my mother in Scrabble!

I felt like pinching myself. I was in love with a guy who had figured out that playing Scrabble with my mother on Christmas Eve was practically the key to world peace. He even invited Sierra to join them, which was even more brilliant. I knew Sierra would say no—she had to play Super Hostess on Christmas Eve, but I could tell she liked being asked.

The nicest news of the evening was that we were going to see Nicky the next day. Sierra had been visiting him every day, and Michael went most days, but the rest of us hadn't met him yet.

"I hoped we could all go this evening," Sierra said at dinner, "but visiting hours in the children's wing end pretty early, and I don't want to be rushed. If we go tomorrow afternoon, we can stay as long as we like."

It's amazing what power a baby has. I mean, Nicky wasn't even there yet, and nobody knew him, but the effect was enormous. My mother had gone shopping today, and there was a Mount Fuji pile of presents under the Christmas tree. Every package had a tag that said "Nicky." My dad had fallen under the spell, too. He spent the morning putting together a pirate ship in the living room.

Nicky even worked his magic on Daniel and me. On our way back to the Golden Nugget after church, we stopped at a drugstore on the Strip. I bought a stuffed duck and a red-and-white striped sleeper suit, and Daniel picked out a sponge frog. Really, that kid was going to get more presents than all the lost angels in Las Vegas, but I really thought he deserved them. He was the reason the whole family was making an effort to get along. It was hard to believe, but a waif who was abandoned in a shopping cart was turning out to be the prince of peace.

Church was okay, too. Saint Andrew's was nearly full, and it actually looked pretty good thanks to a hundred or so poinsettias in red foil-covered pots, the gift of "an anonymous donor." I couldn't help wondering if some misguided Christmas elf had stolen them from Home Depot. The organist had practiced more than usual, and we sang "Oh Come, All Ye Faithful" in English and Tagalog. After the service, Nicky scored another heap of presents from parishioners, including an obviously "pre-owned" Big Wheel tricycle that barely fit in the trunk of Michael's Jetta. It would be a while before Nicky could pedal the thing, but it was the thought that counted.

❖❖❖

It's Christmas, I kept telling myself after midnight, but it was hard to believe. I had never spent a Christmas outside of New England before, unless you count the year we went to New York City with my aunt from Rhode Island. But it's impossible not to get into a Christmas mood in New York City. We window-shopped on Fifth Avenue and went to the midnight service at St. John the Divine. More importantly, we had lunch at Rockefeller Center and watched the ice skaters. What I mean is, it was cold. Las Vegas in December is only chilly. I didn't need a white Christmas to get in the mood, but I was beginning to think it might take something more than a cactus draped with twinkly lights.

Part of the problem was that I couldn't be sure that same cactus didn't have lights on it year-round. As Daniel and I cruised the Strip after church, I tried to figure out what was Christmas and what was everyday Las Vegas, but I failed. The only thing I was sure about was the cone-shaped, color-morphing, fiber-optic tree in front of Caesars Palace—definitely a Christmas addition. But I had no idea whether the faux Brooklyn Bridge was always festooned with lights, same with the trees in front of the Bellagio. And what about those little red lights outlining the top of every hotel tower? Were those airplane beacons or Christmas decorations?

But it was still Christmas, even when I found myself alone in a casino hotel bed. When we got back to the Golden Nugget, Daniel stayed downstairs to play poker. It was possible that he was beginning to understand how important the Victoria McKimber affair was to me. Even so, lying alone in a big strange bed didn't do much toward putting me into a jingle bell mood.

I was just dozing off when Daniel burst through the door. He had a pair of plush antlers clipped on his head and a glass mug of eggnog in each hand. Setting the drinks on the dresser, he took off all his clothes except the antlers. Then, retrieving the mugs, he joined me in bed.

"I'm dreaming of a tight Christmas," he said, handing me a mug and clinking his own against it. "I think if I really want to be serious about poker, I'm going to have to start saying no to all those cute cocktail waitresses."

"Like that's going to happen."

"The eggnog's not bad," he said. "They started bringing it around after midnight."

"And the antlers?" I asked.

"I have no idea how I sprouted those," he said. "I didn't even realize I was wearing them until I saw myself in the elevator mirror."

Fortunately, Daniel had always been a sweet and dopey kind of drunk, and alcohol never affected his powers in bed. Suddenly, it was a season to be jolly, and afterward, I slept in heavenly peace.

❖❖❖

In the morning, we dutifully headed over to the vicarage, where Sierra served a Christmas breakfast that should have won her a Betty Crocker kitchen makeover. After we'd polished off the last perfect maple-walnut cinnamon roll, we headed into the living room and destroyed the wrappings on a couple hundred thousand Christmas presents. Most of them were for Nicky, of course, but my mother had done a good job shopping for me, too. Among a raft of other household accoutrements, I scored a new coffeemaker, a new blender, new wineglasses, and even a full set of new dishes. It was like a bridal shower, and I wasn't the only one who noticed the similarity.

"The groom shouldn't be here," Sierra commented as I opened up a box containing six placemats and napkins, "and we really ought to be playing some silly games."

Fortunately, Daniel isn't flustered by such comments.

"I'm not the groom," he said. "I'm the stud."

It was great! Sierra was the one who blushed, and my parents pretended not to hear. Black family rule number three: If you pay no attention to rude comments or body noises, they never happened.

When all the presents had been unveiled and everyone else had found a good napping spot on a sofa or comfy chair, Daniel and I escaped to my apartment. We only had an hour or so before we were all supposed to head up to the vacant lot at the corner of Craig and Twelfth for "Christmas at the Crossroads." We were going to serve Christmas dinner to the homeless, and then we'd go meet Nicky at Sunrise Children's Hospital. In the meantime, it was actually kind of nice to be in my own apartment, and Daniel was eager to use my computer to catch up on email.

Sekhmet—I still didn't like calling her Delilah—showed up with the top half of a pigeon as I was unlocking the door. It was gross, but I also felt a tiny bit flattered. As soon as she got inside, she stretched out on my TV. She was acting like she was my cat, even though I didn't deserve it.

I had just finished washing and drying my new "authentic French bistro" wineglasses from China by way of Target when Daniel said, "God, aren't you going to love living in Berkeley?"

I looked at him. I could see his smile over the top edge of my laptop screen, nicely illuminated by the glow.

"Me?" I asked. "When am I going to live in Berkeley?"

"I guess I'm asking you to," Daniel said. "I won't know until March or so, but I'm sticking with botany, and the only person I want to work with is Karl Erickson. If I don't get into Berkeley, I'll bum around another year and try again. If that doesn't work, I guess I'll give up and go to med school."

I had just finished setting the last wineglass on the shelf above the sink when I felt Daniel's arms around me.

"It'd be fun, Copper," he said. "We're good together."

I turned around and looked in his eyes.

"Most of the time we're even excellent, Danno," I said. "I love you."

"So, Berkeley, then. Won't it be great? San Francisco a bridge away?"

I kept looking at him as visions of cable cars danced in my head. I'd only been to San Francisco once, and I'd never been to Berkeley. But Daniel knew Berkeley well. He went to sixth grade there when his father spent a year at the university, and he had spent some summers there, too. I think I knew Daniel wanted to go to grad school at Berkeley before I knew his last name.

"You can get a real job there, too," he said.

I pulled away from him. "A *real* job?"

"Oh, come on," he said. "You know what I'm talking about."

Did I? All of a sudden I wasn't so sure. Okay, being the Calendar Girl for the *Las Vegas Light* wasn't the same as being a correspondent for the *New York Times*, but at least it was on the path.

"I mean you can work for a more prestigious paper. It'd be a step up."

I couldn't help thinking about David Nussbaum. He'd pretty much expressed the same idea a few days after I met him.

"Las Vegas is a small media market, but it's got a global reputation," he'd said. "It's a great resume builder—a good place to be from."

"So are you going to leave?" I'd asked David. "Is that your plan?"

"I have no idea," he'd said, and now that I knew about his soon-to-be ex-wife, I thought I understood why. That was around the time he'd shut off the water to her backyard garden.

"I don't know if I want to leave yet," I said.

"Well, it's not for another six months," Daniel said, sitting back down in front of my laptop, "and hell, I don't even know if I'll get in."

"I like Las Vegas," I said.

"I *know*," Daniel said, without even trying to conceal his exasperation. "*It's not what you thought.*"

"Yeah," I said. "And I have stuff to do here that's very important to me."

"Getting your face cut? Hanging out with old whores? Having your apartment trashed?"

Ordinarily, barbs like that would have found their mark, but somehow I felt like laughing.

"Exactly!"

Maybe Las Vegas really had done something to me.

"Right now, though, the important thing is Christmas," I said. "I still have to buy stuff for Richard and Jason McKimber. And serve turkey to the homeless. And go see Nicky."

Daniel didn't say anything.

"You can stay here," I said. "Or I can drop you at the Golden Nugget if you'd rather play poker."

He let out another one of his signature huge, long-suffering sighs. "Let's get going," he said. "You're going to need a Sherpa to carry the ham."

I must have been crazy. I loved Daniel and he loved me. He had just asked me to live with him, for Christ's sake! I thought that was my over-the-rainbow dream!

And what sane person would ever choose Las Vegas when offered a view of the Golden Gate? I didn't just *like* San Francisco when my parents took me there. I *loved* it. We stayed at an entrancingly excellent hotel on Union Square, and we took a ferry to Sausalito. We ate at Fisherman's Wharf, walked around Chinatown, visited museums in Golden Gate Park. If Berkeley was even half as lovely, I was sure I'd adore it. I had always loved college towns, and Berkeley had to be one of the best. It probably had bookstores on every corner and the gold standard in coffee. Why was my heart not leaping at the thought of living there?

Suddenly, two signs appeared in my mind's eye. One was a rusty old motel arrow with lights around the edge and red neon letters flashing "VEGAS." The other was a tasteful granite gatepost with "The University of California" spelled out in nicely chiseled glyphs. Six months before, if Daniel had asked, "Which will it be?" I would have laughed at him.

"Like you think I'd pick *Vegas*?" I would have said with honest incredulity.

So I guess I couldn't really blame him for being surprised now. I was surprised, too, when I thought about it.

◆◆◆

I was actually sort of embarrassed to be a volunteer at "Christmas at the Crossroads," because there were too many of us folks in clean suburban clothes. I felt like a fair-weather do-gooder standing there supervising disposable utensil distribution. It was a job that didn't need doing, and I couldn't help thinking about the other 364 days when there was no food on this corner, and the people we were serving had to fend for themselves.

It gave me the same feeling I'd always gotten back at St. Mark's in New Canaan when we collected money for a mission somewhere in Africa. We'd watch a movie showing emaciated, fly-covered, huge-bellied kids dying of AIDS or starvation. Then everybody would toss a bill or two into the plate, chant a prefab prayer, and zoom over to the country club in their BMWs for oysters on the half shell and prime rib.

I remember my dad saying something like, "You don't help poor people by becoming poor yourself, Copper." I'm sure he had a point. And maybe something was better than nothing, but it never appeased my guilty conscience. I've always thought it would be better to make a real, long-lasting difference to one person than serve turkey drumsticks once a year to a hundred. That's the job Daniel and my mother had been assigned. I was taking a stab at world hunger with a basket of plastic forks.

"Christmas at the Crossroads" was a joint project of the United Christian Charities of Southern Nevada, the Alliance for the Homeless, and a variety of other churches and do-gooder clubs around the valley. Channel 13 showed up, and I kept expecting to see a photographer from *The Light*. It might not have rated a whole story, but ladies who lunched spending Christmas with bums who foraged was a pretty good holiday photo opportunity. I was on my knees refilling my fork basket from a big box under the table when an unexpected voice fell on my ears.

"Copper! Is that you down there?"

I pulled myself to my feet. In between a lanky-haired guy in a grungy army jacket and a bald man covered in tattoos was a familiar smiling face.

"David! What are you doing here?"

"Well, Merry Christmas to you, too. Aren't you going to offer me a fork?"

"Sorry," I said. "I just didn't expect—"

"David!" my mother called from the drumstick station. "Merry Christmas!"

David waved. "Merry Christmas!" he called back.

I could see Daniel's face beyond my mom's. It was wearing an easily recognizable "Who the hell is that?" look. Figuring the forks could take care of themselves for a minute or two, I started moving in the same direction as David.

My mother was already making introductions by the time I got past the mashed potatoes and cranberry sauce.

"Yeah, I graduated in '01," David was saying to Daniel.

I looked at the two of them. I had known they were cut from different cloth, but seeing them side by side was still a jolt. Daniel was nearly a head taller than David, for one thing, but I had never really realized there was such a difference in height. David never seemed short to me, and Daniel never seemed quite that tall. Their clothes were another contrast. Daniel was wearing a stone-washed waffle-knit shirt and long pants with legs that zipped off when the weather called for shorts. David had on a white button-down shirt, corduroys, and a windbreaker. They looked exactly like what they were. Daniel, who still had a slightly sunburned tan, looked like he just got back from a trip through a rain forest, and David looked ready to pull out a notebook and start interviewing somebody. It made me wonder what kind of impression I was making. I had my hair down and was wearing a red turtleneck sweater and black corduroy slacks. I guessed I looked like different things to different people. To my mom and dad, I was still the family baby, and I was pretty much still that to Michael, too. To Daniel, I was at least a little more grown-up. I mean, we did things together that would be labeled "adult" if they were on videotape. But somehow he still saw me as a kid, even though he was less than a year older than I was.

And what was I to David? I wondered. Was I a coworker? A potential roommate? Whatever it was, I didn't think he saw me as an equal. I was just the Calendar Girl, after all. David didn't have to fetch lattes for anybody but himself.

I was still wondering why David had shown up at the turkey feed when he reappeared at the fork station.

"I have something for you," he said.

"What?" I said. "Don't tell me you got me a Christmas present."

He smiled. "Not exactly. It's something from Ed Bramlett."

I rolled my eyes.

"He really wanted you to get this before Monday," David said, holding a manila envelope toward me. "Said it was life or death."

"It's probably anthrax," I said. "The guy hates me."

"Well, don't shoot the messenger," David said. "And anyway, I'm doing you a favor. He wanted your cell phone number, but I told him I'd deliver it."

I stopped handing out forks long enough to peek inside the envelope. Inside was a sheaf of xeroxes and printouts of Web pages, similar to the smaller stack Ed had given me the other day. I caught a glimpse of Julia Saxon's smiling face before I closed the envelope and slid it into my backpack.

"Thanks, David," I said. "Really. Want some dinner?"

"No, thanks," he said. "I usually have Chinese on Christmas. Ancient family tradition."

"By yourself?" I said. "I mean, you could join us for—"

"No, not by myself," David said. "It'll be me and Clint Eastwood this year. I've got *Magnum Force* on DVD. And a big bottle of fancy vodka that Alexandra Leonard gave me. She doesn't drink, and she's very generous with her holiday swag."

"Drinking alone on Christmas," I said. "Pretty sad."

"I told you. It'll be me and Clint."

"Even sadder."

"You're just jealous," David said, and as he walked away, I had to admit he was almost right. Chow mein, vodka martinis, and Dirty Harry really did sound like more fun than another roundtable at the vicarage. Even with Daniel in attendance.

❖❖❖

After we'd finished passing out every last turkey wing, we all drove over to Sunrise Children's Hospital. Sierra had headed there an hour earlier, and when we finally arrived at the right room, we found her ensconced in a recliner, smiling as she held her new son.

"This is a first!" Michael whispered as we drew closer. "They haven't let her hold him before!"

Nicky was sound asleep under a white blanket.

Sierra shifted so we could see his face.

I'm not sure what I expected, but it wasn't what I saw. Somehow, "abandoned baby" had made me brace myself for the worst. I had been expecting to be overcome with a flood of pity for an innocent victim of unspeakable abuse. "I'll love him no matter what," I had been telling myself. "And I'll help him love himself."

But it was a perfect angel whose face peeked over the blanket. His skin was the color of coffee ice cream, and his lips formed a perfect Cupid's bow. His eyes were closed, their long lashes dark against his cheeks.

"He's beautiful," I said, and I swear everyone else said it at exactly the same time. "He's beautiful!"

And then I just stood there, memorizing my new nephew. I looked at Sierra, too, as she smiled down at the little boy. When I finally managed to tear my eyes away from mother and child, I looked at Michael. He was transfixed, a look of wonder in his eyes. I glanced at my parents. They were holding hands. And as I watched them, I felt Daniel take my own hand.

We probably stood there like that for only a few minutes, but it seemed like an enchanted eon. I just kept staring, completely mesmerized. Until this moment, he'd been an abstraction, an idea, a thought. Now he was real. I watched as he turned. His left hand popped out from under the blanket. Sierra leaned forward a little and kissed it. I wanted to do the same, but just then the nurse came back.

"X-ray time," she said, lifting the child from Sierra's arms. We all watched Nicky roll away in a special baby gurney.

Daniel and I stayed long enough to hear that Nicky was gaining weight at a nice rate. His heart surgery was scheduled for the week after New Year's, and his doctors expected an excellent outcome.

"He's going to be absolutely fine," Sierra said, and I couldn't help thinking that Nicky was going to take his new mom with him on the road to well-being. She looked happier than I'd seen her in a long, long time.

"So what do you think of my new nephew?" I asked Daniel as we crossed the hospital parking lot to the Max.

"Cute," Daniel said, but I could tell the glow had already worn off, and he was back to feeling sulky.

"Thanks for coming with me," I said. "And if you don't want to go to the McKimbers'—"

"Just drive to the grocery store and start shopping," Daniel said. "Let's get this over with."

As I had predicted, it wasn't hard to find a supermarket with open doors. The shelves weren't quite as well-stocked as usual, but I still managed to fill up a cart with a huge ham, a couple of salami nightsticks, boxes of crackers, bags of chips, jars of salsa, a log of cheese, three bags of cookies and one of chocolate Kisses, some bottles of sparkling cider, a pound cake, a cherry pie, and several cans of chili, olives, smoked oysters, and nuts. I was about to head for the checkout stand when I realized that the heap of food wasn't going to look very festive in a bunch of plastic Food 4 Less bags. Fortunately, the store had a special on plastic laundry baskets, and I unearthed a roll of red ribbon in an already marked-down pile of Christmas leftovers. The basket was so heavy by the time I loaded it up at the side door of the Max that I was actually glad Daniel was there to lift it.

"I was right," he said. "You did need a mule. That thing weighs more than my backpack when it's fully loaded for two weeks in the jungle."

Chapter 19

As we drove over to the McKimber residence to deliver the Christmas basket, I wondered how much of my motive was altruism and how much was guilt over stealing Victoria's tape recorder and camera. Mostly guilt, I decided, but Heather certainly had something to do with it. I couldn't figure out how she buffaloed me so easily, but I wished she gave lessons.

The house on Chantilly Court looked pretty much the same as it had the first time I visited, except the garage door was closed. Victoria's Taurus was in the driveway, and Heather's black truck was next to it. I parked across the street in the same spot I'd occupied on my last visit.

"Okay," I said. "Operation Santa is now underway."

Daniel hefted the laundry basket out of the Max. It sagged alarmingly under the weight of all those cans, jars, and hunks of meat, but a semester spent lugging scientific paraphernalia through rain forests had served him well. He looked great, even when sullen.

"I'm going to go back and wait in the car after I set this thing down," Daniel said as I punched the doorbell. "This is your party, and I don't want to interfere."

I was about to say, "Chicken!" when the door swung open to reveal two *Penthouse*-quality breasts outstandingly displayed in a red spandex V-neck. That's what Daniel saw, anyway. I saw Heather.

"Daniel!" she exclaimed, locking eyes with him and flashing him a lingering ruby-lipped smile. "Merry Christmas!" How she could make a holiday greeting sound like an offer to unzip a guy's fly, I don't know, but she didn't do it when she greeted me.

"Hi, Copper," she said. "Richard's lying down, but Jason and I are about to have a snack."

Daniel followed Heather's lead, and we stepped inside the front door into a tiled entryway.

The smell hit me first. It reminded me of a time in high school when I left my gym bag in the trunk of my dad's BMW over spring break. Ordinarily, that would have been no big deal, but the can of Vienna sausages I had stashed inside the bag had a teensy hole in it. When I got back from a trip to Cape Cod, my happy nuclear family was on the brink of fission. My dad had hijacked my mother's Camry, and Mom was fighting mad. One whiff of his car, and I couldn't really blame Dad.

While not quite as bad as that, the miasma inside the McKimber house was enough to make my stomach lurch. I glanced at Daniel, and the look on his face told me that he was fighting the heaves, too.

"Whoa!" he said, but it wasn't because of the smell. He was trying to keep his balance. I looked down. We were walking on broken glass, something sticky, and assorted trash.

"Watch your step," Heather said. "I've been cleaning up, but there are still a lot of hazards."

The living room was dim because all the shades were drawn and the lights were off, but I could see that the place looked worse than mine right after the burglars struck. Lamps and shelves were tipped over. Trash was strewn everywhere, much of it consisting of fast-food containers, beer bottles, and Coke cans. The windowsill sported a row of empty Jack Daniel's bottles lined up like trophies. An empty doughnut box on the coffee table was full of used Kleenexes, and next to it, cigarette butts overflowed from an old pizza carton. The TV still worked, though. It was on, and a bony geek was bouncing on a mini-trampoline with a pyramid on his head, explaining how to flush toxins from your body.

"I've cleared a path," Heather said, and we followed her single file into the kitchen, carefully sidestepping a congealed splat of something I told myself was chunky vegetable soup.

Someone had tried to clean up the kitchen. One counter was clear, the sink was clean, and the table was empty enough for Daniel to set down the care basket. The kitchen smelled better, too, in part because there was something baking in the oven.

"Bruschetta," Heather said, using a stack of paper napkins to remove a cookie sheet from the oven. She set it down on some more napkins on the one clear counter.

"I'm going to go find—"

Just then, a door on the other side of the kitchen opened.

"Jason," Heather said. "Good."

I wouldn't have recognized him. He didn't look much like the boy on a skateboard I'd caught a glimpse of the first time I was there. This kid looked clumsier, and his face was puffy. His head was shaved, and he was sporting a fuzzy tuft under his lower lip. Seemingly oblivious to two strangers in his kitchen, he shuffled across the room, slumped into a chair, grabbed a salami out of the care basket, and started peeling it like a banana.

"Hey, save that for later, baby," Heather said. "Look what I made you."

She handed him one of the circles of toasted bread covered with cheese and tomatoes. Jason set the salami back down, grabbed the toast from her hand, and devoured it in one bite. Then he got up, went over to the counter, and ate another one. Then another. Without pausing, he polished off the entire cookie sheet. Tomato juice dribbling out both sides of his mouth, he let out a burp, shuffled back to the table, slumped back into the chair, picked up the salami, and started gnawing on one end.

"Here, baby," Heather said, handing him a napkin. "You need to wipe your face."

Jason didn't say anything, but he bared his teeth at Heather in a sort of distorted grin. I'd been staring at him the whole time he was eating, so I couldn't help noticing his vampire fang of a tooth. Slowly, he pulled himself to his feet, brandishing the salami like a club. Then he stopped, bit a hunk off the end, chewed a moment, and spat out a piece of casing onto the floor. Shuffling over to the door from which he'd emerged, he disappeared back through it. I waited for it to slam, but it closed behind him with an almost inaudible click.

Heather sighed.

"He's a roller coaster, that kid. He's been on new meds the last couple weeks. Richard says they give him the munchies, but he figures eating is better than drinking. I just wish he weren't so zombielike." She sighed again and rinsed the cookie sheet off in the sink. "God, he was the cutest little boy, and smart like you wouldn't believe. He used to read the encyclopedia for fun. And he loved *Jeopardy*. It's hard to believe but that kid could—"

We all heard the crunching sound that meant someone was crossing the living room. A moment later, Richard filled the archway.

"Hey, Heather," he said, and then, "Oh!"

"Friends of Victoria's," Heather said. "They brought you a Christmas present."

Richard was wearing low-slung jeans and a faded black T-shirt. The short sleeves revealed his damaged left arm. A thick web of scars emanated from his elbow. His head was bare, and his alabaster dome almost glowed against the leathery tan of his face. He looked a lot older and wearier than the first time I saw him, but every bit as wary.

"I know you," he said, squinting at me. "You're with the paper."

"She's a friend," Heather interjected. "Victoria trusted her."

"Who's the dude?" Richard said, tipping his head in Daniel's direction.

"Oh," Daniel said, moving toward Richard and stretching out his right hand. "I'm Daniel. Daniel Garside. Copper's—friend."

Richard ignored the hand and let out a nearly inaudible "Hmmph."

"Merry Christmas, Mr. McKimber," I said. "We just came by to bring a little—"

"Come on, Richard," Heather said. "They're *friends*." She put her arm around his shoulder and guided him to a chair at the table. Obediently, Richard sat down. I'm not the only one Heather can boss around, I thought.

"I'm sorry the house is such a mess," Richard said. "It's been hard to get back to normal after—"

"Nobody's blaming you, Richard."

"I should hope the hell not! Goddamn bastards!"

"Copper's helping with that, baby," Heather said, patting Richard's shoulder. "We're gonna nail Bobby Marks. You'll see." She stroked Richard's forehead, but he swatted her hand away.

"I'm not talking about that. I'm talking about the fuckin' home invasion."

"What are you talking about?" Heather asked.

"I'm sure it was Jason's drug-dealing buddies trying to scare him. Because they didn't take anything. Just trashed the place."

"What?" Heather said. "Why didn't you tell me?"

"Hell, I thought I did." Richard slumped back in the chair. His mouth stretched into a half smile under his mustache. "All this time, you've been thinkin' I'm just a crappy housekeeper?"

"When did it happen?"

"I don't know exactly. Couple days after Vicki died."

"When I was in Reno."

"I guess," Richard said. He barked a laugh. "Damn! I still can't believe you thought the house got this gross totally on its own." He rubbed his head with his good hand. "Guess I should've made a better stab at cleaning it up. But—I don't know—it did kinda take the wind out of my sails to come home after wasting a day with the cops to find my house trashed."

"You called the police?" Heather said.

"About the burglary? You've got to be joking," Richard said. "They were already trying to pin Vicki's death on me. If they couldn't blame the burglary on me, I figured they'd find a way to blame it on Jason."

"Nothing at all was missing?" Heather said.

"Nope, just fucked up."

I glanced at Daniel. His face was wearing a look I once saw on a ferret caught by accident in a skunk trap. I'm sure I was wearing a similar look. I'd learned more than I needed to know about the situation, and now all I could think was, "Get me out of here."

"I'm sorry to hear about your house, Mr. McKimber," I said, hoping I could segue into a polite farewell. "I know how awful it is. Something like that happened to me, too."

He turned to look at me across the food basket.

"You bring this?" he said.

"Yeah," I said. "A little Christmas cheer."

"Thanks."

"I've been working with Julia Saxon, too, and—"

"Saxon!" he said. "All that chick wants is her damn tape player."

"What?"

"Some recorder she loaned Vicki. But I don't have it. And I have no idea why it's so damned important."

"Victoria may have taped an interview with some guys from American Beauty," I said. "There might be information in it that Julia can use to make the company pay."

"She told me all that," Richard said, "but it's bullshit. She's just using the missing tape as an excuse. She doesn't want to bother with the case because we're not cash clients, and her chances of ever collecting anything are probably zero."

I was getting more uncomfortable by the second. I was just about to say something about having another appointment when Richard leapt to his feet.

"Shit!" he said, and we all followed his gaze to the door on the far side of the kitchen. Smoke was creeping out from under it.

Richard lurched across the room and yanked the door open. Black billows poured into the room.

Daniel followed Richard, and Heather ran out the back door. I hesitated for a moment, then figured the best thing for me to do was call 9-1-1. I glanced around the room but didn't see a phone. I was reaching for my backpack when Jason erupted into the room with Daniel and Richard right behind him. All of them were gasping and coughing. Then Heather burst in from the garage carrying a huge red fire extinguisher. Daniel followed her back into the smoke.

I pulled my cell phone from my backpack.

"Don't even think about it!" Richard shouted.

"What?" I said. "I was just going to call—"

"9-1-1. I know. Don't!"

"But—"

"Darlin,' I've had just about all the government I can stand." He glared at me. "Put—the phone—down!"

I obeyed just as Heather and Daniel reemerged from the fire zone. "It's out," Heather said. "Only caught the bedspread and the curtain."

"Are you sure?" I said. "I think I should call—"

"No!" Heather commanded. "Don't call 9-1-1. Don't call anybody."

"Why not?" Daniel said. "It'd be a good idea to have them check—"

"No!" Heather and Richard said in unison.

Jason seemed okay, and the smoke was beginning to dissipate.

"Are you sure the fire's really out?" I asked.

"Yeah," said Heather. "That's a very big fire extinguisher. Victoria and I had to get it when we bought inventory insurance for our business, because this is where we store everything that doesn't fit in my trailer. Now I'm glad they made us do it. Jason's room is full of that white crap."

"You okay, Jay?" Richard asked. Jason didn't say anything, but he grabbed the bag of chocolate Kisses from the care basket and tore it open with his teeth. His hands were shaking.

"Guess so," Richard said. "Shit."

"Well, if everything's okay, I guess we'll be going," Daniel said. "We've got some other—"

"Yeah, who'd want to hang around a shithole like this on Christmas?" Richard said.

"We'll be back," I said, not quite knowing what I meant.

Richard snorted. "I don't know, darlin.' Staying away might be your best move."

It hardly seemed appropriate to say "Merry Christmas," so I just picked up my backpack. Daniel and I moved toward the living room, and Heather followed us.

"I still think we should call the fire department," Daniel said as he opened the front door. "Fires can reignite, and it would be wise to—"

"No!" Heather said. We moved outside, and Heather put her arm around Daniel's shoulder. "You don't get it, do you, baby?" she said.

I don't get it, either, and he's not your baby! That's what I wanted to say, but I figured it would only make things worse.

"Firemen are the man, and we can't have the man around here."

"Huh?" Daniel said it, but I was thinking it, too. *Huh?*

"They'd take one look at Richard and the disaster in that house and take custody of Jason on the spot. He's only fifteen. Get it now?"

I guess we still looked blank, because Heather went on.

"This house is bad, but let me tell you something. Being a kid in the foster care system is worse. In Jason's case—hell, I don't even want to think about it. You saw his room, Danny. You know what he was doing in there."

Danny! She called him *Danny!*

Suddenly, I was the one who had to get out of there, and no amount of Heatherness was going to stop me.

"Come on," I said, tugging at Daniel's arm. "We've got to go." For a second, Daniel was the rope in a two-woman tug-of-war, because Heather hung on to his other arm.

"Um—" Daniel said.

"Come *on,*" I said. "We're supposed to be at the vicarage." I let go of Daniel's arm. "I'll be in touch," I said to Heather in what I hoped was a confident tone. I headed toward the Max, fighting the urge to look back at Daniel. I'd already unlocked the driver's door by the time he joined me.

My heart was hammering as I jammed the key into the ignition, and I wasn't even sure why I was so upset. A house nearly burning down isn't something minor, but there was more to it than that.

"What *was* he doing in that room?" I said to Daniel as I pulled out.

"What do you think?" he said. "It was classic funeral pyre. Smoking in bed."

"Tobacco?"

"Like you have to ask."

Of course it wasn't tobacco. I don't even know why I asked that, because my mind kept thinking "meth lab" and "crack pipe," neither of which I knew anything about except that they involve flame.

"He was smoking a joint, listening to tunes, playing an electronic game, and—"

"Gnawing on a big salami?"

"You've got the picture." He paused. "You know, Copper, I'm not sure we shouldn't call the fire department. The house really could still be on fire."

I had just reached the end of Chantilly Court. I looked over my shoulder before turning left onto Riviera Lane. Heather had gone back inside. The house looked peaceful and normal. There wasn't the slightest hint that anything was the teensiest bit wrong. Even so, Daniel had a point. Even if the fire was out, Richard and Jason were close to meltdown.

"I don't want to," I said.

"What?" Daniel said. "You don't *want* to? What the hell is that supposed to mean?"

"I'd rather respect their wishes," I said slowly. I was still trying to figure out exactly what was keeping me from making a call that might save lives.

I glanced at Daniel as I waited for the gate to swing open at the end of Riviera Lane. I didn't like what I saw on his face. After I'd pulled onto the main street, I slowed to a stop next to the curb and shifted the Max into park.

Daniel turned a gaze on me I'd never seen before, the sort of look you might have if you were watching someone drown kittens.

"What would have happened if we hadn't been there?" I asked. "They didn't ask us to come." I paused. "Well, Heather sort of did, but Richard certainly didn't. I just can't bring myself to be a meddling intruder."

"What about a Good Samaritan, then?" Daniel said. "It's not about whether we were invited. They need a lot more help than a hard salami."

That hit home. I gripped the steering wheel and bit my tongue.

"I'm calling 9-1-1," he said, fishing in his pocket for his cell phone. "What's the address back there?"

"Guess you should've been paying more attention."

"You're not going to tell me?"

I put the Max in gear and pulled away from the curb. Daniel twisted his head around, but there were no street signs in sight.

"You should've waited in the car," I said as I stopped for the light at Blue Diamond Road. "Like you said you were going to."

"Fuck you," Daniel said.

"*What?*"

"You heard me."

I couldn't quite believe it, but I had.

❖ ❖ ❖

It had been a Christmas of firsts. My first nephew, my first house fire, and now, to cap it off, my first "fuck you" from my first true love. I got on the freeway and headed north. It was the right direction to get to the vicarage, but I was feeling singularly reluctant to arrive at Christmas dinner in my current condition.

"Want me to drop you somewhere?" I asked Daniel.

Ordinarily, this would have been a cue for him to say something conciliatory, but I wasn't surprised by his reply.

"Yeah," he said. "Someplace on the Strip."

"Where on the Strip?"

"I don't care."

He wouldn't talk, and I wasn't in a mood to cajole him. I was still reeling from the "fuck you." That's never a nice thing to hear, but somehow it's worse when it comes from the lips of someone who actually has fucked you.

We covered the distance to Las Vegas Boulevard in silence, and I pulled into the main entrance of Mandalay Bay, the southernmost casino on the Strip. Daniel slipped the eggplant jacket off and left it on the seat when he got out.

"You're on your own to make amends with my family," I said. "I'm not making excuses for you." He slammed the door and disappeared into a crowd of Asian tourists.

A taxi behind me started honking immediately, and I tailgated the limo ahead of me until I emerged back out onto Las Vegas Boulevard. I turned left, and then I was cruising the Strip alone on Christmas. Alone in Sin City in a car that seats seven with dedicated seat belts. I couldn't help thinking about all those stories I'd read about suicide rates soaring over the holidays. Not that I felt suicidal. Disgusted was closer to it, although I couldn't deny a strong current of sadness running right through the middle of it.

It was just beginning to get dark, which is a very pretty time in Neon Land. The sky was a clear dark royal blue. The lights on the huge marquees look more understated at dusk than they do against the night sky, like they're just waking up and getting ready for a big night of partying. While the crowds milling along the sidewalks weren't any smaller than usual, they weren't any larger, either. If I hadn't known it was Christmas Day, nothing would have given me much of a clue, unless you count the two old ladies in Santa hats weaving through the sidewalk throngs on a tandem tricycle.

For the first time, I truly understood why people who can't stand the holidays come to Las Vegas. Las Vegas doesn't destroy days like Christmas. It just hides them in 364 other days with equal wattage. As I moved past the MGM Grand, I was seized with a sudden desire to park somewhere, duck into a casino, and buy myself a martini.

I kept driving, but when I reached Flamingo, where it would have made sense to turn right and head for the vicarage, I didn't. I couldn't bring myself to show up there alone and feeling awful. Not only did I not want to make up a story about Daniel, I was still upset about what I'd seen at the McKimbers' place. Daniel wasn't wrong when he said they needed more than a salami, and he was probably right about calling the fire department, too. I hoped their house was still standing, but I still wondered if Heather was wrong about "the system" being such a terrible place for Jason. How could anything be worse than that cesspool of a house?

Another thought nagged me, too. What if Heather wasn't really a dear friend of the McKimber family, but rather a Mensa-smart opportunist? Sure, everything she said and did looked supportive of Richard, but maybe something more sinister was motivating her. How would I ever know? Pretty much everything I knew about Heather came from Heather herself. The only thing I knew for certain, I suddenly realized, was that this Christmas was winning a prize for being the most depressing one ever.

It wasn't long before I was on the northern stretch of Las Vegas Boulevard, the humbler section north of the Stratosphere Tower, where you can get married without getting out of your car, and you can pay by the hour for your honeymoon motel. I watched a cop chat with a streetwalker at the corner of Charleston. Business as usual.

I toyed with the idea of heading to the Golden Nugget, but I'd spent too much time alone in bed there already, and I knew it would just make me want to call Daniel and try to patch things up. And I didn't know what to say. I wasn't sorry for how I felt, even if I was sorry we were having a fight on Christmas. And not only a fight, but the worst fight we'd ever had. It really bothered me that Daniel had said "fuck you." We'd never spoken that way to each other before. I felt as though something had dried up between us that would never spring to life again. It reminded me of David Nussbaum's backyard.

Chapter 20

I drove to *The Light*, which isn't far from the Nugget. Neutral turf sounded good, and I figured I could look over the stuff Ed Bramlett had collected for me while I decided whether I could face Christmas dinner at the vicarage. The old coot had made such an effort to get it to me "before Monday," so I figured maybe I should look at it before Monday, too.

The guard at the security kiosk, a young black woman wearing a Santa hat, was watching TV, painting her nails, and blowing big pink bubbles. She said "Merry Christmas!" before raising the gate, and I parked closer to the building than I ever had before. The lot wasn't empty, though. There were at least fifteen other cars, and another one pulled in next to me as I got out.

The parking lot wasn't deserted, but most of the building was. I didn't see even one other person as I made my way to my cube. Good, I thought. Alone at last. No Christmas, no Daniel, no family, and not even any coworkers.

And also no jacket. The building was freezing and I'd forgotten to put my blazer back on when I left the Max. I didn't want to go all the way back downstairs, so I headed to my cube, hoping a confined space might be a little warmer.

I stopped by my mailbox, where, by amazing good fortune, I found a red hooded sweatshirt stuffed in alongside the usual assortment of envelopes and slips of paper. It was a promotional gimmick for a comedy show, and it was size extra-huge, but I didn't care. I slipped it on immediately and pulled up the hood. I was actually grateful that it hung down to my knees.

It was time to muster my courage and phone my family, but I decided to postpone the task a little bit longer and make myself a cup of tea. I was half-afraid I might run into Ed Bramlett in the lunchroom, but the lights were off, and nobody was lurking in the darkness. While my water was heating up in the microwave, I bought a package of cheese and peanut butter crackers from the machine in the corner. Christmas dinner. I munched one while looking out the window onto the smokers' patio, and as I stood there, raindrops began spattering the glass.

Rain! It's a rare but serious phenomenon in Las Vegas. Most of the time, everything is so utterly arid, you can't imagine precipitation could ever occur. When it does, usually with no warning I ever notice, it won't be a gentle drizzle. Either you get a few fat drops that vanish as mysteriously as they appeared, or else it's the Johnstown flood. Really, it's like heaven's Hoover Dam busts open, and enough water to fill Lake Mead comes crashing down. Five minutes later, all the major thoroughfares are navigable by oil tankers, and helicopters are performing "swift-water rescues" of people stranded on the roofs of cars. Okay, the part about the oil tankers is an exaggeration, but I'm not making up the part about the rescues. Flash floods are real. When I first got to Vegas, I got caught by a flash flood in a grocery store parking lot. I finished seven chapters of *The Da Vinci Code* before a dove showed up with an olive branch.

By the time I had finished another cracker, it was obvious this wasn't just a few fat drops. Rain was sheeting off the eaves over the patio, and the beds around the trees looked like wading pools. I'll be here awhile, I thought, but at least I had an excuse for missing dinner at the vicarage.

I used that excuse, too. Michael answered the phone, and I told him that Daniel and I were trapped in a flood on the east side of town. "I wanted to show him some of the countryside," I said, "but I hadn't planned on a hailstorm."

"A hailstorm!" Michael said. "That's weird. It's only raining here."

"It's pouring here now," I said. "I don't know when we'll be able to drive."

"Well, get here when you can," he said. "You wouldn't want to miss the beef Wellington."

"I hope you'll save us some," I said, hoping even more fervently that the storm would be a long one.

It was a cop-out, but I just wasn't in the mood to reveal to my family that Daniel and I were having a spat. Or maybe I was just following family tradition, the way a good Black should. My parents were having a huge spat, after all, and talking about it was the last thing they'd ever do.

Back in my cube, I turned on a light, rummaged in my backpack for the envelope David had delivered for Ed, and dumped the contents out onto my desk.

A quick look confirmed what I had already noticed. It was all about Julia Saxon. Printouts of newspaper stories, a couple of police reports, some court documents, copies of minutes from City Council meetings, photographs, and even two Xeroxed pages from the 1983 Valley High School yearbook. The first one, which featured a large photograph of a big-haired Julie Bigelow in a white gown and mortarboard, listed her accomplishments, including a stint as junior class president and a role as an attorney on the school's mock trial team. She'd also played tennis and starred as Ado Annie in *Oklahoma!* But it was the second page that made me start paying real attention. A montage of photographs identified the Class of '83's "Superstars," a boy and a girl in each category. Duly noting the "Cutest Back Pockets" and "Most Likely to Sleep in the White House," I learned that Julie Bigelow and a boy named Jasper Cutler were the "Most Likely to Rob a Bank Together." Oh, come on, I thought. Maybe Sierra and Michael were right. Julia didn't deserve suspicion because of a silly label in her high school yearbook.

The next page that caught my eye was a set of minutes from a City Council meeting about a year ago. I scanned it, and sure enough, Julia Saxon had been on the agenda, representing a client who wanted to build houses on a property on the north side of town. The city rejected the petition because of "hazmat ground contamination" caused by two ancient, leaky underground gas tanks left over from an old filling station on the site.

Next was a newspaper article about the Willow Lake property next to the wastewater treatment plant that the Alliance had wanted to buy. The treatment plant was enough of an environmental problem that the city wouldn't let the adjacent land be used for houses. The City Council did grant a variance when it looked like the Alliance was going to acquire the property. Still no homes, they said, but it was all right to build "multiunit housing, including apartments, dormitories, or temporary housing for the homeless." Why all this was okay if houses weren't, I couldn't figure out, but I guessed it was because they figured homeless people wouldn't notice the smell.

I still couldn't see why Ed had been so eager for me to get this pile of info before work on Monday, but when I looked at my watch and realized nearly an hour had passed, I was actually grateful to him. I hadn't thought about Daniel or Christmas even once. I picked up a court brief, thinking I might as well read that next.

"Whoa! It's a big red Smurf!"

I almost knocked my mug onto the floor in surprise.

"David! What are you doing here?"

I pulled the red hood back and hoped my hair wasn't too much of a mess.

"I should be asking you that! You're the one who celebrates Christmas."

"Yeah, well ... I thought you had a date with Clint."

"Oh, I do, but I ended up spending more time downtown than I expected today. I ran into some friends from back home on Fremont Street, and we had a few beers at the Main Street Station brewpub. I had to let the drinks wear off before I could drive, so I hung out in the coffee shop at the Golden Gate for an hour. Had the place practically to myself. But anyway, I just stopped by here to check my mail before I head home. Oh, and here's something you might want to know. There's a chance the cops are going to pick up Bobby Marks tonight."

"Really? For Victoria's murder?" I asked.

"Possibly. It could just be for assault, though. The Nye County Sheriff is involved, which means he did something in Pahrump."

"Where the brothels are."

David nodded. "Don't know anything more. We'll just have to wait and see."

Somehow, that news cheered me up a little. If Bobby Marks killed Victoria, then Heather was probably the McKimbers' real friend.

"Has the rain stopped?"

"Nope, but it might be showing signs."

David leaned against the partition.

"What *are* you doing here, Copper?"

Damn. I didn't feel like talking to David about Daniel, but the story I'd concocted for my family wasn't going to work.

"I'm sort of homeless again," I said, hoping it sounded sufficiently vague.

"Hmm. Weird situation for a WASP on Christmas."

"Yeah, well, holidays aren't immune to weird situations."

Our eyes met. David may talk loudly, and he may speak his mind, but he also thinks carefully. I watched him consider what to say next.

"Is this what Ed sent you?" he asked, looking at the pile on my desk.

"Yeah," I said. "I'm still trying to figure out why, though."

I opened my file drawer.

"Ed also gave me these," I said, pulling out the pages he had delivered in person. "I haven't had a chance to do anything more than glance at them."

"Want some help?"

"Um …" I said. Did I really want to bring David into what was already an uneasy blend of family, boyfriend, work, and career aspirations? I kind of liked keeping him as a separate refuge, but on the other hand …

"Yeah," I said. "I'd actually love some help."

"Well, look," David said. "It's freezing here. Why don't we go to my place?"

I had to pause. If I drove all the way to Green Valley, I'd definitely be blowing off beef Wellington at the vicarage. I'd be pretty much blowing off Daniel, too.

"Will Clint be okay with that?" I asked. "I wouldn't want to horn in."

"Copper," David said, "it would make his day."

❖❖❖

So I decided to go, even though I had no toothbrush, and I was pretty sure that if I drove all the way across town I wouldn't be coming back in only an hour or two. But who knew? And who knew what Daniel was doing? Screw him, I figured. I could use David's insights on the Ed Bramlett intelligence, and his house did feel like a refuge. This had been a lame Christmas anyway. Except for meeting Nicky, it had been worse than a regular day. Although I was grateful to my mom for the bridal shower of household gifts. Really, that was sweet.

I was on my way down to my car when I realized I had to brave another phone call to the vicarage. If I didn't make contact, my mother would probably make the police issue an Amber Alert.

Yes, she's over eighteen, I could hear her say, *but she's my baby! You've got to find her!*

I considered calling Michael's cell phone, but then decided I better straighten my spine and call the house. "I'm sorry, but I'm not going to make it tonight," I practiced out loud as I punched numbers on my keypad. No, wait! No "I'm sorry," even though skipping Christmas dinner felt as rude as missing my own wedding.

The phone rang three times before the answering machine picked up.

Yay! Another Black family tradition! My parents' strictest dining room rule was "No phone calls, in or out." Michael and Sierra didn't adhere to the custom, but tonight they were apparently kowtowing to the ancients.

I waited for the beep.

"This is Copper," I said. "I'm sorry, but"—*damn!*—"I'm not going to get there tonight. Merry Christmas, and I'll call in the morning. Bye!"

I clicked my phone shut and smiled. Except for the "I'm sorry," I'd pulled it off! And better yet, as I passed Russell Road, the freeway under me was suddenly bone dry.

When I got to David's house, I parked on the street and rang the doorbell. As I stepped into the entry hall, I noticed that the wedding picture in the alcove next to the door was gone. The only evidence that it had ever been there was a little bent nail in the wall.

It was weird, but the absence of that photograph made me feel as though David's marriage really was over. He'd removed Rebecca from the holy shrine, and in her place—nothing. Somehow that seemed more final than a court document. It should have seemed sad, too, but that's not the feeling that started wrapping itself around my stomach. That was a giddy feeling, an excited feeling.

Except he *is* married! I reminded myself fiercely. *Don't let sentiment blur the cold hard truth!* Still, I couldn't help thinking as I followed David into the kitchen, he was in the process. He was moving on.

"Are you hungry, Copper?" David asked.

"Kinda," I said, still grappling with the new feeling the naked bent nail gave me. "And—thanks for inviting me over, David. It's been a really strange day."

"Well, I guess that sweatshirt is the right outfit for you, then," he said. "I'm not used to you as Little Red Riding Hood."

"What big teeth you have," I said.

"And nothing to eat with them," David said, his head stuck inside the refrigerator. "I was going to get take-out Chinese on the way home, but I forgot to tell you, and you gave me my key back. I didn't want you to beat me here and have to wait."

"You could have called."

"True." He pulled a package of ground beef out of the refrigerator. "But I remembered I hadn't had a chance to make you a meat loaf."

I was very glad David was still rummaging in the crisper drawer when he said that, because it made a tear jump up in each of my eyes. It was just so damn sweet that somebody wanted to make me meat loaf. I pulled off my sweatshirt, surreptitiously wiping my eyes with it on its way over my head.

"So Ed Bramlett's flirting with you now?" David asked as he located a bowl, a can opener, a knife, some celery, and an onion.

I rolled my eyes, but it was a wasted gesture. David was too busy opening a can of tomato sauce to notice.

"It's a bunch of stuff about Julia Saxon. He hates her."

"A lot of people do."

"But she always seems so professional and civic-minded to me. She's helping the Alliance for the Homeless, and she took on Victoria McKimber pro bono. And I just read a story about how she helped a neighborhood downtown get a skateboard park, and she's on the board of the Humane Society—"

"A real champion of underdogs and nonprofits."

"Well, yeah!" I said. "So why do so many people despise her? Because of her dad? Because she's a strong woman?"

"Her father didn't help her reputation much, but I think she's made her own enemies." David was chopping up an onion now, and wiping his eyes on his sleeve. I liked watching him. All I'd ever seen him do in the kitchen before was make coffee.

"You hate her, too?"

"No. I don't know her. I just wouldn't trust her."

"I guess that's what Ed is trying to tell me. But I can't figure out what I'm supposed to do about it."

"Want some help?"

"You asked me that before," I said, "and I haven't changed my mind."

"Well, look, then," David said. Why don't you spread everything out on the dining room table, and as soon as I get dinner in the oven, I'll join you." He wiped his hands on a paper towel, opened the refrigerator, and pulled out a beer.

"And Merry Christmas," he said solemnly as he handed it to me. "I'm sorry you're not with your family, but I'm not sorry you're with me."

And damned if that same little thrill that took hold of me when I saw the empty marriage shrine didn't wiggle its way into my belly again. I was still sorry Daniel was mad at me, but I wasn't sorry at all that David had just diced me an onion.

Beer and backpack in hand, I moved into the dining room, where the table was clear except for two silver candleholders that had to have been wedding presents.

I was still arranging everything when David emerged from the kitchen and turned on an overhead light.

"Thanks," I said.

"Yikes," he said. "This is quite a pile."

"I'm organizing it chronologically," I said. "As much as I can, anyway. Some things don't have dates."

"Damn!" David had found the yearbook page. "Look at that eyeliner!"

"Wait'll you see the page underneath."

"*Most Likely to Rob a Bank Together*," David read. "Cute." He looked more closely. "Hmmm," he said slowly. "That's Jaz Cutler."

"Jaz?" I said. I'd heard that name—where was it? Oh, my God! On Julia's mystery tape.

"Well, it says Jasper here, but it's Jaz, all right. I'd recognize that schnoz anywhere."

David handed it to me. Jasper Cutler did have a distinctive nose. And I'd seen it before, I realized with a jolt. It belonged to the guy who was with Julia the night we went to Mondrian. Same curly hair, too, except without the bald spot. I wondered again if he'd been my attacker.

David was working his way through a stack of articles from *The Light*.

He shook his head. "I don't get it," he said.

"What?"

"Why Ed gave you this stuff. He must have spent hours collecting it all. What for?"

"He loves me," I said. "Or he hates me. Hell, I don't know."

"I'm not sure it has anything to do with you, Copper."

"Gee, thanks."

David kept poring over the stories. "Did he say anything? Write you a note? Explain anything?"

"Nope." I thought back to the time Ed had almost coughed himself to death in my cube. "He's known Julia for a really long time, though."

"Not surprising," David said. "He's one of the few native sons at *The Light*. He was actually born in Las Vegas."

Without talking much, David and I kept reading stories, scanning court briefs, and looking at grainy photographs. The only obvious theme in all of them was that Julia fought like a bulldog for her clients, and in many cases, she won. That kind of record could definitely inspire the enmity of her opponents, but did it really make her a bad guy? Maybe Ed Bramlett hated her for the same reason he called the Sekhmet Temple women "a bunch of ball-busting dykes." He was a card-carrying misogynist, and Julia Saxon was the kind of woman he despised the most. But that didn't explain why he'd made such an effort to give me all this stuff. Ed was mean, but he wasn't stupid. I was the stupid one. Something was staring at me, and I just couldn't see it.

I was reading a story about Julia's fight to keep the city from closing a shelter for battered women when the oven timer went off. David retreated into the kitchen to rescue his meat loaf.

"Dinner's almost ready," he called.

"Want me to set the table?" I asked, joining him in the kitchen.

"Sure!" David said, handing me one of the two martinis he was holding. "Let's eat in here so we don't have to move all your Julia stuff."

I arranged plates and silverware on the kitchen table, and as soon as the food was ready, David went back into the dining room. When he returned, he was carrying the two silver candleholders, which he had furnished with new white tapers. God, not only was he a guy who made meat loaf, he was a guy who bought candles. He found a match, lit them, and flipped off the ceiling lights. "Too dark?"

"No."

"Too romantic?"

Yes! I felt like shouting, but I didn't. I didn't even look at him. I just sat there a moment, trying to let my heart rate slow back down.

"If I had to guess," David said as he cut me a slice of meat loaf, "I'd say Ed was building a case. He knows something about Julia, but he doesn't have proof. So he's looking for guns and hoping he'll find one that's still smoking."

"Why would he give all that stuff to me?"

"That is something I wish I could tell you," David said. "Ed Bramlett isn't known for sharing."

"You can tell me who Jaz Cutler is."

"He's the heir apparent of a family that owns large chunks of downtown. He calls himself a developer, but he's really just a flat-footed old rich boy who plays a lot of golf."

"Flat-footed?"

"Well, I don't know what's wrong with his feet, actually, but something is. Sometimes he uses a cane. Always wears comfortable shoes."

I thought about the white running shoes again. They were unusual to wear with a tuxedo, but not for someone who might need to be fleet of foot after committing a felony. Even so, dorky shoes alone were no crime, and staying friends with a high school chum was hardly a smoking gun. They obviously hadn't robbed a bank together, or Ed would have provided documentation.

"Sorry I haven't been much help," David said.

"Oh, but you have," I said. "I still don't have any answers, but I feel as though I've got better questions."

After dinner, David and I tried to read more stories about Julia, but somehow we'd lost our focus.

"Okay, enough old news," David finally said. "Time for an old movie. Want to watch *Magnum Force?*"

"I guess," I said. "Or maybe I should head home."

"You have a home?"

Damn. I sure didn't feel like I had a home, even with all my new loot. I looked at David.

"Sorry," he said. "None of my business."

I sighed.

"Well, you're welcome to stay here if you want to, Copper," David said. He paused and shot me a little smile. "Truth is, I've missed—" He paused again. "I've missed beating you at backgammon."

David sat on the sofa to watch the movie, and I took his recliner chair. Ordinarily, sitting in a recliner guarantees that I'll be sound asleep by the end of the opening credits, but not that night. David's presence was like a continuous, low-level electric current, and it made me wish I hadn't been so quick to jump into a one-person chair. Then again, maybe I was lucky I did. It was getting harder and harder to hear that little voice whispering, "He's married."

My restlessness was heightened by a nagging question. What was up with Daniel? Where was he? He hadn't called me, and even though I try not to play too many games, I couldn't shake the feeling that he was the one who should make the next move.

I can't say Dirty Harry is my favorite hero, but I caught every last nuance of his personality along with every last lip curl and squint. When the film had run its course, David stood up.

"It's pretty late, Copper. Are you sure you want to drive home?"

"No," I said. "If your fold-out's available, I'd like to take you up on it."

I was looking straight at him when I said it, and as soon as the words were out of my mouth, I felt my face begin to burn. *Damn!*

I am positive David noticed my sudden pinkness. I know what I look like when I blush, and it isn't subtle.

"I was hoping you'd say that," he said quietly. Our eyes met.

"Thank you," I said, mostly to keep myself from saying, "I was hoping you'd ask."

"You're always welcome, Copper," David said. Our eyes met again, and I'm pretty sure his face had more color than usual, too.

"Always."

Chapter 21

Lying there in David's ex-wife's ex-study, I couldn't sleep. As I looked around, I noticed the sewing machine had vanished along with the red-flowered hat and the books about marital sex.

Daniel hadn't called, and the more I told myself to forget about it and go to sleep, the more wide awake I became. Finally, I threw the covers off, turned on the light, and rummaged in my backpack for my phone. I obviously wasn't going to get any rest until I broke down and called him.

I checked my phone. *Four missed calls?* I checked the ringer, but it wasn't turned off. *Damn!* Why hadn't my phone rung?

The first call was my mother.

"Copper! We're worried about you! Please call!"

The second was Mom again.

"Copper! We just got your message! Are you sure you can't get here tonight? It's Christmas, darling, and we miss you. Well, we hope you'll get here when you can. Love you!"

The third was Daniel.

"Hey. Thought I'd call to see what's up. Call me back. Bye."

I sighed. The words didn't sound particularly apologetic, but his voice did. I felt my shoulders loosen a little.

Oh, Daniel. I don't want to fight with you.

The fourth call was from Daniel, too. It had come in at about midnight, but that time he left no message.

I punched Daniel's number immediately, but after four rings, his voice mail answered.

"Hi—it's Copper." I paused, wishing I had thought about what to say before I called. "I'm—I'm—" Why wasn't he picking up, anyway? Where was he? But I guess that's what he was wondering about me. "Call me, okay?"

Even though I was sure I'd never fall asleep, I set the alarm on my phone for six. I figured that would give me enough time to figure out how to make myself presentable enough to go to work. Neither my apartment nor the Golden Nugget sounded very appealing, but I was going to need a shower, and …

❖ ❖ ❖

Monday, December 26

A horrible dream woke me up five minutes before my alarm would have. I was hiking up a steep mountain to a house surrounded by a tall chain-link fence topped with razor wire. When I reached the house, no one was there. Suddenly I was on the outside of the chain-link fence, clinging to it. Rocky cliffs dropped off below me to water hundreds of feet below. I tried, but I couldn't climb up. I would have to try to climb down.

Then, suddenly, I heard Daniel's voice. I looked up, and he was clinging to the fence above me.

"Don't worry," he said. "I'm here."

He inched down alongside me, but before I could say anything, he smiled and—let go! He twisted into a dive, and he was gone!

I clung to the fence as the realization dawned that I could never get away alive. My arms were already weakening, I was alone, and—I woke up, my heart pounding.

The room was dark, but I could see light under the door. Good. At least David was up.

I threw on the bathrobe he had loaned me and joined him in the kitchen. He was wearing boxer shorts and a "Race for the Cure" sweatshirt.

"Hey," he said, smiling at me in a way that almost made me feel better. "Want some coffee?"

"Maybe," I said. "I'm still recovering from a scary dream."

David filled a Harrah's mug and set it on the table.

"Do you remember it?"

"Sort of," I said. "Basically, I was about to die, so I woke up instead."

"Sounds like a wise choice."

"I got four calls last night, but my phone never rang."

"Oh, I should have warned you about the little vale of silence on Palm Treasure Drive," David said. "Cell service is notoriously weak right here. Drives me nuts."

I took a sip of coffee.

"I think maybe I should have let that dream kill me," I said.

David sat down across the kitchen table from me, his mug in front of him.

"Copper," he said, "if there's anything I can do …"

"You've been great, David," I said. "I owe you."

David smiled. "And don't think I won't collect," he said.

❖ ❖ ❖

I couldn't face going to my apartment before work, and the Golden
Nugget was out of the question until I resolved things with Daniel.
That left going to work in the same clothes I wore Christmas Day,
but fortunately there was some very nice herbal-smelling shampoo in
David's downstairs bathroom, and I found a hair dryer in a drawer. I
always keep some mascara in my backpack, so only my teeth needed
attention. I figured I'd stop at a drugstore on my way to *The Light*,
but the first thing on my agenda once I was out of the no-cell zone
was to call Daniel.

He answered on the first ring.

"Hey," he said.

"Hey," I said, trying to match his careful nonchalance. "You okay?"

"I'm fine," he said. "Where are you?"

"On my way to work. Where are you?"

"Golden Nugget."

It was one of those horrible conversations where every time you
say a word it feels like you're throwing a raw egg, and every time you
hear a word, you feel like you have to catch one without breaking it.
But in the end, we managed to agree that I'd pick him up at noon
at the Golden Nugget and we'd get "a bite to eat." Things had to be
less awkward in person.

My second call was to the vicarage, where Michael answered the
phone.

"What happened to you?" he said. "We were worried."

"I'm sorry," I said. "I just couldn't get there."

"Turned into a real ice storm, eh?" Michael said.

"That's a good metaphor for it."

"Well, I hope you can come to dinner tonight, Copper. It's Ted and
Jackie's last night in town, you know."

"I know," I said. "I'll come right after work." I paused. "Thanks, Michael."

"We're just glad you're okay, baby sister. See you tonight."

The "baby sister" grated, but when I think of all the justifiably outraged things he could have said, I decided it was a minor transgression. I hoped Sierra would be as forgiving.

A quick stop at a drugstore equipped me with a toothbrush and toothpaste, and I put them to use in the women's restroom on the way to my cube.

I was just finishing up when Alexandra Leonard joined me at the sinks. She was the only person in the building who didn't look like she'd overdone it at the wassail bowl. She was her usual perky chipmunk self.

"Hi, Copper," she chirped. "Happy Boxing Day!"

"Hi, Alexandra," I said, shaking off my toothbrush.

"Heard about Ed Bramlett?"

"What about him?"

"He got taken to UMC yesterday afternoon," she said. "Intensive care. Pneumonia. May not make it."

"What?" I tried to sound less surprised than I was.

"He's really had a hard time with the chemo this time," she said as she dried her hands. She smiled at me in the mirror as she smoothed her hair. "Well, anyway, have a great day!"

Ed Bramlett had *cancer*? I knew he was in bad shape, but—why hadn't I heard about it before?

In my cube, I tried to get started on my morning calls, but thoughts of Ed Bramlett kept haunting me. He'd been gravely ill when he tried to get my cell number from David. Making sure I got that envelope might well have been the last thing he did before he was hauled off to the hospital. He wanted me to read it before Monday. Was something bad going to happen today that I was supposed to prevent? Or was he just trying to beat his own clock?

I sighed and reached for the phone. Mondays are busy, even the day after Christmas. Might as well get started. But the phone rang as I was about to lift the receiver.

"Copper!" Damn. It was Heather.

"Richard got swarmed this morning," she said. "When I got here, there were eight cop cars crammed into the cul-de-sac. I counted. *Eight.*"

"God, what happened?"

"Somebody reported a gunshot, but Richard says he just slammed the door hard when some dude from the homeowners' association came around to harass him."

I thought back to the day Richard aimed a hose at the guy who'd tried to videotape him washing his car. It wasn't difficult to imagine a dork like that telling the police that a slamming door was a gunshot.

"The cops hung around awhile and took a couple of Richard's guns. They finally left, but they saw the house, including the new disaster area in Jason's room."

"Did they take him?"

"No, but it doesn't mean they won't. Copper, we've got to get him out of here. It really is only a matter of time before—"

"Okay, Heather," I said. "Let me make some calls, and—" I had no idea what I was going to do, but getting Heather off the line was definitely the first step.

"Shit," Heather said.

"What?" I could hear crashing and shouting in the background.

"Okay, bye," she said, and the line went dead.

At least she said "okay," I thought, and even "bye." The shouts and crashes probably weren't life-threatening.

I had actually succeeded in making a call to the Silverado about their January events calendar when David materialized in front of my desk.

"I've got some Ed Bramlett news," he said.

"I've heard," I said.

"That he died?"

Oh, my God!" I said. "No! I just heard he was in the hospital."

"Yeah, well ... "

"Really? He's dead?"

David nodded.

"Damn," I said.

"Yeah," David said. "You weren't finished with him, were you?"

I looked at him, and our eyes locked.

"No," I said. "I wasn't." I sighed and ran my hands through my hair. "He was incredibly vulgar, and then he gave me that pile of stuff. Now he dies."

"A bastard to the end."

"I really wanted to talk to him today," I said. "I was counting on it."

"I know," David said. "Hence my presence in front of your desk."

"You have some new ideas?"

"No, but if there's anything I can do, Copper, please—"

"Why didn't you tell me Ed had cancer?"

"I didn't know, Copper," he said. "We all knew he was sick, but—"

"Alexandra Leonard knew he had cancer."

"Alexandra Leonard knows everything." David shrugged. "Ask Norton Katz if you don't believe me. Whenever he's short of good gossip for his column, he goes straight to her."

David didn't stick around. We both had way too much to do. As soon as he left, I checked my email and found a message from Greg Langenfeld, Editor-in-Chief.

"I regret to report that Edward Bramlett passed away at University Medical Center early this morning. I will let you know funeral details when they become available."

And then it seemed as though everyone in the building felt responsible for informing me of Ed's death personally. By the time the visitations began to diminish, I felt as though I were Ed's grieving girlfriend instead of his last victim. Even J.C. Dillon, Ed's obvious successor as resident male chauvinist, stopped by.

"He liked you, Copper," J.C. said.

"Right," I said. "He was practically in love."

"He called me yesterday morning," J.C. said. "Told me he was giving you his Saxon file."

J.C. had my attention now.

"You want to hear what else he said?"

Yes! I wanted to scream, but I limited myself to a noncommittal nod.

"He said, *I got Saxon down to the end zone, old buddy, but I couldn't score. I never dreamed I'd have to pass to a blonde, but she's the only one with enough reason to take it over the line.*" J. C. paused. "Then he said something about Saxon screwing your brother. Does that mean anything to you?"

"Screwing my brother?" I said. "He said that?"

J.C. nodded.

"Yes," I said. "It means something to me."

"Good," J.C. said. "And by the way, nice work on that movie review. I wish I'd read it before I wasted two hours watching the flick. Your line about the pockmarked butt was perfect."

What? J.C. Dillon was giving the Calendar Girl a compliment? But he was gone before I could thank him, and I had more pressing things to think about anyway.

❖ ❖ ❖

Ed's time had run out, but mine hadn't. Not quite, anyway. Unless—I suddenly thought back to the night we had dinner at Mondrian. Julia had practically ordered Michael to meet her the next day, even though it was a Saturday and even though it was Christmas Eve. And Michael had agreed, I was sure of it. Was he already "screwed?"

I thought long and hard about everything I knew. Between Julia's cryptic tape and the envelope of stuff Ed had given me, the only scenario that made any sense was that Julia—and presumably Jaz and Johnny—were doing something shady with the Alliance's real estate deal. *Damn!* I wished Ed had stuck around long enough to tell me what he suspected. I wished that about Victoria, too. This was the second time in two weeks that somebody had given me a pile of papers and then died.

I called the vicarage, but the answering machine was on. I called St. Andrew's, but Michael's recorded voice answered there, too. It didn't surprise me, because Monday was his day off. I tried his cell phone. Voice mail there, too, and I left a third message to "call me as soon as you can. It's important."

I sighed. Like it or not, I had to call Sierra. The receptionist at Accolade Realty put me right through.

"Sierra. It's Copper."

Silence.

"I'm sorry about last night."

More silence.

"Are you there?"

"Yeah, I'm here."

"Look, I'm really sorry, and—something's come up."

"What now? You've been caught in a hurricane? No wait, I know. There's been a major earthquake on Fremont Street."

"I'm sorry, Sierra. I really am. But—this is about Michael. He could be in big trouble."

Silence.

"I'm not making this up. There's evidence that Julia Saxon is doing something shady with the real estate deal. I could show you—"

"Evidence! I'll give you evidence!" I held the telephone receiver away from my ear. "You've been polluted by all those assholes at the newspaper. They've always been out to get Julia, and you know why they haven't succeeded? *Because they have no evidence!* Your so-called evidence is just a big pile of shitty rumors, and I can prove it."

"I know you're probably right," I said, "but could you make sure everything's okay anyway? Just to be sure?"

"Who do you think I am, Copper? I work in a real estate office, in case you hadn't noticed. Of course I can check things out."

She hung up, and I couldn't help smiling. Yeah, she was mad, but I could handle that if she was also going to dig into the Alliance's property deal. Except—I called her back, hoping she'd take my call after that last interchange.

"Sorry to bother you again," I said. "But when are you going to check into the deal?"

"I'm doing it right now, Copper," Sierra said. "And I'd be making more progress if my phone didn't keep ringing."

"Okay," I said. "And thanks."

A huff preceded the slam.

God, I thought. Even a double-size bottle of designer vodka wouldn't fix things this time. I called Michael's cell phone again, but he still wasn't answering. I couldn't think of anything else to do on the Julia front, and after I'd worked halfway through a stack of press releases, it was time to head up to the Golden Nugget to meet Daniel.

❖❖❖

Daniel opened the door in nothing but boxers. He was smiling.

"I missed you," he said.

"I missed you," I said.

He moved aside. On the bed was a big tray of sushi, a bowl of grapes, a plate of brownies, and a bottle of champagne sticking out of a plastic ice bucket.

"You're incredible!"

Daniel kissed me. "I thought it was time to get back to the way we were," he said. "Feel like some horizontal sushi?"

Horizontal sushi. It was a phrase and a habit we'd enjoyed back at Princeton. California roll never tastes better than between the sheets.

"Where did you find sushi?" I asked.

"Asked the front desk first," Daniel said, "but then the taxi driver said he knew a better place. I was surprised he spoke English, and downright amazed that he was interested enough to recommend a sushi bar. Never would have happened in D.C."

"They actually have to take an English test here," I said. "And maybe he got a kickback, but I think it's only strip clubs that pay a bounty for customers."

I looked again at the smorgasbord on the bed. The spread looked pretty tempting.

"I'm starving."

Daniel picked up a pair of chopsticks and smiled. "May I pincer you up a salmon roll, ma'am?"

There's something about a hotel room that lets you shut out the rest of the world—and even the rest of your life—for a little while. And Daniel had spent all morning playing caterer. That was unbelievably sweet, and I told him that at least a hundred times.

"I wish I didn't have to go back to work," I said as we finished off the brownies. I'd limited myself to one glass of champagne, but it had been enough to erase all career ambition. "I'm off tomorrow, though. All day."

Daniel drained his glass, set it on the nightstand, and rolled over to face me.

He was about to say something when my phone rang.

"I have to get that," I said. "Just a minute."

It was Chris Farr, and he sounded unusually harassed.

"How soon can you get back here?" he asked.

"I'm headed there now," I said, jumping off the bed and grabbing my clothes. "What's happened?"

"Beaucoup changes in Dazzle, and since you're not going to be here tomorrow—"

"I'll be right there, Chris, and I won't leave until everything's under control."

Daniel was still studying me when I hung up.

"We've still got to talk," he said.

God, those are ominous words when they come out of a man's mouth. A woman says them, and all it means is, "Let's hang out." But from a guy, they're like Dirty Harry's gun.

"Okay," I said. "Pick a topic."

"Where were you last night?"

"What? Oh, I stayed with a friend." But damn my ears. They're worse than Pinocchio's nose, and I wasn't even lying. "Where were you?"

"Here. Alone." He drained his glass and refilled it. "Is the friend someone I've met?"

I looked at Daniel. He knew as well as I did that he had met only one person in Las Vegas who qualified as a "friend."

For a moment, I was sorely tempted to say no. But what was the point? I hadn't done anything to be ashamed of. I hadn't even sat on the sofa with David to watch *Magnum Force*, and it irritated me that Daniel was making me feel like I'd spent the night having torrid sex with him.

"I stayed at David Nussbaum's." I was tempted to add "in his wife's study," but I didn't. I shouldn't have to, I kept thinking. That's not the way it's supposed to work. I'm not guilty of anything, and I shouldn't have to prove my innocence.

Daniel got up, found a pair of jeans, and pulled them on. He had a T-shirt over his head when I spoke again.

"I don't think I should have to apologize for that."

His head poked through, and his face was wearing the same look as it did when I wouldn't tell him Victoria's address.

"I love you, Daniel," I said. "I wanted to be with you. But you didn't want to be with me, and so when David offered, well … "

Daniel just stood there.

"Will you come with me to have dinner with my family tonight?" I said. "My parents are leaving tomorrow."

For a horrible moment, I thought he would say no, and it felt like near death. Our whole relationship swirled in front of my eyes. Was this it? Were we done? Damn it! David and I hadn't even so much as smooched!

Daniel wouldn't look at me at first. When he did, I saw tears standing in his eyes.

"Daniel, I'm—" Tears jumped to my own eyes. "I hate this. I love you."

"I love you, too, Copper."

"I'll pick you up as soon as I can after work," I said. "Okay?

Daniel didn't say anything.

"Please? I'll get here no later than five thirty. I promise."

He finally nodded, and I left.

Back at *The Light*, I attacked the stack of notes and press releases Chris had waiting for me, and I managed to power through most of them. When I went into the lunchroom to get some coffee, I found myself checking the corners for Ed Bramlett. *Damn!* It was almost like I actually missed the old guy.

Chapter 22

I made a point of getting to the Golden Nugget at five fifteen. If Daniel and I had any hope of patching things up, I really couldn't be late.

When we arrived at the vicarage, my dad was drinking bourbon in the kitchen, and Michael was doing a bad job of fixing dinner. Dad immediately struck up a conversation with Daniel, and before I could ask where Sierra was, my mother spirited me out the back door.

"Copper, I need to use your computer again," she said, closing the kitchen door. "I need to send some email."

"Mom, I—"

I couldn't bring myself to let her make another email mistake.

"What's that?" my mother interrupted. She was pointing to the far side of the yard, where some obvious action was taking place under a dense boxwood hedge. We watched as Sekhmet emerged on her belly.

"She's carrying something," Mom said.

It was pretty dark, but there was no denying the cat had something white and furry hanging out both sides of her mouth.

"What is it?" Mom asked. "Is it alive?"

Oh, God, I thought. What if it's some poor kid's bunny?

I crossed the lawn to see.

"It's not alive," I said, pulling the thing out of Sekhmet's mouth. "It's a muff, I think—no wait—it's a cuff!"

Yes. It was a white rabbit-fur cuff lined in satin. It even had a large rhinestone-studded cuff link.

The cat complained loudly as my mother and I examined it.

"I wonder where she found it," I said, turning the thing over in my hands. "It certainly doesn't look like something from a garbage can."

"She's a very odd kitty," my mother said. "Yesterday, I had to stop her from stealing a bra out of Sierra's laundry basket."

"Yeah, she's weird, all right," I said. "She's been leaving me strange gifts ever since I started feeding her." Like men's briefs, I was thinking, and maybe Sierra was right about the cinnamon roll. The only pervert in the neighborhood was my own cat.

"Well, anyway, may I use your laptop again?"

"Mom, I've got to tell you something first," I said. I took a deep breath. "The last time you used it—"

"I broke something? I'm sorry!"

"No! You didn't break anything. You just—" I looked at her. "You left a copy of your message in my outbox, and a reply came to my inbox."

"Oh." She was silent for a minute or two. "Copper, there's something I should tell you."

About time, I thought.

"You know Patrick."

"I do?"

"Yes. Patrick Cluff."

"Mr. Cluff? From St. Mark's?" Mr. Cluff was an old dude who taught Sunday school at our church and planted rosebushes in the Memorial Garden every spring. At least I always thought of him as an "old dude" because his wife had died and he seemed kind of grandfatherly. He was nice enough, but the thought of the freckly old guy getting a boner for my mother was unsettling. I actually preferred the mental image of her getting nailed by a virile young potter.

"Are you and Dad splitting up?" I asked.

"I don't know," Mom said.

Wait a second! I wanted to shout. You're getting it on with another man, and you aren't sure your marriage is on the rocks?

"It really depends on how things go with Graham," she continued.

"Graham? Who's Graham?"

"Your father's boyfriend."

What?

I couldn't have been rendered more speechless if she had kicked me in the stomach.

"Patrick's getting me through this," she said softly.

I just stood there.

"He was a friend. I didn't expect to fall in love with him."

I still didn't know what to say. A lifetime of training in silent denial hadn't prepared me for a conversation like this.

"I better go in and help Michael," I said at last. "Does he know about—you and Dad?"

Mom nodded. "I told him today. Sierra knows, too." She brushed a curl off her forehead. "I was going to tell you, too—the right way. I'm sorry you had to find out by—"

"It's okay, Mom."

It wasn't, though. I could only hope that someday it would be.

"Where's Sierra, anyway?" I asked, following family tradition and changing the subject.

"She called earlier. She's held up at work."

I headed inside.

"I'll be right in," Mom said. "Give me a minute."

I left Sekhmet's fur cuff on the washing machine on my way through the laundry room. In the kitchen, my father was engaged in animated conversation with Daniel. I couldn't help staring at them. God! Fifteen minutes ago I would just have been happy they were having a good time. Now, I couldn't help noticing how my dad was standing. Weight on one foot, hip thrust out, and he touched Daniel's arm when he laughed.

For a fleeting second, I felt like grabbing the frying pan on the counter and smashing him on the head. Damn it, Dad! Did you have to make our whole family history a big fat lie?

Since I couldn't exactly shout out the question without ruining the evening entirely, I tried to concentrate on helping my brother make spaghetti sauce. With luck, he wouldn't bring the subject up. I needed time to get my head around our new family dynamic.

"Sierra should get here any minute," Michael said as he tried to slice a mushroom. The knife slipped, almost costing him the end of his thumb.

"Here, let me do that," I said. "Spaghetti sauce is a lot better without blood in it."

Michael happily relinquished the knife and turned over the sauce-making project to me.

"Sierra had something a lot fancier planned, but when I asked her how to get started, she changed the menu."

Wise of her, I thought.

"Did you meet with Julia on Saturday?" I asked.

"No," Michael said, slightly surprised. "Why?"

"Just wondered," I said.

"I was supposed to, but I put her off until today. I was about to leave for her office when Sierra called. Told me to use any excuse to get out of the meeting. I don't know what's up, but Julia was pretty upset when I told her I couldn't make it."

Just as Mom came in from the backyard, Sierra called from the living room. "Michael, are you here?"

"Yes!"

Michael headed out of the kitchen and a second later called out, "Copper! Come here!"

I joined them in their bedroom. Sierra was sitting on the edge of the bed hyperventilating.

"I've got it all," she said, patting a file folder on her lap. "Copper, you were right."

"What?" Michael said. "Will somebody tell me what's going on?"

"Julia's a crook," Sierra said.

"What?" Michael said again.

"Look, we've got to do dinner with your parents," Sierra said, her voice beginning to return to a more normal pitch. "Once they're gone, I'll explain everything."

"Dinner's just about ready," I said. "Just have to boil the spaghetti."

"Thanks, Copper," Sierra said. "I'll set the table."

Doing our best to appear calm and normal, the three of us headed back across the living room.

"What the freaking hell is this?" Sierra's voice shrilled from the laundry room, where she'd gone to retrieve some clean napkins.

"Oh! I forgot to tell you," I said. "It's another cat trophy."

"Damn!" Sierra said. "Do you have any idea where she got it?"

"Copper and I saw her drag it through the back hedge," Mom said. "I thought it was alive."

"God," Sierra said. "Do you have any idea … ?"

"What's the big deal?" I said. "It looks like something a Chippendales dancer would wear."

"Look at this." Sierra held the cuff out, and we all gathered around. She pointed to the rhinestone cuff link. "That's an 'L,'" she said, "See it?"

She was right. The capital cursive L traced out in glittery stones was plainly visible now that I was seeing it in brighter light.

"A rhinestone 'L' means only one thing in this town," Sierra said. "I think this belonged to Liberace."

"Really?" my dad said, suddenly much more interested. "Is that possible?"

"You'd be amazed what I've seen in people's houses around here," Sierra said. "Lots of people collect memorabilia—they go to auctions any time a show shuts down or an old casino's going to get imploded. Hans and Dustin—the two gay guys down the street who got burglarized—that's how they built their collection. I'm going to call them in the morning. If this is theirs, maybe our kitty knows where to find more."

Sierra set the cuff down on the little phone desk, and soon dinner was on the table. I'm not sure I talked much while we ate. All I remember is my mind jumping back and forth between my parents' crazy relationships and whatever Sierra had in her manila file folder. And what was happening between Daniel and me? Was my whole world on the verge of disintegration? How could that be, when everything seemed so smooth on the surface?

After dinner and Greek coffee in the living room, my parents began getting ready to leave. They had an early flight the next morning, and a rental car to return.

"You never sent your email," I said to my mother as she pulled on her sweater and picked up her purse. "Want me to send a message for you?"

"No, that's okay, darling," she said. "I'll call from the hotel." She hugged me. "I'm sorry things are tough, Copper, and I'm proud of you."

Proud of me? What for?

"Just take care of yourself, Mom," I said. I picked up the tray of demitasses and headed toward the kitchen.

My father was standing alone near the little phone desk. His right arm was stretched out in front of him, and on his wrist was the Liberace cuff. He was looking at his reflection in the window.

I froze as realization hit me like a truck. My father was gay. He'd been gay all his life. Oh, my God, I thought. What's it like to be locked in a closet for more than half a century? I couldn't imagine. I remembered what he had told me about his mother the day we went to the Liberace Museum. "For her, being homosexual was simply not an option." Oh, Daddy. What you really meant was that it wasn't an option for *you*.

The cuff was off, and Dad was facing me. Our eyes locked. He knew that I knew. I set the tray down, walked over and kissed him on the cheek.

"Think it's real?" I said.

"I'd like to believe it," my dad said. "I—" he paused, and our eyes met. He reached out and ruffled my hair. "I love you, kiddo."

"I love you, too, Daddy-o," I said, and I ruffled his hair back.

❖ ❖ ❖

Sierra was all business as soon as the door closed behind my parents. "Daniel, if you'll excuse us, Michael, Copper, and I have got to have a little meeting. If you want to watch TV—"

Thank you, Sierra! I'd been dreading telling Daniel myself.

"You can go up to my place," I said. "You can have my laptop." I turned to Sierra. "Let me go set it up, okay? I'll be right back."

Daniel followed me up the stairs. "I'll be back as soon as I can," I said after I'd made sure Daniel had Internet access.

"Whatever," Daniel said, sitting down at my desk. I didn't like his tone. It almost made me wish he'd said, "We've got to talk" again. I sighed.

"I won't be long, I promise."

Back in the vicarage, I found Michael and Sierra at the dining room table. Sierra had spread out a bunch of papers, and Michael had a tragic look on his face.

"So what's the deal?" I said.

"After you called, I pulled all the background on the Alliance's transactions," Sierra said. "And it all looked perfectly fine. Landmark Properties owns the Bluebird Motel, and it still looks like a perfectly good property for the Alliance. But since you seemed so convinced Julia's up to something, and I was so sure she wasn't, I did a little more homework. I pulled the background on Landmark."

Sierra moved some papers to the top of the pile.

"Again, everything looked good. Landmark is a limited liability corporation, and the partners are Jasper Cutler and John Kusick. The officers are people whose names I didn't recognize except for one that seemed familiar: R. Taylor Higginbotham. Recognize that name, Michael?"

"Maybe ..."

"The 'R' stands for Rachel."

"Julia's assistant," Michael said slowly.

"Yeah," Sierra said. "And that wasn't a good sign. So I got the whole file from the Office of the Secretary of State. Took a couple of hours, but it turned out to be worth it. Guess who another director of Landmark Properties is."

"Julia Saxon." Michael and I both said it, and Sierra nodded.

"It gets worse," she said. "As long as I was checking, I figured I might as well see what was happening with the original property—Willow Lake." She riffled through some more papers. "It's nice to have friends at title companies. I found out that another limited liability corporation has made an offer on it."

More paper shuffling.

"This one's called Triple J Ranch Partners. I checked out who the officers are and didn't recognize any names, but I got the full list of directors anyway. Sure enough, the three Js are there. Jasper, John, and Julia."

"If it was that easy to find out what was going on," Michael said, "how come nobody noticed before?"

"Nobody bothered," Sierra said. "Julia obviously thought they didn't have to work very hard to pull this off."

"What's the real crime, though?" I said. "What do they get out of it that they couldn't have gotten above board?"

"I was wondering that myself," Sierra said, "and I think it comes down to two things. One is, the Bluebird property probably has some major defects they've neglected to disclose. Hazmat, if I had to guess. Old leaky gas tanks are common up there, and it costs a fortune to clean them up. But that's just a guess."

"It's a very good guess," I said, remembering the articles Ed Bramlett had given me.

"Yes, but it could also just be a run-down property they've managed to get some inflated appraisals on. What I'm almost positive about is that they want to buy the Willow Lake property for the price the Alliance was going to pay. Now that it's been rezoned for multi-family units, it's worth a lot more, and if they move fast they can swoop in before any other offers come in."

"There's still something bothering me," I said. "A reporter at the newspaper was convinced that somehow you were going to 'get screwed' by all of this, Michael. And—just a minute. I've got something you've got to hear. I'll be right back."

Julia's tape recorder was in my car. I glanced up at my apartment as I retrieved it from the glove box. The lights were still on.

Please be patient, Daniel, I prayed. You were right. We really do need to talk.

Back in the dining room, Sierra and Michael were still poring over all the papers.

I set the recorder on the table and clicked it on. This time, as I listened to Julia chat with her accomplices, everything made perfect sense. They were angling to get the Willow Lake property, and Julia had set it up so—if nobody looked very closely—it would be "all clean."

But there was still one troubling problem. What did Julia mean when she said Michael had been "taken care of?"

"*Isn't it great to have God on our side?*" Sierra repeated as I clicked the recorder off. "That bitch! How could she?"

"But what does it mean?" I said. "I know it's underhanded of them to take the Alliance's property deal, but how does Michael get hurt?"

"That bitch!" Sierra said. "That fucking bitch!"

"I think I know," Michael said, and we both looked at him. His face was the color of a hospital sheet. "I've got something to show you."

"That fucking, fucking bitch," Sierra said.

Michael came back with an envelope in his hand and sat back down.

"Julia sent this to me by courier today. She said the courier would wait while I signed it." He opened the envelope and slid something

out. Sierra and I leaned across the table. It was a cashier's check for
$300,000.

"It's made out to you!" I said.

"Yes," Michael said. "Julia told me somebody at Landmark screwed
up and had the check made out to me instead of to the Alliance. It's
supposed to be a donation—it was part of the deal. So she wanted
me to endorse it. I asked her why Landmark couldn't get a new check,
and she said this would be a lot faster and accomplish the same thing."

"That fucking bitch," Sierra said.

"I asked her if I should endorse it over to the Alliance for the
Homeless, and she said, 'No, it's going into an escrow account. Just
sign it.'"

I waited for another "fucking bitch," but Sierra seemed to have
run out.

"Yeah," she said. "'Just sign it, and later if I need to, I can show
the world you got a personal kickback of $300,000 for guiding the
Alliance away from a valuable property and into a bad one with an
artificially inflated price.'"

That fucking bitch!

"But I didn't sign it," Michael said. "I was about to, though."

"Why didn't you?" I asked.

"Well, I had only stopped by St. Andrew's to meet the courier, but
any time my car's parked in front of the church, it guarantees activity.
Mrs. Carrington showed up with the latest dire news about the altar
guild. When I got her taken care of, my cell phone rang."

"Me?" Sierra said.

"Yup."

"I'm going to be a lot nicer to Mrs. C. from now on," Sierra said.
"The old bat can show me as many photos of her neurotic dachshunds
as she wants."

"I kept the check, sent the courier away, and called Julia. She was pretty upset, but I told her everything would just have to wait until tomorrow. I guess I dodged a pretty big bullet," Michael said. "Thanks, sweetheart. Julia may think she's got God on her side, but I'm happy to have you."

Sierra didn't say anything for a minute.

"Actually," she said at last, "you should be glad you have Copper."

Sierra looked at me, and I realized I had just heard the biggest apology ever to emerge from her mouth.

"It took us all," I said, "and we're not through. I think we've avoided the screw job, but there's still the property deal. Wouldn't it be better if the Alliance got Willow Lake?"

"Yeah," Michael said. "I was willing to make the best of the Bluebird property, but the location's not nearly as good."

"Willow Lake's a far better investment," Sierra said, "even if Bluebird isn't an outright liability."

"This tape," I said, tapping the recorder, "gives us the leverage we need to make Julia set everything straight. Let's pay her a visit tomorrow."

"I already told her I'd show up at ten," Michael said.

We spent some more time working out the details, and by the time I was on my way up to my apartment again, I had agreed to go with Michael to confront Julia the next morning. He wanted a witness, and Sierra thought it would be better if the witness weren't his wife.

"I'm his sister, though," I said.

"I know," Sierra said, "but you're also the press."

Had I heard right? Sierra was calling me "the press?"

"She's got a point," Michael said. "I'm glad we have the press on our side."

And my pompous big brother was, too!

Before I left, I almost asked them what they thought about Mom's revelations. No, I told myself. There would be plenty of time to dissect my parents' issues after we got Julia Saxon, Esquire, taken care of.

❖❖❖

The only light on in my apartment was the night-light in the bathroom. Daniel was sound asleep on the bed. As quietly as I could, I slipped off all my clothes and slid in next to him. He moaned softly and turned. His arms slipped around me, and his body curled around mine. I sighed. *Oh, Daniel. This is so good. You and me together, sleeping like spoons. This is how it's supposed to be.*

My mind whirled with thoughts of Julia and the face-off Michael and I had planned for tomorrow, but Daniel's rhythmic breathing soon slowed me down. And just before I fell asleep, I felt the soft thump of a cat's paws landing on the end of the bed. The whole family's here, I thought as I drifted off. My parents might be philanderers, and my brother a stooge. My cat might be peculiar, and I myself may have my priorities mixed up. But right that very minute, and for a few more hours, everything was perfect.

❖❖❖

Tuesday, December 27

It stayed perfect, too. Daniel and I woke up before dawn and we made love.

"I love you, Copper," he said as we lay there in the dark. "I miss you."

"I love you, Daniel," I said. "And you can't miss me because I'm right here."

But the truth was, I missed him, too. What had happened to us?

"All I wanted was to spend a week with you," he said. "But right now, I'd settle for a day."

"Daniel—"There was no point in postponing the inevitable. "I wish I didn't have to but—"

Daniel pulled away from me and sat up.

"Let me guess," he said. "You've got an appointment with a pimp at Kmart."

"Come on," I said.

"Come on what?" he said, standing up. "Come on, let's go get some breakfast? Somehow, I bet not."

"This won't take long," I said.

"Oh, you mean like last night," Daniel said.

"Do you want to hear what it's about or not?" I asked.

"I've done a lot of listening lately, Copper," Daniel said. "When does it get to be my turn to talk?"

"My brother's in trouble," I said. "I have to help him."

"Well, that's a step up from a dead hooker, at least."

Right then, my phone rang. I looked at the number before I answered.

"It's Heather," I said.

"Oh, great. The *live* hooker."

I sighed and took the call.

"Copper, a detective was here last night asking Richard a bunch more questions. He's a mess this morning. Have you gotten anywhere with Julia?"

"No, but I'm seeing her this morning." I didn't see any point in telling Heather my meeting had nothing to do with Victoria.

"Good. I think I've found a ranch school in California that will take Jason, but I'm going to need at least ten grand to get him settled. Tell her that, okay?"

Out of the corner of my eye, I saw Daniel pull his cell phone out of his jeans. He retreated across the room and made a call.

"I'll do what I can. Any idea what the cops suspect?"

"Richard's afraid they might think he killed Victoria."

"Oh, no!"

"They asked questions about Marks, though. And American Beauty, so who knows?"

Daniel finished his call before Heather hung up.

"Want some coffee?" I said.

"You have time?"

"Yeah," I said. But unfortunately, my cupboard was bare. It had been a while since I'd done any grocery shopping. "I'll have to go borrow some coffee from Sierra." I was about to add, "I'll be right back," but I restrained myself. No reason to reignite the war just yet.

Sierra was in the kitchen pouring a cup of coffee from a full pot.

"Oh, hi, Copper, "she said. "I've been thinking things over, and I think we should—"

"May I borrow some coffee?" I said. "It's kind of an emergency."

"Beans or already made?" she said. "Are you okay?"

"I'm not sure," I said, not even sure which question I was answering.

"Is everything okay with Daniel?"

"No."

Without another word, Sierra pulled two mugs from the cupboard above her and filled them from the pot. "Sugar?" she asked. "Cream?"

"No, black's fine," I said. "Thanks." I picked up the mugs. "I'll be back soon," I said. God, it was becoming my favorite lie.

I was halfway across the driveway when a taxi pulled up at the curb. Daniel appeared at the top of my stairs. We met at the bottom, and I kept up with him as he walked purposefully to the curb.

"You're leaving?" I said.

"Yeah."

"Leaving Las Vegas?"

"I'm not sure yet. Thought I'd have breakfast and think things over."

"Will you call me? We really should talk."

Daniel made a gulping sound. A laugh? Or was it a sob?

"I love you," I said.

Daniel looked at me, but he didn't say anything. Then he opened the taxi door and disappeared inside.

The cab pulled away, leaving me standing there at the curb in my bathrobe holding two rapidly cooling mugs of black coffee.

Chapter 23

Sierra and Michael were at the kitchen table, heads together in heavy conversation when I joined them. I refilled my mug and pulled up a chair.

"I've been up all night thinking," Michael said. "The way I see it, I've got to let Julia know what we know and give her a chance to make it right."

"We should take the tape," I said. "That's the smoking gun."

"I'm way ahead of you, Copper," Michael said. "One of the things I did while I wasn't sleeping was make a copy." He got up and retrieved a boom box from the kitchen counter. "I tried to do it with my computer, but I'm not enough of a geek." He punched the play button, and the three Js started talking. The recording was a little rough, but still completely intelligible. Michael clicked it off. "Finally, I just turned on the little recorder and let it play with this old boom box set on 'record.' It's not perfect, but it'll do. And Sierra's going to take the original to work with her."

"And put it in the office safe," Sierra said.

"What about the check?" I said.

"I took a picture of it," Michael said, "and I'm planning to tear it up in front of Julia." He chuckled. "Sure never thought I'd rip up a check for a third of a million dollars—made out to me."

"There's one thing that worries me," I said.

"One thing?" Michael said. "That's nothing. I can think of a million."

"Julia likes to tape stuff," I said. "She might tape us."

"Well, we aren't going to say anything incriminating, are we?"

"We don't intend to, but—well, she's really smart, and we know she's dishonest. That's a dangerous combination. I mean, think about what she could do with the tape."

"You're right," Sierra said. "Too bad you can't use sign language."

"Hmm," I said, thinking. What if we took some paper along, and wrote down whatever we wanted to say to Julia instead of saying it out loud? It seemed kind of silly, but I floated the idea out to Michael and Sierra anyway.

"Julia will think it's weird," Michael said, "but making her a little uncomfortable isn't a bad idea."

"Wait," Sierra interjected. "As long as we're going to be paranoid—I'll be right back."

She returned with what looked like a picture frame and a couple of felt-tipped markers.

"Whiteboard," she said, turning it around. "You can write on it and then wipe it off. No annoying evidence!" She smiled. "What do you think?"

I think we all felt silly, but there didn't seem to be anything to lose by taking the whiteboard along.

Michael got up to refill his coffee mug, and before he sat back down, his cell phone rang.

"Good morning, Julia," he said, his eyes meeting mine. "Yes. Yes. I'll be there at ten." He paused. "No. Ten." Another pause. I could hear Julia's voice but not her words. "It's really going to have to be ten, unless you want to push it into the afternoon." Julia's volume increased a few decibels. "Okay, then. See you at ten."

"Good work," I said. "She can be pretty hard to resist."

"All of a sudden, I'm finding it a lot easier," Michael said.

❖❖❖

At a quarter of ten, I pulled up right behind Michael's Jetta across the street from Jackman, Sarnoff, Saxon, & Cline. Their offices were near the county courthouse in a neighborhood that used to be residential. All the houses had been made over into offices, mostly inhabited by attorneys, architects, and CPAs.

I gave my name to the young Asian woman at the front desk, and she escorted me to a small office with two upholstered chairs, a wall of shelves and filing cabinets, and a secretary behind a desk. Michael was sitting in one of the chairs. The whiteboard was sticking out of his briefcase on the floor next to him, and the old boom box was in his lap. The secretary was on the phone. I sat down in the vacant chair and looked around. Whoever had done the decorating was fond of synthetic houseplants and paintings of boats, I noted. The shelves were full of the usual fat books with gold lettering on the spines you'd expect to find in a law office.

My eyes fell on an overfull trash can beside the secretary's desk. Next to it was a cardboard box, and I could see that there were several old cassette tapes inside it. A black one with silver writing on it was on top.

"May I get you anything?" the secretary asked after she ended her call. "Coffee? Tea?"

"I'd like some water, please," I said.

"Nothing for me, thanks," Michael said.

"With ice, please," I said. Michael looked at me questioningly as the secretary departed.

As soon as she was gone, I stood up and moved closer to the box next to the trash can. I picked up the black cassette. *The Phantom of the Opera. Original Broadway Cast.* It was exactly like a tape my father had loaned me years back and I'd never returned. *Damn!* Could it be? I turned the tape over. Sure enough. There was the little stick-on address label my dad put on everything he lent to people. I checked the box again. Two more of my dad's tapes were from my apartment, too—*Jesus Christ Superstar* and *Annie.* I hadn't missed them because I hadn't listened to them in ages. I don't even own a cassette player anymore.

The fourth tape wasn't mine, and it took me a moment to decipher the scrawl on its label. "Jason McK. as George Washington. 2nd grade. Mrs. Davis."

Damn! Julia was not only behind my trashed apartment, she was responsible for the disaster at the McKimbers' house, too.

Moving back across the room, I held the *Phantom* cassette out to Michael.

"Recognize this?" I asked.

"It's Ted's!" Michael said, looking at the little sticker. "But how—?" He looked at me and realized the truth at the same instant.

"I think whoever Julia hired took these to prove they'd really done the job even though they couldn't find what she wanted."

"Damn!" Michael said.

"Yeah," I said. *That fucking bitch!* If she wanted her precious tape that badly, she was going to have to pay for it.

I had just enough time to stuff the cassettes into my backpack before the secretary came back with my water. My heart was pounding so hard I was afraid she might hear it as she handed me the glass.

"Hi, Michael!"

Julia Saxon strode out of her office, but she stopped abruptly when she saw me.

"Copper! Hello! What a nice surprise." She looked from me to Michael and back at me. "Come on in."

I was shaking as I passed her, and I prayed it didn't show.

Julia shut the door behind us, moved behind her desk, and sat down. Michael and I each took a chair facing her on the other side. It was a big dark hardwood desk, so shiny that Julia was almost reflected in it. She folded her hands in front of her.

"Do you have the check with you, Michael?" she said.

"Of course, Julia," my brother said. He set the boom box on the desk. His briefcase was in his lap. He pulled out the whiteboard, the two felt-tip markers, and two tissues. He handed me a marker and a tissue. Our eyes met, and Michael picked up the board. Before he could write anything, I grabbed it out of his hands. Michael was surprised, but he didn't say anything.

"What are you doing?" Julia said.

I scribbled on the board and turned it toward her.

WE'RE GOING TO WRITE INSTEAD OF TALK.

"Okay ... " She dragged the word out, like a question. Good. We'd definitely caught her off guard. I turned the board around, rubbed out the words with the tissue, and started writing again.

"Michael—what's going on?" Julia asked. But Michael was busy watching me write.

WE HAVE SOMETHING WE WANT YOU TO HEAR.

Michael punched the play button on the boom box.

I watched the color drain from Julia's face as she recognized the voices. I started writing again.

YOU'RE GOING TO FIX THE PROPERTY DEAL.

"Okay," Julia said, "Okay. But Michael, the check—"

Michael reached into his briefcase. This was the part where he was supposed to shred the check, but—*hold on!* I grabbed Michael's wrist, took a deep breath, and spoke out loud.

"The Alliance is very grateful for Landmark's generous donation."

"What?" Michael and Julia said it in unison.

"Copper—"Michael said, but I squeezed his wrist until my knuckles turned white. He let the envelope slip back into his briefcase.

"Michael has endorsed the check over to the Alliance, and he'll deposit it today," I said. "The money will be in the Alliance's account by the end of the day, just as Landmark intended."

I sneaked a glance at Michael. His mouth was open, but he still didn't say anything.

Michael reached for the whiteboard, but I turned it toward Julia again and pointed to each word.

YOU'RE GOING TO FIX THE PROPERTY DEAL.

Turning it back, I erased the board and wrote:

WILLOW LAKE. NO MORE BLUEBIRD.

"Okay, okay," Julia said. "But Michael—"

"We really appreciate all you've done, Julia," Michael said. "You've been nothing short of brilliant." I looked at him in amazement. He was actually getting into the spirit of things. So was I. I erased the board again and penned my next demand.

CLOSE BEFORE THE 31ST, OR THE D.A. GETS THE TAPE.

I had no idea if the D.A. was the right person to rat her out to, but her reaction was satisfying.

"We'll get everything straightened out," she said. "There's plenty of time."

Her forced smile looked more like a grimace, and I saw her hands shake before she hid them under her desk.

"I guess that's all, then," Michael said. "And thanks again—" I poked him in the ribs.

THERE'S ONE MORE THING, I wrote.

"What?" Michael and Julia asked in unison.

I NEED A CHECK FOR $25,000 RIGHT NOW.

"*What?*"

I erased and kept writing.

CASHIER'S CHECK TO RICHARD MCKIMBER.

"$25,000?" Julia said. "What for?"

JASON'S SCHOOL. IT CAN'T WAIT.

"It's too much," Julia said.

"So was this," I said out loud. I pulled Jason McKimber's cassette out of my backpack and held it up.

$25,000 OR IT GOES TO THE COPS, I wrote.

"That's extortion," Julia said in a tone so self-righteous I felt like laughing.

I pushed my chair back and stood up. I shrugged.

"Okay," I said. "Come on, Michael." I picked up the boom box and shoved the whiteboard under my arm. "Let's get out of here."

I actually made it to the door.

"Hold on, both of you," Julia said. "Just hold on."

I turned around. I pulled the whiteboard from under my arm and yanked the cap off my felt-tip pen with my teeth.

"Will you cut it out with the message board?" Julia said. "I'm not taping you. You're being unreasonable."

It took all my willpower to prevent myself from writing FUCK YOU on the whiteboard.

But Julia was sitting at her desk again. Two phone calls later, a check was in the works.

"You can leave that with me," she said sweetly, pointing at the boom box.

I sighed and pulled out the whiteboard again. I uncapped my pen.

"Okay, okay," Julia said. "*Okay.*"

The forty minutes we waited for the cashier's check to be delivered from the bank seemed like fifteen years, and as we navigated our way back out to the street, I kept expecting a goon to conk us on the head and take all our stuff. But nothing happened.

When we reached our cars, Michael said, "You were pretty scary in there, baby sister. And I'm still not so sure I should take Landmark's money—"

"You aren't. You're accepting it for the Alliance. I couldn't see one good reason to let those thieves have their money back after what they did. Can you?"

"It's blood money, in a way."

"Launder it by using it for a good cause."

❖ ❖ ❖

Fortunately, the main branch of the Bank of Nevada was less than a mile from Julia's office. I followed Michael in the Max, still on the lookout for goons. We parked side by side and went in. There was no line in the bank, and less than twenty minutes after leaving Julia's office, the Alliance's coffers were fatter by $300,000.

"Phew," Michael said when we were back out on the sidewalk.

"Hold the sigh of relief," I said. "I've still got Richard's check to take care of."

"Could you at least take 30 seconds to clue me in, Copper? Who is he?"

I filled my brother in on the details of the McKimber saga he didn't already know.

"I'll tell you more later," I said. "And you can tell me whatever fairy tale you've concocted for the other Alliance board members."

Michael groaned.

"Copper, I think you committed extortion in there."

"Let her prove it," I said. We climbed into our cars. As I watched him pull into traffic, I hoped that whatever we had committed in Julia's office wouldn't come back to hurt my brother. If anyone ever deserved being named after an angel, it's Michael.

I called Heather while I was driving. She answered on the first ring.

"Hey, it's Copper," I said. "I've got Richard's cash. Can you get him and meet me at his bank?"

A moment of silence.

"Really? You got ten grand?"

"I got twenty-five."

"*Awesome!*"

Heather and I agreed to meet at the Bank of Nevada on Warm Springs. It wasn't Richard's branch, but Heather said it would be easier to find. I liked the fact that it was in a large, busy shopping center. I was still feeling paranoid about whatever thugs Julia might keep on retainer for situations like this. I probably looked in my rearview mirror more than I looked though my windshield the entire way across town.

When I pulled off Warm Springs into the shopping center, I spied Heather's truck immediately. Victoria's blue Taurus was parked next to it. Both vehicles had American Beauty decals on the back windows.

Heather jumped down from her cab as soon as she saw me pull in, and Richard McKimber began to haul himself out of the Taurus. Jason had come along with Richard, but he stayed in the passenger seat, his eyes hidden behind mirrored sunglasses.

Without much fanfare or conversation, I handed the cashier's check to Richard. He stared at it, then looked at me.

"What do I have to do for it?" he said. "Sign off on something? Cut off an arm?"

"Nope," I said. "I think you can consider it a personal gift from Julia Saxon."

"Awfully generous of her," Heather said. "But I know better than to ask too many questions."

"Just get it into your account," I said to Richard. "I'm not going to relax until I know it's securely yours."

Richard grunted and headed into the bank.

"Copper," Heather said. "Have you got that picture you showed me of the two guys from American Beauty? The cops were back this morning, and I'm getting kind of concerned. I get the distinct impression they might arrest Richard."

"For killing Victoria?" I said. "But that's crazy."

"Maybe they won't, but I think that photo might take the heat off. Or at least give them a couple other faces to suspect."

"What about Marks?"

"He's vanished. Classic rich-boy behavior. He's probably sunbathing in the Cayman Islands while he waits for it all to blow over. But he isn't the perp, anyway. I found out he went to the Wild Horse after he left the Beavertail the night Victoria died. That's the brothel next door. Stayed there until morning. But anyway, American Beauty has a better motive."

In fact, I had the photograph Heather wanted in my shoulder bag, but I was reluctant to give it to her. I had stolen it, after all, and the last thing I wanted was to have to answer police questions myself. Especially now that I was an extortionist.

"I'll call you later," I said. "I've—I've got another appointment."

"Where's Daniel?" Heather asked as though she had read my mind. "I thought he was sticking around for New Year's."

"Yes, that was the plan."

Heather studied me a moment.

"Well, if there's anything I can do to help."

God. Help from Heather was a scarier thought than prosecution for theft.

"Thanks for getting the money, Copper. Cottonwood Ranch is going to be perfect for Jason."

"Where is it?"

"Newberry Springs. Near Barstow."

"I guess he can't get into any trouble in the middle of the howling desert."

"You'd be surprised what's out there. They've got a lake. He can go waterskiing, even."

I glanced at Jason as I walked back to the Max. He was studying his teeth in the rearview mirror. He sure loved that little vampire fang of his.

My phone rang while I was still in the parking lot. It was Daniel. He was at the Venetian on the Strip, and he asked me to meet him there.

❖❖❖

Daniel was leaning on a balustrade over the Grand Canal when I spotted him. The white wedding gondola was floating by, and a Danny DeVito clone in a red-and-white-striped T-shirt was singing "Volare" to a tiny Asian bride in a huge white dress and a sixty-something white guy in a tight black tux.

"That's *amore*," I said to Daniel, moving in next to him.

"Hi." But he didn't look at me. "I moved out of the Golden Nugget."

"Where's your stuff?"

"At the front desk."

"You're leaving?"

Daniel finally looked at me.

"I've got to do something," he said. "But hey, this is Vegas. I've got a lot of choices."

I turned away. Tears were welling up inside me, and there didn't seem to be much I could do to stop them.

"Gamble. Get drunk." He paused while the gondolier finished his song to a smattering of applause. "Get laid."

"Daniel." It came out with a sob.

"Yeah?"

I gulped. "Can't we really talk?" I put my hand on his arm and looked at him. There wasn't any point in trying to hide my tears.

"Copper—" He paused. "I've tried. I think I'm done."

"But you waited for me here. I thought—"

"I've been waiting for you the entire time I've been in Las Vegas."

"I'm here now."

"Yeah? For how long? Until something more important happens?"

"I'm sorry."

"No, you're not."

"I'm sorry we're like this. I really am."

"Copper, do you really like this fake canal and phony twilight sky and Disneyland gondolier?"

"That's a trick question."

"Maybe," Daniel said, "but the trouble is, everything's 'trick' with us these days. It's like we have an illusion of a relationship, but when you take away the smoke and mirrors ... " His voice trailed off.

"Look—may I buy you lunch?" I said. "Real food?"

And it was real food, even if it was served by a fake Italian waiter on an ersatz St. Mark's Square under an artificial dusk.

Not that we ate much. We mostly just sat there watching a guy, completely dressed in white, fool passing tourists into thinking he was a statue. Ordinarily I kind of liked that sort of thing, but then it just reminded me that Daniel was right. Our relationship looked convincing enough to the outside world—and to me, too, most of the time. But to be honest, sometimes I did wonder if it was just an illusion I kept up for appearances. I'd had role models for that, after all. My own parents had preserved a façade for decades. That thought made me sad—panicky even. Was I capable of a solid relationship, or was I doomed to settle for a charade? Then, as I watched the guy in white, his arm trembled. You can't stand still forever, I thought. And it's way too exhausting to try.

We barely touched our pasta, and our conversation flowed about as well as cold lava. By the time we let the waiter have his table back, we had agreed on only one thing: We would drive to the Golden Nugget, where I would gather my things and check out while Daniel claimed his luggage from the concierge.

"Where to?" I asked when we were back inside the Max. "The airport?"

"I don't know," Daniel said.

"Well, you're going to have to make up your mind," I said. "If you want to stay, we can go to my place. But I should warn you. My phone will ring. Victoria's family and my brother might still need me. I have to go to work tomorrow. I've probably committed a crime—maybe more than one. My cat's a kleptomaniac, my mother's having an affair, and my father's gay."

Daniel looked at me. Our eyes met, and in an instant so short there's no word for it, every emotion I've ever felt rushed through me. I wanted to scream. I wanted to cry. But what I did was laugh. So did Daniel. And then we both cried.

"I love you, Copper." Daniel said, and I wish he had stopped there, because I would have said, "I love you, too," and maybe somehow …

"I really do."

How is it that a phrase that sounds like assurance always signals trouble? I waited for the inevitable.

"But … "

Yeah, *that!* I waited for the "but."

"But what?"

"Come on, Copper. You know it's not working out."

"We could work it out if we tried. If we wanted to."

"Things are just different. Nothing has been what I expected."

"You mean *I* haven't been what you expected."

Daniel looked at me. "Yeah." He shook his head. "But Vegas, too. Like you said."

Well, you haven't been what I expected, either, Daniel, I wanted to say. I guess I had you mixed up with some guy who could accept me for who I am. But Daniel's disappointment was like an elephant between us, and I couldn't summon the energy to try to push it away.

"The airport, then?" I asked.

Daniel nodded, and we pretty much didn't talk again until after he had bought a standby ticket to Phoenix. From there, he could get a flight to Austin, and with luck, he'd be at his parents' house before the next day.

"Bye," I said when we reached the security checkpoint. What else was there to say?

"Bye *for now*," Daniel said.

I looked at him. A snowman on the Strip had a better chance of survival than our relationship.

"Bye, Daniel," I said.

"Bye *for now*, Copper."

We hugged, and he hefted his backpack onto his shoulder. Before he disappeared beyond the security gates, he was already talking to a woman with long braids who was carrying a guitar.

As I walked back through the airport, I kept expecting to cry. I still loved Daniel, and I couldn't believe he didn't love me, too. We'd been so good together, and we'd had such sweet plans. But as I made my way to the parking garage, the grief I was anticipating never came, and by the time I was back behind my steering wheel, I realized it wasn't going to. All I felt as I pulled back onto the freeway was a huge wave of relief.

Chapter 24

David Nussbaum called to tell me that *The Light* would be running a story the next day about Victoria McKimber. They'd been following the case, but nothing had run for a few days because nothing reportable had happened. Only now, something had. Just as Heather suspected, the police had decided that Richard McKimber was a "person of interest."

"They've got a terrible picture of the guy, Copper," David said. "It won't do much to vindicate him in the public eye."

It wasn't hard to imagine a bad photo of Richard McKimber. All you'd have to do to capture a Pulitzer-worthy snarl would be to knock on his door and say you were from the paper.

It also wasn't difficult to jump to the conclusion that he'd killed his wife. I'd tried the theory on myself, and even without an insurance policy to motivate him, it was easy to imagine that being married to a self-proclaimed hooker would be enough to make a guy snap.

"He's really not a bad guy," I said. "He spends most of his time trying to take care of his son. The only person he might murder is the president of his homeowners' association, but so far, he's only sprayed him with a hose." I paused. "Actually, American Beauty has more to gain from Victoria's death. Do you know if the cops are looking into that?"

"All I've heard is that they have shifted their attention from Bobby Marks to the husband," David said, "but if I hear anything else, I'll let you know."

"Thanks."

"Oh, and Ed Bramlett's funeral is Thursday morning at Davis Mortuary. His gay daughter is organizing it, and a couple of other family members have shown up from Utah."

"His *gay* daughter?"

"Yup. They hadn't spoken since she came out of the closet a couple of years ago, but I guess he didn't quite disown her. I heard through the grapevine that she's already taken up residence in his house."

"So I guess he must have had a wife somewhere along the line?"

"Yeah. Charlotte Inman of Hurricane, Utah. They divorced in 1984. I've got the obit in front of me. Want to hear the rest?"

"No, thanks." God. Old Ed had a lesbian daughter, and I have a gay father. It's almost like we had something in common.

"Anything new on the Julia Saxon front?" David said.

I hesitated. I trusted David, but he was still "the press." He proved it with his instant suspicion.

"I smell a story," he said.

"I'm not ready to talk," I said. "I've—I've had a very tough day."

"Are you alone?"

"What do you mean?"

"I think you know what I mean."

I sighed. David really is a born newshound. "Yeah. I'm on my own."

"Well, if you need anything, you know how to reach me," David said. "I've got another date with Clint tonight, but he's very understanding. Never complains a bit when I mute him."

"Clint again? You going steady or something?"

"Yeah, we're getting serious. Tonight I'm watching *The Bridges of Madison County.*"

"You're joking."

"I am. But if I weren't—?"

"I've got to have dinner with Michael and Sierra," I said.

"The gauntlet," David said.

"Well, not exactly," I said. "But I do need to talk to them."

"No, *The Gauntlet*," David said. "That's the Clint flick I really do have for tonight."

After we hung up, I dug through my backpack and found the pictures from Victoria's old camera. I flipped through them, considering their value as evidence. The two men in the dark restaurant were easily identifiable. Heather had already recognized one of them, and I had a name that probably went with the other. But would the pictures be helpful enough to the police to risk being outed as a thief? Did they prove anything more than that two guys who worked together were in a dark restaurant at some point on December 15th? The only thing that suggested Victoria had taken the pictures was her tape recorder sitting on the table. The date stamp was suggestive, though. I checked to make sure that December 15th was the day before Victoria's body was found.

I looked through the rest of the pictures again. They all had date stamps on them, including the ones of Jason.

I looked more closely at the vampire boy in his mirrored sunglasses. Heather was right. It was easy to see that Jason had taken the pictures himself. His hand and the camera were reflected perfectly in his lenses.

I was about to go back to the other photos when I noticed something else. Behind Jason's head, on the back window of the car, I could see a round decal. It looked familiar, even though it was reversed.

Damn! I'd seen that decal that morning! It was the American Beauty logo. There were beads hanging from the rearview mirror. I'd seen those this morning, too. When Jason took that picture, he was in his mother's car, in the driver's seat. On December 15th.

I pulled the negatives out of the film envelope. He had not only taken the pictures on December 15th, but he'd taken them sometime after Victoria had snapped the American Beauty dudes. Jason's self-portraits were the last two shots on the roll and, judging from the light, they were taken around dusk. I noticed one other thing as I looked at the pictures again. In one of them, a shoulder and part of an arm in a black sleeve were barely visible on the far right-hand edge. Somebody had been in the passenger seat.

Well, so what? I asked myself. It wasn't weird for a kid to be in his mother's car, even if it happened to be the day before her body was discovered.

Except it *was* weird. Victoria wasn't at home that day. She was at the Beavertail quarreling with Bobby Marks after meeting the men from American Beauty. The pictures were telling a story, but it wasn't one that I could make sense of.

❖ ❖ ❖

Daniel called. He had made it to Austin.

"Just wanted to let you know I'm okay," he said.

"Thanks," I said.

"Bye for now."

I had tried to talk him out of the "bye for now" earlier, but damned if it didn't sound nice now. Except—hadn't we broken up? The guy walked out on me—couldn't even hang around for New Year's. Right?

Oh, Daniel. What the hell happened to us? Couldn't we make room in our relationship for ourselves *and* our lives? If we didn't, maybe Victoria was right all along. Maybe we were just a hooker and a john, getting together for no-fuss sex.

Damn it. We never did talk. Not really. I wondered if we ever would.

❖❖❖

Dinner at the vicarage was a very casual affair. Sierra had picked up a pizza on her way home. She asked if Daniel would be joining us.

"He's playing poker at the Golden Nugget," I said. I just wasn't up for telling the truth. Fortunately, my little lie was enough to ward off further questions.

Michael had been home most of the afternoon, on the phone trying to convince all his board members and donors that he really knew what he was doing.

"I've been worried all day that Julia was going to figure out a way to weasel out of our agreement," Michael said, "but at about four thirty, she sent a new set of escrow instructions by courier, just as we agreed this morning. Sierra's got to look them over, but as far as I can tell, the Willow Lake deal's together again, and it'll close by Friday."

"I delivered Richard McKimber's check, too," I said. "Now he can afford to send his son off to Cottonwood Ranch."

"Really?" Michael said. "That's where he's going?"

"You've heard of it?"

"I've been there. It's got a good reputation for helping troubled kids."

"Well, this kid's definitely troubled," I said. "It was bad enough that he's bipolar. It didn't help that he found out his mother was a prostitute a couple of days before she died."

"So now you can bow out of the whole sordid mess?" Sierra asked.

"We still don't know who killed Victoria," I said.

"Might be best to leave it to the cops, baby sis—Copper," Michael said.

"Maybe," I said.

But I wasn't about to let somebody get away with murder.

❖ ❖ ❖

Wednesday, December 28

The story in the morning *Light* made me sad. David was right about the unflattering photo of Richard McKimber. He looked like a raving lunatic. And he wasn't wearing a hat, which made him look older and nuttier than he actually was. The story also included quotes from neighbors who seemed all too eager to say things like, "We've always been suspicious of him," and "Richard McKimber has a hair-trigger temper. I won't let my kids go anywhere near him."

The story also included this disturbing tidbit:

> *McKimber left his home Tuesday afternoon with his son Jason, 15. According to a neighbor, the two were carrying luggage. "It wouldn't surprise me if that's the last we see of him," said the neighbor, Al Ternullo, 74. "And I say good riddance."*

The piece closed with a boilerplate request for anybody with information helpful to the police to call "Secret Witness," a program that promises that the identity of tipsters "shall remain protected and anonymous."

The pictures from Victoria's camera tugged at my conscience. If they provided clues about Victoria's last hours, did I have the right to withhold them from the police? I toyed with the idea of turning the pictures over to Secret Witness, but it seemed like a cop-out. Besides, they would have lost half their value if I weren't around to explain the timeline and say where I'd gotten them.

Damn. I couldn't say I wanted to, but I needed to make another trip down to Chantilly Court. Old Mr. Ternullo was going to be very disappointed, but I was willing to bet that his neighbor would be back tonight after dropping his son off at Cottonwood Ranch.

I had lunch in the lunchroom with David Nussbaum. It felt great to eat a sandwich without worrying whether an old lecher was going to ask if we'd made a mattress squeak.

"Want to go to Ed's funeral with me tomorrow?" David asked.

"I can't say I *want* to, exactly, but sure," I said. "I have the day off, so I guess I'll meet you there. It's at ten, right?"

"Yes," David said. "We could have lunch afterward."

"I'm afraid I can't," I said. "I've got an errand."

David looked at me questioningly.

"In fact," I said, "I've got stuff I should be doing right now."

It was risky to keep hanging around David. I knew myself well enough to know I might reveal too much about my involvement with the McKimber family.

"How about dinner tonight?" David said.

"What? No date with Clint?"

David leaned forward and lowered his voice. Even without Ed Bramlett around, the lunchroom had a lot of attentive ears.

"I was hoping for a date with you."

There it was, out in the open—kind of like a flower bulb that finally sends a leaf above ground. We'd been flirting with the idea, of course, but until David popped the bare question, we could pretend we weren't really doing it.

"I can't tonight," I said. "I'm sorry." And before he could come up with another offer I might not be able to refuse, I fled to my cube.

He didn't follow. He didn't call. With luck, I told myself, I'd escape at five without bumping into him.

The irony was that I would have liked nothing more than to bump into David. Truth be told, I wouldn't have minded bumping into him for a good long time.

❖ ❖ ❖

I saw them as soon as I turned the corner onto my street. Not one but *two* cop cars in the vicarage's driveway. My heart stopped beating, I stopped breathing, and I had an almost irresistible urge to pull a U-turn and start driving to Connecticut. All I could think was that Julia Saxon had decided to nail me for extortion. That or somebody had figured out I was withholding evidence in the Victoria McKimber investigation. Either way, the law was there to arrest me. I looked at my hands. They were shaking even though I had the steering wheel in a death grip.

I slowed to a halt and took a few deep breaths. Gradually, my world came back into more realistic focus. Maybe the cops were there because they had figured out who had broken into my apartment. That was a much more pleasant thought, especially if they had connected the break-in to Julia. I liked the image of her in handcuffs, preferably on the front page of *The Light*.

A couple of neighbors were standing on the front lawn of the house across the street. They were all looking at a silver Lexus, and it was easy to see why. The front end was up on the sidewalk and crunched into a pine tree. As I pulled closer, one of the cop cars in the driveway began backing out. As it turned and passed me, I caught sight of a face through the back window. Jaz Cutler! And wasn't this the same silver Lexus that chased me down Dean Martin Drive?

I let the other police car pull out, parked in the driveway, and headed toward the house. The front door was ajar, and I heard voices coming from the kitchen.

I found Michael and Sierra there.

"Copper," Sierra said. "Are you okay?"

"Sure," I said. "What about you?"

"We've had some excitement around here," Sierra said.

"So I gather," I said. "What happened?"

"Michael and I both came home about three hours ago to work on letters to Alliance board members. All of a sudden, somebody started pounding on the door and yelling."

"Jaz Cutler?"

"Yes!" Sierra said. "Michael tried to calm him down, but he was drunk. He kept calling us thieves and demanding his money back."

"Sierra managed to sneak off and call the police," Michael said, "which turned out to be a good thing. The guy pulled a knife on me."

Whoa! Sort of like what he did to me at the liquor store in Green Valley.

"Then, when he heard the sirens," Sierra said, "he jumped in his car and tried to drive away."

"Didn't get very far," I said.

"Good thing that pine tree's as big as it is," Sierra said, "or he might have gone right on into the Stecklers' living room."

"It was good in another way, too," Michael said. "In addition to assault and battery, the cops nailed him for drunk driving. He had an open quart of tequila in his car. Oh, and a gun."

"It didn't help that he called the male cop the N-word and the female cop the C- word," Sierra said.

"God," I said. "I'm glad you're okay."

"We're fine," Michael said. "And a tow truck is supposed to come and haul the car away."

"When I saw the police cars, I thought maybe Julia had—"

"You and Michael must've really terrorized her," Sierra said. "The deal's set to close on Friday, no problem."

And Jaz Cutler was on his way to jail. Things were definitely looking up. I thought about telling Michael and Sierra the whole story about Jaz and me, but decided to save them the angst. Plus, I didn't want them telling Mom, who'd be even more upset. Justice had been served, and I was happy to leave it that way for now.

"Where's Daniel?" Sierra asked suddenly.

"In Texas," I said. No point in lying again. "Family emergency." Well, maybe just a little.

I knew Sierra didn't buy it, but she didn't pry.

❖ ❖ ❖

Thursday, December 29

Ed Bramlett's funeral wasn't bad, all things considered. The best part was that the body had been cremated, so there wasn't any plasticized mannequin to gape at. Ed's daughter read "O Captain! My Captain!", and a minister of the nonspecific Protestant variety gave a eulogy so flattering it sounded as though he thought Ed should be deified. Then a man who had gone to high school with Ed spoke briefly, ending with the line, "He was the best man who ever lived."

I had a hard time believing my ears. David and I looked at each other, which was a huge mistake. We both had to feign major coughing attacks to cover our laughter. Then I noticed that quite a few other people in the assembled multitude suddenly had throat problems, too.

I thought about what Ed Bramlett himself would have thought about a line like that. He would have laughed, too, but he wouldn't have tried to cover it up. He would have just guffawed, and to hell with what anybody thought.

Ed Bramlett might not have been the best man who ever lived, but as we all sat there trying not to snicker, I appreciated Ed for the first time. He was an unapologetic, opinionated, politically incorrect curmudgeon, and his last few deeds on earth included saving my brother's ass. He might not merit deification, but maybe he deserved membership in the brotherhood of excellent old bastards.

After I said good-bye to David, Chris Farr waylaid me on my way back to the Max.

"Copper, I'm glad I caught you. I just wanted to say—well—thank you for how you handled Ed. I know it was tough."

"I had no idea he was dying."

"Very few people did. That's how Ed wanted it."

"Sounds like him, all right."

"Look, is there any way you can stop by *The Light* this afternoon? I know you're on vacation, but—"

"I have an errand I can't postpone, but after that I guess I can," I said. "What needs to be done?"

"Oh, nothing!" Chris said. "I just forgot to give you your share of the New Year's swag yesterday."

It turns out the arts and entertainment editor is second only to Norton Katz and Alexandra Leonard in terms of how many "comps" he gets offered. If I made it to *The Light* before he left at five, Chris would let me paw through whatever tickets to New Year's Eve parties were left. Too bad Daniel cut out early, I thought. But Michael and Sierra might enjoy a night at a fancy club. Especially if the Alliance's property deal really did close on Friday.

❖❖❖

I called Heather to get a McKimber update.

"Yeah, Richard's back home," she said. "Things went as well as we could hope at the school. Jason isn't thrilled, but he didn't fight it, either."

"Are you driving?" I said. I thought I could hear highway noise in the background.

"Yeah, I'm on my way to Reno. Life and business must go on." She paused. "Thanks for getting the money from Julia, Copper. I don't know what you did, but I swear Victoria's smiling at you from heaven."

"I'm hoping to get Julia to keep up the squeeze on American Beauty."

"Me, too, but the important thing was to save Jason and Richard from their meltdown. Everything else can wait. Richard has decided to stay in business with me, by the way, although I'm pretty sure he's going to sell that house. Some people just aren't cut out to live with homeowners' associations."

"Yeah. He needs to be able to wash his car without getting in trouble."

"You saw him wash a car?"

"Yeah," I said. "Victoria's Taurus. In the driveway."

"Weird. They always took it to a car wash on Blue Diamond. He's pretty crippled, you know."

"Yeah, well, maybe he was just rinsing it off."

But Heather was right. It was kind of weird. His wife's body had been discovered just the day before, and he was washing her car?

Chapter 25

When I arrived at 1075 Chantilly Court, the street was quiet. No news vans, no cops. But the blue Taurus was in the driveway, which meant that Richard was probably home.

I rang the bell. The drapes moved a minute later, and Richard opened the door. He was wearing a laundered shirt, I noticed, and he'd shaved recently.

"Hello, Copper," he said. "Come on in."

Resisting the urge to hold my nose, I stepped inside. But as my eyes adjusted to the dimness, I realized the stench was gone. The floor was no longer an obstacle course, and all the furniture was upright. The living room was far from a showplace, but it was so much better than the last time I'd seen it, I couldn't help commenting.

"Wow!" I said.

"I wish you didn't sound so surprised," Richard said.

"I'm happy to see you've recovered from the break-in," I said. "I—"

"Thanks for getting the money, Copper."

"I'm glad it helped."

"Victoria's death is being ruled accidental," he said. "I just found out this morning."

Our eyes met, and I saw the question in his gaze.

"Oh," I said. "You're probably wondering why I'm here."

"Would you like a Coke or something?" he asked. He started moving toward the kitchen, and I followed him.

"Sure," I said. "A Coke would be great."

The kitchen actually looked clean enough to eat in. The table was clear, and I sat down in one of the chairs.

"I've got something to show you," I said.

Richard handed me a can of Coke and sat down opposite me.

"What?" he said.

I pulled out the envelope of photographs.

"Victoria took these," I said, spreading them out.

"That's Rick Mack. He's a V.P. at American Beauty," Richard said, pointing at the same man Heather had identified. "I don't know the other guy." Then his eyes fell on the last two pictures.

"Damn! That's Jason. Where'd you get these?"

"Victoria gave me lots of stuff," I said, evading his question. Richard picked up one of Jason's photos and peered at it.

"December 15th," he said. "She died that night."

"Yeah," I said. "So she talked with the American Beauty guys in the morning?"

"Yes. She met them someplace on her way to the Beavertail."

"Did she come home that day?"

The look on Richard's face reminded me of a cornered fox.

"No."

"Then how did those pictures of Jason get on her camera?"

"I don't know."

"Look at them. He was in her car when he took them."

"How did you get these again?" Richard said.

I took a breath and let it out.

"I stole Victoria's camera the first time I came here."

"*What?*"

"It was in her shoulder bag on the driveway. When you went inside, I took it."

There it was, my big confession.

Richard was silent for a full minute, and by the time he spoke again, I had identified three escape routes from the house.

"You know I can't do anything to you for stealing her stuff," Richard said. "So just give the pictures back and leave. Let that be the end of it."

I stared at him.

"No," I said. "I'm not leaving until you explain it to me. If you don't like it, call the police."

Richard glowered at me.

I just sat there.

"Okay, then," I said. "Have it your way." I unzipped the side pocket on my backpack and fished out my cell phone. "I didn't call 9-1-1 the last time I was here, but—"

Richard still didn't speak. I punched the numbers into my phone. Each beep made Richard's frown a little angrier. I paused. I raised my finger over the call button.

"Victoria came home that day around four," Richard said softly. I clicked my phone off and set it on the table. "She wasn't supposed to leave the Beavertail, but I asked her to come home anyway. Jason was having a particularly bad episode, and I needed her help."

He looked at me and blinked a couple of times. For a second, I was tempted to threaten him with my phone again. But as we stared at each other, I realized he wasn't stalling. He was pulling his thoughts together. He wanted me to know the truth.

"She got him calmed down, even though a big part of his problem was her. A few days before, when she told him about her—profession—he was upset." Richard rubbed his head and sighed heavily.

"But what really enraged him was that she had lied to him. He just couldn't seem to get past that. Anyway, they seemed to have worked things out, and Jason asked her to take him out driving. He just got a learner's permit, and she was teaching him. She was a much better teacher than I am. I just get pissed off and start swearing." Richard picked up one of the pictures of Jason again. "That kid knows just how to push my buttons."

Richard stopped talking, but and I didn't know what to say. I picked up my Coke, intending to take a sip. I set it back down. My stomach was too turbulent to trust.

"They left. An hour or two later, Jason came back. Alone."

"What happened?"

"Darlin,' if I knew that—" He paused. "I don't know. Jason was in worse shape than before Vicki arrived. I tried to get him to tell me where she was, but all he would say is, 'She can just walk the fuck home!' I forced him to go with me to look for her, but he was confused, and it was dark by then. We never even looked along the right road. *Damn!* I should have kept looking. I should have—" He dropped his head into his hands.

"Why didn't you report her missing?" I said. "I know you hate the cops, but—"

"She was AWOL from the Beavertail. If they found out, she would have lost her job. If she was unhurt, she never would have forgiven me for blowing the whistle on her." Richard stood up and started pacing. "I told myself I'd call in the morning if I hadn't heard from her. First the Beavertail, and then, if I had to, the cops. But the early news beat me to it."

We both just sat there for a while. My head swirled as I tried to process what Richard was telling me.

Suddenly, his head popped up, he gathered the photographs into a pile, and stared at me.

"These are mine," he said. "You had no business taking them."

"I know," I said. "I'm a thief. So press charges."

"God damn it."

"Did Jason kill his mother?"

"It was an accident. I still don't know all the details, but Jason's remembered bits and pieces. He has nightmares. But other times he knows nothing at all."

"There was evidence on the car, wasn't there?"

That surprised him.

"You were washing it when I showed up."

"They had a fight. She told him to pull over—let her take over driving." He paused, looking down. I waited, wondering if that was all the story I was going to get. He sighed and went on. "He did pull over. Vicki got out, but Jason didn't. And while she was walking around the car, he took off."

He sighed again and shook his head.

"Jason didn't realize that he hit her, but the mirror on the passenger's side was broken. The autopsy showed that Vicki died from losing blood from a wound to her neck and shoulder. Their best guess was that she was hit by a car, which is why the police are calling it an accidental death. Well, they're right. It was an accident."

He shot me a look that felt like a challenge.

"What I know for sure," he went on, "is that if the police knew all of this, Jason's life would be a bigger hell than it already is, and I'd lose him forever. I've already lost Vicki. I can't lose Jay, too." He stared at the floor. "They can arrest me. They can lock me up. They can shoot me full of poison. I don't give a flying fuck. They're just not going to get their hands on my son. This isn't his fault."

I looked at Richard McKimber. I had no doubt that he meant every one of those words with his whole heart.

"I've got to go out to my car," I said. "I'll be right back."

Richard followed me through the living room and stayed at the front door while I crossed the street to the Max.

This was it, I told myself as I opened the door. There was no going back, no changing my mind later. I opened the glove compartment and pulled out a new white business envelope. Shutting the door again, I walked back across the road to join Richard McKimber.

"The pictures are yours, Mr. McKimber," I said. "And so are these." I handed him the envelope, and he peeked inside.

"The negatives."

"Happy New Year," I said.

❖ ❖ ❖

I can't remember driving from Richard's house to *The Light*. Seriously, I don't know whether I took I-15, Dean Martin, or some other route entirely. A vortex of what-nexts, what-ifs, and what-nows whirled around one enormous "What have I done?" in my head.

Because, really—what *had* I done? I had just given physical evidence to a guy who might have murdered his wife. After all, I only had Richard's word that he drove around looking for Victoria. He could have deliberately left her to die in a ditch. Heck, he could have found her and mowed her down. Even if he had told me the truth, Jason might be a premeditated murderer, not just an upset, inexperienced driver. But somehow, I knew none of that was true.

I made a mental list of everything I was sure of. I was sure Bobby Marks didn't kill Victoria, and I was sure the American Beauty suits didn't, either, or anybody from the brothel. None of them knew where she was that night.

So who really killed Victoria McKimber? Maybe Jason. Maybe an anonymous hit-and-run driver. But it seemed to me as I sat there in her kitchen that the real question wasn't "Who killed Victoria McKimber?" It was "*What* killed her?" It took a whole chain of events, starting with the accident that crushed Richard's arm. If that hadn't happened, and if Jason hadn't had such expensive medical problems, Victoria wouldn't have gone to work at a bordello. Richard would still be working at Nate's Crane, and he wouldn't have entered Victoria in the American Beauty contest. She wouldn't have won, and she wouldn't have had to tell her son what was really paying his bills …

But that's all moot. All those things did happen. So, should her death go unavenged?

My head was spinning. Forcing Julia and her pals to donate money to the Alliance for the Homeless and for Jason McKimber's therapy seemed like a better penalty than anything a judge and jury might have handed down in either of those cases. And Jaz Cutler was in jail. The criminals had been punished. There had been moral reckonings.

But you're a criminal yourself, Copper! That silent accusation kept repeating itself in my mind. You've stolen, you've extorted, and you've withheld evidence important to a police investigation.

But another voice kept winning every argument. It was a quiet, little voice, but I heard it loud and clear every time I let my mind slow down. I heard it whenever I stopped thinking about laws and rules and what a judge might say.

Victoria loved her family. Yes, she liked notoriety and she traded sex for money. When I met her, I couldn't believe she had a husband. Now, I couldn't believe how much she'd been willing to do to take care of him, and how much both of them loved their son. No, the family wasn't "up to code." But hell, neither was mine anymore. I wasn't sure any family was, if you poked beneath the surface.

Victoria died. Her husband and her son had suffered. I could have made life worse for them. Instead, I decided to make it better. Whether or not Victoria was "smiling at me from heaven," I had no doubt that she would have approved of what I did.

Chapter 26

I pulled up in front of the vicarage around five thirty. The front door was standing open, and I heard voices and laughter as soon as I stepped inside. I dumped my backpack on the sofa and headed to the kitchen to find out what was going on.

"Copper!" Michael said. "I'm so glad you're here!"

"I was just going to call you!" Sierra said. "Do you know Hans and Dustin?"

"Yes!" I said. "We met at the Armstrongs' garage sale when I first got here. How are you?"

I shook Dustin's hand first. He was a cute, curly-haired Kewpie doll of a guy, and tonight he was wearing a red velvet jacket that made him look like a Christmas elf. Hans was taller and beefier, and his handshake could have squeezed a grapefruit.

"Champagne, milady?" Dustin said. "We're celebrating!"

"Sure!" I said. "So—the deal closed?"

"Recorded at 4:52," Sierra said. "I don't think I've ever been that close to the wire."

Hans handed me a flute and clinked his own against it.

"Happy New Year!" I said. "A little early!"

"And a happy new year to you, too!" Dustin said, "But there's yet another splendid reason to shout huzzah! Sierra my darling, do you want to spin the tale or shall I?"

"Go ahead," Sierra said, laughing. "You'll do a much better job."

"Once upon a time," Dustin began, "a lonely Dutchman was wandering the streets of Provincetown—"

Hans laughed. "Whoa, Dusty. We don't have all night."

"Oh, don't we?" Dustin said. "Sad. Okay, the police have caught the blackguard who stole our Liberace collection."

"Really?" I said. "That's great!"

"Indeed it is, my sweet," Dustin said, "and we owe your fine feline friend a hefty debt of gratitude."

The police hadn't been very interested in solving the mystery of the missing Liberace collection, but when the fur cuff appeared, they'd perked up.

"As luck would have it," Dustin said, "Hans observed your sweet kitty emerging through a hole in a house over on Maria Elena that should have been occupied by a—what was the object, Hans?"

"A dryer exhaust hose," Hans said. "And she was dragging the gold lamé cummerbund. I recognized it immediately."

"The policemen came at once!" Dustin cried. "They said something about 'probable cause,' and they went inside and arrested a repellant young ruffian—what was his name?"

"Gary Bruno," Hans said. "We know his mother! I was taking her some fruitcake when I saw your cat. It was so awkward!"

"We didn't even know Dorothy had a son," Dustin said, "and she had no idea that he was carrying off her neighbors' possessions.

"Including your parrot?" I asked.

"Mr. Simms!" Dustin and Hans exclaimed in one voice.

"That's the most brilliant news of all!" Dustin said. "Simmikins is fine! Gary didn't like him, so he gave him to a boy down on Oakey who broke his leg snowboarding. We're sharing custody until he gets out of traction."

"Pâté?" Hans said, handing me a plate. "And the Stilton is fabulous."

"I still can't believe Gary tried to convince the police that he was a victim, too," Dustin said. "As though anyone would want to steal used briefs enormous enough to cover that bottom."

I didn't say anything, but I almost choked on my champagne. Another mystery solved! Sekhmet wasn't partial to Liberace. She just liked going over to Gary's place and carrying off whatever he had left lying around, like underpants and cinnamon rolls.

Before we were finished, we'd drunk toasts to Sekhmet, Mr. Simms, Liberace, and the police. We'd raised glasses to the Alliance for the Homeless, baby Nicky, and the approaching new year. Three bottles were empty when I finally staggered up my stairs.

❖❖❖

Later that night, I sat on my couch and let Sekhmet knead my thigh while I looked at two tickets to the New Year's Eve party at Mandalay Bay. I had tried without success to give them to Michael and Sierra. They declined because Michael had to get up early on Sunday for church.

"You go, Copper," Sierra had said. "New Year's Eve on the Strip is fun! Invite a friend and have a blast."

Would it be terribly rude, I wondered, to call David Nussbaum? It was nearly midnight.

I realized that, on top of all my other crimes, I was about to break a law I'd always held even more sacred. Theft, extortion, withholding evidence—they all paled in comparison. In my whole livelong life, I never dreamed I would ask a married man out on a date.

There was no answer, but he'd know I'd called. Damn caller ID.

❖❖❖

Saturday, December 31

My phone rang around ten the next morning. Oh, God, it's David, I thought as I fished my phone out of my backpack. I was suffering serious remorse for having called him at midnight. It was the champagne, I told myself. And I was tired. Maybe I could claim that I'd dialed his number by accident, or—but I didn't recognize the number on my screen. And when I answered, I didn't recognize the voice.

"Hello," it said. "I hope I'm not bothering you."

"Who is this?" I said.

"Richard McKimber. I got your number from Heather. I hope that was okay."

"It's fine," I said. "How are you?"

"I'm fine. I just wanted—I just wanted to tell you we're having a memorial service for Vicki. Out at the Sekhmet Temple. Next Saturday night. We're going to scatter her ashes."

"I'll be there."

"Good."

"Thanks, Mr. McKimber."

"Richard."

"Thanks, Richard."

"Thank *you*, Copper."

Twenty minutes later, my phone rang again. This time, the number on my screen was all too familiar.

I greeted David.

"Did you call me last night?" he asked.

My heart immediately began revving up.

"Yeah."

"What's up?"

"Um, well, it's like—"

"*What?*"

"I know this is kind of short notice, but, well, um—"

This time he just waited.

"I've got tickets to the New Year's Eve party at the Foundation Room."

Silence.

"Well, um, would you like to go with me?"

"I have another date."

Damn, damn, *damn!* Why in hell had I thought I could get away with asking him at the last minute? It was New Year's Eve, for Christ's sake!

"It's with Clint—*The Good, the Bad and the Ugly* and quite a nice bottle of champagne."

"You're joking."

"Not about the champagne."

"So—you'll go?"

"It would be my great pleasure, Ms. Black. Allow me to go unearth my tuxedo."

After I hung up, I walked to my closet and pulled out the strapless bronze minidress Heather had given me. Whatever the new year might bring, I was going to ring it in wearing a terrific dress.

Acknowledgments

This book is what happens when you move to Nevada and begin to realize that it really is just a little different from other American locales. For all who have shared interesting historical tidbits, recommended books, told me stories, introduced me to unforgettable personalities, and given me a glimpse beyond the veneer of stereotype, my thanks.

Thanks in particular to Pat and Peggy Whitten, whose tales of life in Storey County provided background and inspiration, and to Laraine Russo Harper, whose innovative policies allowed me to observe firsthand a few things normally hidden from view.

Endless gratitude to Mark Sedenquist. He's not only the wind beneath my wings, he's also the giant turbine at my back.

My deepest appreciation to Margaret Sedenquist for encouragement, inspiration, example, and support.

To Maureen Baron and Nancy Zerbey, thanks for being wonderful editors. For a captivating cover and elegant design, thanks to Sue Campbell.

To Ruth Mormon, Brian Rouff, Eric Chiappinelli, Stephen Glass, Sandy Glass, Jeffrey Goldman, Michael Dickman, Tom Herbertson, John Tsitouras, and Jeff Tegge, my thanks for advice and encouragement.

Lastly, and with fond memories, I am grateful to Allan Fleming and Carolyn Hayes Uber for giving me a glimpse of life inside the *Las Vegas Review-Journal* of yesteryear.

About the Author

Megan Edwards likes to travel, as evidenced by her peripatetic life that included nearly seven years "on the road" all over North America. She also enjoys life in Las Vegas, a city that attracts travelers from around the globe. Whether she's venturing forth to see the world or staying home while the world comes to visit, she's always on the lookout for colorful characters and their stories. This is her third novel.